11/11

Retribution

Jos. R Walsh

11/11

Retribution

Jos. R Walsh

PRODUCTIONS

Binghamton, NY, U.S.A.

Publisher: RxDx Productions

ISBN: 979-8-3494-4117-2

Printed in the United States of America.

Contents

Chapter 1
14th Street - First Shots

November 11th in New York City brought intermittent bright sunshine through occasional cloudiness. New York City winters could be rather gray and bracing. Today, however, seemed a pleasant break. It was nearly 40 degrees shortly after sunrise and a cool but pleasant day loomed. Everything but the weather would soon change.

This date then, 11/11, marked to many of the members of Al Qaeda, al-Nusra, ISIS, and other Middle-Eastern Islamist Jihadists as their 'Date of Infamy'. It marked the day that victorious Western imperialists set out to redesign the world map to their liking without regard to the opinions or intentions of the people who inhabited those lands.

In July 1922, the League of Nations entrusted Great Britain with the Mandate for Palestine, yet another example of Western imposition upon Eastern citizens. Resentful and indignant Arabs could hardly bear the insult and degradation imposed by Western imperialists that land owned by families for generations was now a 'Protectorate', or even worse, now shared by 'Outsiders'. This resulted mostly in wars, battles, and endless attacks by the aggrieved parties.

As he walked through the 14th Street Subway Station, Scott Warren wasn't certain if he'd be able to remain calm upon encountering police, but he was fairly confident he could pray and maintain composure as he'd been repeatedly trained. He was wrong.

When he spotted Transit Police Officers Hamilton and Brown approaching, trailed by another rifle-bearing cop and another with a dog, he felt as if cardiac arrest was imminent.

The New York City Transit System has more than 7 million daily customers and approximately 250 officers and supervisors assigned to counter-terror operations in the NYPD Transit Bureau. Their job is to protect the customers and infrastructure of the system from *Terrorist Attack*. *Terrorist Attack* these days was a pervasive possibility.

This day, Officer Peter Hamilton and his patrol partner Officer Stephanie Brown were part of that assignment, patrolling the IRT Nos. 4, 5, and 6 Trains and platforms. They were assigned to a New York City Transit Police Bureau that served more transit customers than at any time in the city's history. Today the officers were conducting Counter-Terror/Transit Order Maintenance Sweeps (CT-TOMS). Peter Hamilton was a decorated sharp-shooter and U.S. Army Combat Vet. Today, as was often the case, he was armed with a Heckler & Koch MP5 Submachine Gun. This 'HK' was fitted with a 25-round clip and fired up to 1,600 RPM. Fully prepared for an extended gunfight, another 14-round clip was attached to his belt and he also bore a 17-round 9mm Semi-Automatic Pistol.

Stephanie Brown, his smaller, but nonetheless ferocious partner, was carrying a Glock 19 Semi-Automatic Pistol holding 17 9mm rounds of immediately available ammo. She too, bore extra clips, just in case…

Hamilton was the shooter. Brown, a wrestling champ back at the Academy, was the tackler. Both were on patrol in full CT uniform today and sported blast-resistant helmets and bullet-proof flak jackets. They were part of a six-person team. Four were in uniform. Two more 'stragglers', also heavily-armed with concealed weaponry, were in plain clothes. One of the uniformed officers handled an explosives-sniffing dog. Once again, non-specific info warned counter-terror personnel in New York of intel citing activity which indicated the possibility of *Persons of Interest* making their way to the city for *Reasons Unknown*, but nonetheless *Suspicious*.

Scott Warren was 26 years old, American-born, raised since age five in the U.K., having family and friends on both sides of *The Pond*. With much travel back and forth, Warren had dual U.S.-U.K. citizenship and travel papers. He posed no discernible distinction nor security threat in either country. The front he presented was, however, quite different from his actual character and intent. Scott Warren was an angry young man.

All noise in the station was amplified by the somewhat grimy, but still quite attractive white ceramic tile. The volume of noise rose and fell in sync with the arrival and departure of trains. A fairly steady, audible level of crowd noise between trains, and then a louder tone combined with the grinding, screeching whoosh of an arriving or departing train, and then a return to the regular murmur as train noise subsided.

The station was crowded at this time of the morning rush-hour, with the flow of human traffic moving steadily. Most of the travelers were regular commuters, knowing where and how to proceed, always quickly, as 'The Regulars' moved swiftly through their daily morning commute. The others, visitors and tourists, wandered about perplexed at the vastness of the underground station and array of signs and directions.

The scene was expected to be repeated in reverse order as The Regulars headed up from the trains in the afternoon-evening homeward-bound commute. But today, unknown to the masses, things would be tragically different by this afternoon.

Warren's everything-on-the-fly childhood, his disconnect to anything solid and stable, left a huge and persistent void in the center of his soul. Something was missing. At heart, he was bitter and aimless. Then he met the al-Nusra sympathizers of London, and eventually Muhammad, Achmed, and 'The Seekers'. From the beginning, Warren was fully attentive and sympathetic with the anti-capitalism, anti-imperialist rhetoric of their radical Islamic rebellion. Being aimless with an angry and vengeful energy, the focus he found in their 'Brotherhood' and camaraderie was oddly enough, fulfilling.

Scott Warren's lifestyle involved shifting about from shore to shore, living with not only his parents, but various relatives as life went on and Mother and Father resumed their professional and academic pursuits. Warren had a sister, Karen, three years his junior and the time they shared together was substantial early on. By the time he was 12 though, they saw each other infrequently. Their constantly shifting upbringing had left Karen too, with some childhood confusion and resentment issues. By the time she was 20, Karen was addicted to opiates and turning tricks in London to get dope. This further enraged the already angry Scott Warren, and he was further infuriated that despite all that he tried to save her, he was powerless to arrest her addiction and its consequences.

Scott Warren was 5 ft. 9, 195 lbs., sandy-haired with a fair complexion and fairly good-looking. He was well-educated, but anxious and depressed. He was resentful, moody, and adrift. When needed, he could be rather charming and engaging; he was not unintelligent. Though his anger was not upfront, it brooded alive and kicking just below the surface. His personality came across as that of an even, educated, smooth young man. As Warren grew into his mid-20s, that anger matured, gained intent, and sought focus.

He crossed paths with the Jihadists in London. Warren, still stung by his sister Karen's tragedy, wandered about seeking some substantial, meaningful direction. As he grew closer and more and more in line with their incendiary, revolutionary, and ultimately, jihadist philosophy, he felt focused, worthy. The persistent feeling of powerlessness was now also gone. Now, he was the powerful one. All the power he craved was now his, and it was packed into 'The Vest'.

The intensive 'Commando' training in Pakistan indoctrinated in Scott Warren was for him to remain calm and pray to the One True and Merciful God, Allah, upon any potential encounter with law enforcement 'Agents' during his mission. If, however, an encounter appeared inevitable, one should immediately detonate the 'Special Vest', thus killing enemy agents, delivering final justice to the rabble, and ensuring the martyr's immediate transition to eternal paradise.

It was as if by some mysterious karma that both Brown and Hamilton locked onto Scott Warren at an exact instant. Both felt, as much as saw 'bad juju' with this one. Even his very gait appeared awkward. Instantly, instinctively, both officers peered into his eyes. Even from 10 yards away, the result of that observation was alarming: The eyes they looked into were twitchy, nervous, almost panicked. The coat was bulky, clumsy. In a barely perceptible motion, Brown glanced over at her partner Hamilton. In sync, Hamilton had received Brown's nod. 'Got him' he said in response.

Scott Warren could barely remember Allah's name, much less any prayers as he saw the police approach him. But he knew, he knew one thing, more than anything. He knew he had to detonate the Vest, or all would be lost.

At that same instant, NYPD Transit Officer Pete Hamilton knew, more than anything else at that moment, that if he did not kill the 'Target', something very ugly would happen. Having served in combat in Iraq, he was all too experienced with the tragic aftermath of a suicide bomb attack. "You, Stop! Hands Up!" Even as the words are shouted, Scott fumbles for the detonator switch in his right-hand coat pocket. "Stop!"

Bam-Bam, firecracker-like loud explosions reverberate off the ceramic tiles of the train station, increasing the ferocity of the initial reports. In the next instant, he had gotten off two kill-rounds and the target was down.

Scott fell back, killed instantly by a shot into the skull above the nose, and an instantaneous second shot into the larynx. The detonator switch was now out of the coat pocket dangling precariously. Half the crowd ran screaming hysterically out of the station. A lot of the rest of the crowd, no strangers themselves to shots fired in New York City, reflexively fell to the ground, some covering their heads with their arms, upon hearing the echoing gunfire eruption.

Officer Hamilton had all he could do to stifle the sudden surge of adrenaline and keep his finger off the trigger as he gaped wide-eyed at the detonator. Hamilton's partner, Officer Brown raced over to the sprawled body on the ground, one hand on the Glock, the other reaching for handcuffs in her belt. Like Hamilton, alertly, intently, her eyes locked onto the detonator switch. In an even tone, she informed her onrushing colleagues—"we've got a situation here…"

That message was then transmitted to Transit Bureau Police Department Operations:

Shots Fired—Target Down! Notify Bomb Squad forthwith—we have a situation here! The NYPD Special Operations Desk was then immediately notified, alerting the Emergency Services Division, including Bomb Squad, for Priority Response to the station. Nearby Transit and Street Patrol Units were notified for immediate response.

This activated an intricate, previously arranged reaction of NYPD, FDNY, and E.M.S. Units. Citywide resources were dispatched for Emergency Mobilization. All across the massive sprawl of the five boroughs that comprise the immense metropolis that is the City of New York, Police, Fire, and Emergency Medical Service Units bullied their way through the organized mess that is the Morning Rush Hour, in response to the city-wide alert.

Transit Emergency Crews were rushed to assist with the emergency evacuation of the thousands of morning Rush Hour commuters in, and arriving at, the crowded station.

Along with the multi-faceted, multi-task operation necessary to achieve the complete evacuation of a crowded and busy transfer station of the NYC Subway System, another series of top-level, lifesaving decisions needed to be made very quickly: How much of the city's Subway System needed to be shut down?

The Rapid Transit Operations Control Center on E.54th St. in Manhattan is home to the 'heart and soul' of New York's oft-maligned Rail Transit Division; operator of the MTA's Subway System. At the moment of alarm from the Union Square Station, FDNY 9th Battalion Chief Frank Watson responded to the RTO to manage the Fire Department's and FDNY/EMS response to the 'Situation'. Chief Watson was a 14-year veteran of the department, and as a Transit Liaison Officer, had expert, special operations training in the unique specifics of the New York City Transit System.

Also *en-route* was NYPD Special Operations Lieutenant Steve Palmer, responsible to manage all NYPD response including Emergency Service, Counter-Terror, Bomb Squad, and Patrol Task Force Units. Lt. Palmer, like Chief Watson, had special training dedicated to Transit Operations.

Chapter 2
The Route to Grand Central

James Waters was, as directed by Muhammed, riding the No. 6 Lexington Ave. Uptown Local. After many hours of soul-searching and agonizing consternation, he was now on his way to execute the mission. He'd left the Lower East Side safe-house and was on his way to fulfill his destiny. Allah, or whomever, be praised, James was on his way.

He still remained mostly indifferent to Allah being the source of his epiphany. However, he did understand this: Muhammed and fundamentalist Islam had invigorated what he supposed was his soul, and his Islamic experience in Pakistan had elevated him to a conviction of his beliefs. The militant training he'd undergone there propelled him into action. This day, there would be tremendous, dramatic change.

So he sat this glorious morning, not just another passenger in the crowd, on the A.M. rush-hour Uptown train. This particular passenger was about to bring some justice to an unjust world. The 'Special Vest' he wore would be the instrument of justice. The vest bore violent suffering and death for many in New York City. Today, it was once again time for this pagan world capital to bear the cost of rampant injustice.

James had been able to identify the crushing injustice of the world, and his own inability to act to initiate dramatic change. He came from a past which left him acutely attuned to, and personally pained by, the imposition of authority from a father he deemed distant and indifferent. He resented the dominance wielded by the rich and, like his father, self-indulgent. James saw them as greedy and authoritarian, wielding power over poverty-stricken, marginalized individuals and populations.

The specific date chosen by the terrorist conspirators, 11/11, was significant. Precedent had been established by previous attacks, New York City on 9/11, and London, on 7/11. The date also bore some ironic significance: On 11/11, 1921, an unknown World War I American soldier was buried in Arlington National Cemetery. Similar ceremonies occurred earlier in England and France, where an unknown soldier was buried in each nation's highest place of honor (in England, Westminster Abbey; in France, the Arc de Triomphe). Each of these memorial gestures took place on 11/11. Thus followed universal recognition of the celebrated ending of World War I fighting at 11 a.m., November 11, 1918 (the 11th hour of the 11th day of the 11th month). The day became known as "Armistice Day." It also marked the day that the victorious imperialist Allies would set about carving up the Middle East as they saw fit.

James Waters had, over time, come to accept that he was a vessel. There were others this morning too, James knew, that were serving as vessels with their own instruments, to bring radical justice, once again, to the money-hoarders and the criminally indifferent masses of New York City.

James boarded the train this morning at the Bleecker St. Station. He was to travel six stops, to Grand Central Station. There, his statement would be made, his special testimony announced. The powerful explosives loaded into the Special Vest would bring about enough chaos and misery to make their point. Unbeknownst to his fellow passengers, Grand Central was to be the last stop for many this day. This was God's will after all, wasn't it? Yes, he was certain it was; it is. James had had a long and arduous journey to this moment, physically, mentally, spiritually. But now it was here. This was, is, indeed, the moment God, Allah, whatever He be called, had intended for him.

James had come to this moment after years of searching. That search had come to its fruition upon meeting Muhammed. It had begun quite unremarkably with several discussions during, after, and then between classes at their World Religions Course at NYU.

James at first satisfied his curiosity and sense of mission by volunteering at a non-profit agency purporting to be of non-sectarian, emergency relief/social services. Further investigation by various parties found this claim somewhat dubious, and that was fairly well known. The 'Social Services' group claimed they provided humanitarian relief services to "all persons in need" in "distressed areas in the Middle East." The 'buzz', however, both official and non, was that the group was a front, to shuffle money to jihadi 'warriors'. These allegations, however, further piqued, rather than inhibited, James' commitment to the cause. James, under the sway of perceived injustice and persecution of Muslim groups, became dedicated to the group's commitment to "relief of distress".

His volunteer experience, and ongoing discussion with Muhammed, progressed to attendance and participation in prayer, lecture, and meditation sessions at Al Farooq Mosque in Brooklyn, a place well-known for its radical jihadist extremism. Then long, spirited conversation of fundamental Islamic beliefs and practice, frequently going on well into the late and early hours, with Muhammed, Achmed, Mehmet, and the other 'teachers'.

Eventually then to London, Istanbul, and finally Pakistan. Now, this glorious day, Muhammed, Mehmet, and several other of the followers, had sent out the 'martyrs', as vessels of justice, prepared with their instruments of destruction, on the path to everlasting glory. So it was, that James found himself this morning, 11/11, on the trip to Grand Central, to deliver justice. The other 'vessels' had their stops this day as well: Carefully selected thriving New York City commuter hubs, targeted for Allah-inspired, man-made chaos and suffering.

The Uptown No.6 now roared into Union Square Station. James had four stops to go. And quite soon, this very place, Union Square, would know the furious destruction of one of the Seekers' Special Vests. Death and misery would soon be the order of the day here, and at Grand Central Station, and elsewhere throughout this wretched city of greedy infidels.

Muhammed, the operations officer of the Jihad Militia Group, was responsible, together with Mehmet, the recruitment/personnel officer, for determining each recruit's readiness and assignment for the mission. Each recruit needed to demonstrate their readiness and potential along each phase of orientation and development and training. This was after all, a suicide mission. Therefore, each individual had to demonstrate total commitment and personal willingness to proceed to the next phase of training, and a commitment to die for 'the cause' if chosen.

As such, it needed to be determined when they were recruited in New York, if each recruit was ready, and willing, for the next phase in London. And in London, readiness for Istanbul, and in Istanbul, Pakistan. The London jihadi phase was meant to further indoctrinate the recruits. Istanbul, for further radicalization, and review and testing to gauge the trainees' intention and willingness. Pakistan then, for more specific combat training, and overall evaluation.

Once there, the 'new commandos' were introduced to weapons training. At first, handguns – pistols, both automatic and semi. The recruits, several of whom had previously never fired a weapon, underwent an intensive and rigorous period of repeated instruction and practice, until proficiency could be readily demonstrated. Eventually then onto rifles, and then shoulder-fired rocket-propelled grenades (RPGs), and other bazookas. At each phase, demonstrated proficiency was required. Then on to mortars, improvised explosive devices (IEDs) and finally: the 'suicide vest' all the while continuous, constant, radical fundamentalist, Islamist jihadist, lecture and meditation.

Chapter 3
The Ascension of Jihadi Warriors

While in Pakistan, the commandos were judged on their readiness and willingness under fire in actual terrorist/combat operations. As a requirement for successful completion of training, the 'New Commandos' had to participate in a live fire operation. This was not merely practice with live rounds, which was already an almost daily drill, but an actual combat mission with successful access to, operation at, and withdrawal from a chosen objective. With live combat and other terrorist operations ongoing across the Pakistani border in Afghanistan, there was plenty of opportunity for *practice*.

At one point in their training, the New Commandos joined with an al-Qaeda combat team for an infiltration mission across the border into Afghanistan. The team conducted a midnight expedition to an Afghan border village. Arriving pre-dawn, they attacked a government-allied militia outpost. Emerging from the darkness, they launched rocket-propelled grenades and directed automatic weapons fire into the garrison, ultimately racing into the outpost to execute survivors. Mission accomplished, they fled back to the Pakistani border and crossed safely back at sunrise.

By this point, the *Vessels of Destruction* had reached an elevated, actually revered status among Jihadi warriors. Here was a group of men, no matter their past level of devotion to Islam and Jihad, who were now offering themselves to literally give their lives for the cause.

They were revered in various ways; not only for their devotion to self-sacrifice, but also for their actual value to the group, as they'd pledged to sacrifice themselves in action. It was exactly the kind of attention and respect they'd craved and had been denied for years. It was precisely why they were here.

Although Jihad has been a somewhat recent tragedy in the U.S. and the West, its roots are hundreds of years old and deep. Jihadists' more recent history dates back to the actions in the Middle East of Western empires, most particularly but not exclusively, Great Britain and France, with the U.S. playing a minor, conciliatory role.

In an effort to disentangle themselves from the maddening and puzzling social and religious maze that is the Middle East, these dominant international empires began drawing artificial lines on the map of the world, designating this area or that in the Middle East as a kingdom, state, territory, or protectorate, mostly without the consent of the people who lived in and around these 'Lines of Demarcation.'

The most obvious and persistently troublesome example has been the creation of the State of Israel in 1947. However, Israel is not a lone example. Iraq, Iran, Kuwait, and other Arab states can trace much of their geographic origins to the map-makers of historic Western empires. The recent crumbling of strong-arm governments in Afghanistan, Iraq, Egypt, Syria, as well as Libya, created areas of opportunity for violent, fundamentalist Jihadist terrorists to organize and create havoc.

Modern trans-national terrorism in the Middle East can be traced to *The Great Arab Revolt* of 1936-39, when one of the most famous of the Muslim Brotherhood's leaders, the Hajj Amin al-Husseini, Grand Mufti (Supreme Muslim religious leader) of

Jerusalem, incited his followers to a three-year war against the Jews in Palestine and the British who administered the mandate. In 1936 the Brotherhood had about 800 members, but by 1938, just two years into the *Revolt,* its membership had grown to almost 200,000, with fifty branches in Egypt alone.

During the *Great Arab Revolt* of 1936-39, which al-Husseini helped organize and which Germany funded, the swastika was used as a mark of identity on Arabic leaflets and graffiti. Arab children welcomed each other with the Hitler salute, and a sea of German flags and pictures of Hitler were displayed at celebrations.

By the end of the 1930s, there were more than a half-million active members registered, in more than two thousand branches across the Arab world. In British Mandatory Palestine alone there were 38 branches under the leadership of the Hajj. To achieve that broader dream of a global jihad, the Brotherhood developed a network of underground cells, stole weapons, trained fighters, formed secret assassination squads, founded sleeper cells of subversive supporters in the ranks of the army and police, and waited for the order to go public with terrorism, assassinations, and suicide missions.

The overwhelming defeat of Germany, and thus its regional allies in the Middle East, and subsequent occupation of Arabian, Palestinian, and Egyptian territories by victorious American, British, and French forces, led to a vacuum of support for Jihadi terrorists. Eventually, though, it all boiled down as it had since the time of The Crusades: East vs. West, Christianity vs. Islam; Jihad.

The Special Vests themselves were a product of years of Jihadist devotion to mass destruction. These terrorist explosives were the result of persistent trial and development of mass-casualty weapons. They were used repeatedly and improved upon by various Jihadist terror-attacks in London, England, Iraq, Israel, Afghanistan and Pakistan, Syria, Chechnya, and most recently, Paris and Brussels.

These instruments of horror were the latest and most destructive devices recently developed in the halls of hell that are Jihadi bomb factories. Their lethality and capacity for mass injury were multi-pronged. The first and foremost component of these weapons of destruction was the ferocious explosives.

Chapter 4
Constructing the Instruments of Terror

Explosives technicians and other investigators of the New York City Subway incident knew that the most recent and highly favored explosive of choice for terrorist groups worldwide has been triacetone triperoxide (TATP). Besides its high-energy, mass-force explosive properties, it is difficult to detect. Only the most sophisticated, high-tech detection devices can recognize the substance, and even then, only under favorable, managed conditions. TATP's base ingredients—drain cleaner, bleach, and acetone—can be bought easily and without attracting suspicion; its chemical composition is simple, and in its finished form, it is almost undetectable.

For the same reasons that Hamas uses TATP to send suicide bombers undetected into Israel, the al-Qaeda network has adopted TATP for its terror missions abroad. The substance was included as the trigger in the shoe bomb that Briton Richard Reid tried to detonate on a flight from Paris to Miami in December 2001.

Counter-terrorist forces, such as the NYPD, understand that one of the tricky detection problems is that TATP itself is an organic substance. Thus, there is a need for a detection device that can clearly identify it in a mass of other organic matter, like, for instance, a busy and crowded subway station. TATP, though, is a highly volatile substance, prone to detonation by outside variances like friction and temperature. It is for this reason that terror and counter-terror operatives alike have called it 'The Mother of Satan'. However, it has proven manageable enough, and successful enough, to create targeted destruction if handled correctly and used quickly.

The next layer of destruction built into these particular vests was shaved magnesium and magnesium powder. Magnesium is another organic, difficult-to-detect, metallic substance. It is more easily detectable in bulk form and under managed conditions, but again, in a busy train station, encased in a variety of metals itself, subject to the sway and fro of the crowd, wind and other atmospheric variances blowing down into and venting up out of the station, calls for some pretty sophisticated, bulky, and expensive instruments.

Magnesium, ignited by the high-energy explosion of the TATP, burns as a super-heated, nearly molten metal. Propelled into the surrounding vicinity of the TATP explosion, it is rocketed through the air as an expanding cloud of burning shrapnel. It is an ugly, monstrous scene. Burning magnesium binds to anything it comes in contact with, be it human or artificial. As it sears into whatever surface it has landed on, the metal continues to burn at super-high temperatures, not only burning the surrounding oxygen like some sort of jet fuel, but also giving off a toxic vapor while consuming O_2. It cannot be extinguished by water and must be smothered either chemically or physically. It is deadly, difficult, and gruesome.

The other toxic ingredient of the Special Vests was the deadly poison, cyanide. Another tricky and volatile substance which requires special handling and care, but has been found to be manageable enough for manic terrorist bombers. Cyanide is a popular weapon of modern warfare. Because it, and similar poisons are seen as 'Weapons of Mass Destruction' and terrorism, all the forces that utilize it rampantly deny having anything to do with cyanide. Iraq used chemical weapons (thought to include hydrogen cyanide), against Iraqi Kurds, who were considered opposed to the regime of Saddam Hussein. The most notorious such attack was the killing of 5,000 Kurds, including many civilians, in the city of Halabjah in 1988.

Its effects, however, are self-evident, and it is highly traceable after it has been deployed. Before the explosion, though, it too, is a substance requiring sophisticated technology to detect. Oddly, despite much modern technology, explosives-sniffing dogs are seen as the single-most efficient detection method.

The explosive cylinders in the vests were specially configured with cyanide-laced cardboard discs. During the process of the TATP and magnesium explosion, sulfuric acid is introduced into cyanide at high temperature and under pressure, creating hydrogen cyanide. Hydrogen cyanide gas was the agent Nazi mass murders used in the gas chambers at the infamous concentration camps, and the agent produced by the Special Vests.

As cyanide is inhaled, it causes coma and seizures, apnea, and cardiac arrest, with death following in a matter of seconds. At lower doses, death may be preceded by general weakness, headaches, vertigo, confusion, and difficulty in breathing. At the first stages of unconsciousness, breathing is often sufficient or rapid, although sometimes accompanied by pulmonary edema, which can often lead to fatal respiratory distress.

As a result of this multi-layered mix of flammables and toxins, the 'kill-zone' was not only at once highly effective, the area of detonation and the immediate area around that point for 40-60 feet, would remain poisoned for hours, and at some points days to come. Also, the chemical-protective clothing worn by rescuers would be contaminated upon exposure. The CPC gear would have to be showered off after contact, further delaying victim search and rescue operations.

Because of the military demand for cyanide, the product is readily available in many areas, in various forms. And it was not as if the United States was unaware either. A recent Congressional investigation found that the U.S. is a virtual supermarket for terrorists and foreign governments seeking high-end military technology. Components that can be used to build nuclear weapons and equip militants fighting US and British troops are fairly available. The Government Accountability Office told a congressional panel: The lack of restrictions over sales of these items, and the difficulties of inspecting packages and individuals leaving the United States, "results in weak control, that does not effectively prevent terrorists and agents of foreign governments from obtaining these sensitive items."

And little, if any, meaningful reforms have been enacted and enforced in the time since, to prevent the proliferation of these dreadful weapons. Actually, the polar opposite of controlling war weapons marketeering, and monitoring became accepted practice. Potentially dangerous persons in the U.S. were, mostly unrestricted.

The free-marketing of weapons, and keeping them available to the vast majority of 'customers', was the law of the land.

Prior to this 11/11 mission, hundreds were killed, and several hundred were injured and maimed in a Paris terror attack. Soon thereafter, a radicalized Muslim man and wife killed over a dozen people and seriously wounded dozens more in a San Bernardino, California massacre.

The very next day, the U.S. Congress voted down legislation that would make it illegal for persons on U.S. 'No-Fly' lists to purchase weapons, and also bills that would strengthen and lengthen the background check waiting period for persons to buy guns in the U.S.

In essence, the United States Legislature, just weeks and days following terrorist, mass murder attacks, said that suspected or potential terror suspects could not fly on airplanes in the U.S., but they were free to legally purchase a wide variety of firearms. And the day following mass murder in California, the U.S. Congress voted that it was not going to require a law that would enable more comprehensive and thorough criminal and psychiatric background checks of those wishing to buy guns in the U.S.

The procuring and smuggling then, of weapons of mass destruction was essentially a *free-market* business.

As this plot to attack New York City once again came into operation, it was decided that the compilation and construction of the Special Vests should occur within a manageable distance of their targets. It was decided then, that the bomb 'factory' would be in lower Manhattan.

There were five vests to be constructed and transported for delivery to the 'martyrs', without being detected. This involved compiling these toxic and hazardous ingredients at the factory, and assembling the deadly components of the vests. This was by its very nature, extremely dangerous and sensitive, precise work. There was complicated and sometimes heated discussion on how exactly to go about this work.

The bomb-maker, Fasil al-Marsi, wanted all the components already compiled and stored at a specific location. Muhammed, the Operation Commander, did not. Aside from the inherent power struggle over who should eventually rule on this point, was the matter of detection and exposure. Not only the matter of actual exposure to the various chemicals, as far as Muhammed was concerned that was al-Marsi's problem.

But there was the matter of any attention the collection of that amount of materials might garner, and the exposure of all of the bomb components being lost at once should anything go wrong. After some emotional discussion and then concession all around, it was agreed that al-Marsi should have the components of more than one device at a time available for him, but that he did not necessarily need to have them all at once.

Chapter 5
From Soviet Foes to American Enemies

The Operations Officer and overall Commander of this mission, Muhammed, had followed a path well-known to those tracking terrorist 'operators'. Originally a Muslim Afghani tribesman by family origin, Muhammed's family became Pakistani citizens when Great Britain, compelled by years of civil war in the region, drew new borders on the map. For years, Muhammed's family and their community seethed under the yoke of what they viewed as European imperialist impositions on their nationality and citizenship.

Over time, the villages in the Safed Koh tribal regions of Pakistan, with deep Afghani roots, generally disregarded the national boundaries as much as they could. Pakistani officials and agencies frequently enforced their domain over the population, with results ranging from disinterested cooperation to armed resistance. As time passed, Pakistani officials learned they could only govern the area with a significant armed presence, which they occasionally deployed in a show of force.

The village tribesmen knew that ignoring Pakistani rule came with its own risks, but often chose to take these risks. It was in this environment that Muhammed was raised, immersed in strict Islamic obedience and jihadist fanaticism. He first attended, and later preached at, a madrassa. He also became a combat-hardened veteran, having served in bin Laden's army opposing the Soviet invasion of

Afghanistan. Following the withdrawal of Soviet troops and the collapse of Soviet influence in the region, Muhammed's sponsors and allies dominated.

After the Soviet retreat, Muhammed's Taliban brethren and their al-Qaeda allies took control of Afghanistan. All Soviet sympathizers, or those suspected of Soviet sympathies, were brutally eliminated. After years of evading Pakistani threats, Muhammed and his allies ruled a country. However, this changed when Muhammed and his cohorts decided to engage in war with the United States of America, culminating in a massive and multi-pronged terrorist attack.

Not long after their grand and devastating scheme, they found themselves without a homeland. After years of hiding, combat, and constant relocation, Muhammed and his compatriots ended up in the remnants of what was once known as Iraq. Following a poorly-planned and under-supported American intervention in Iraq, Muhammed and his comrades found a new base of operations.

By the time of the 11/11 operation, Muhammed was 45 years old, fully radicalized, and deeply contemptuous of Western society, as well as most non-Taliban-aligned Muslims. He had inherited his father's and grandfather's legacy of discontent and brutal vengeance.

Chapter 6
Transporting Terror
Across the City

A one-room workshop was rented in downtown Brooklyn to store and distribute the various bomb ingredients. Once adequate portions were compiled, they were transported under the cover of a standard, slightly-used minivan to the 'factory', an artist's studio in Greenwich Village.

The materials were transported in increments, undetected over the Manhattan Bridge—one of the city's toll-free East River crossings. This made the Manhattan Bridge, and occasionally the Brooklyn Bridge, favorable choices for crossing into Manhattan. The absence of a toll plaza meant there was no point where traffic halted, allowing continuous observation and monitoring.

These bridges were only sporadically monitored for suspicious substances. The difficulty in detecting the bomb ingredients, coupled with the small amounts being transported, practically ensured safe passage. And, if not, such were the risks incurred in such dramatic operations.

In the Brooklyn warehouse, three commercial standard refrigerators stored the bomb components. To avoid drawing attention, components were acquired in moderate amounts and refrigerated to keep them 'fresh'. The cooling provided stabilization for the inert chemical ingredients of the poison bombs. This refrigerated stabilization not only made the volatile ingredients more stable but also harder to detect.

Thus, the refrigerated and discreetly covered components easily slipped through temporary hazardous chemical monitors occasionally deployed by the city on the two bridges. In Manhattan, moving pads and blankets were laundered for reuse. After being used a second time, they were washed again, then burned, and the ashes scattered at various locations around the city late at night.

At the East Village studio, the components were assembled into deadly individual devices by al-Marsi, and then delivered one at a time to each of the 'Martyrs' Sanctuaries'. These 'sanctuaries' were actually illegal single-room occupancy apartments scattered throughout Greenwich Village and the Lower East Side of the city. These apartments had been secured weeks in advance by Muhammed and his team, paid up in cash, no questions asked. Due to the apartments being in violation of city housing regulations, a 'No Questions Asked' policy was strictly observed throughout the rental term: *Don't Ask—Don't Tell.*

Chapter 7
The Vest on the 6 Train

On the I.R.T. 6 Train, James carefully twisted his body, taking care not to disturb the explosive vest hidden beneath his coat, as he peered into the crowd awaiting the subway. He didn't see mere fellow commuters or fellow New Yorkers; instead, he saw a gathering dominated by the greedy and the criminally indifferent—many of whom would soon become casualties. It was harsh, but justified in his mind. *They should have been more aware of the surrounding suffering and misery. They could have intervened or at least voiced their concerns. Instead, they carried on with their trivial pursuits, oblivious to the hardships fostered by the West's capitalism and materialism.* Today, these deplorable beings would inadvertently serve a higher purpose. Their suffering would spotlight the cause for the Greater Good. Worship and serve God Allah, not the Almighty Dollar.

At 14th Street/Union Square, an NYPD Transit Bureau Officer entered the subway car occupied by James and his vest. Suppressing panic, James prayed silently. He knew that showing signs of distress might draw unwanted attention. By appearing meditative and detached, he hoped the officer would overlook him—and she did. After a brief glance, she dismissed James as just another face in the crowd and moved on to the next car.

As intended, James seemed ordinary, a nondescript working-class New Yorker, just under six feet tall with a medium build. He inherited his mother's light brown hair and green eyes, and his father's handsome features softened by his own modest smile. The sudden presence of a police officer was indeed distracting, but he had been trained well—he stayed calm and focused on his prayers. The Transit Officer continued her rounds, heading into the next car.

Allah provides—the mission continues. James, like the other chosen vessels, had been specifically groomed for this role. To the untrained eye, he was just an average New Yorker commuting to his destination, unaware that only two minutes after the Uptown Local departed, the entire mission was at risk. Upstairs, Scott Warren was down.

Across from James sat a petite, olive-skinned woman with striking features. Thirty-year-old Miriam Bednar was naturally reserved and distant, a demeanor shaped by her survival through devastating experiences that had claimed the lives of others around her. She, along with her parents and younger siblings, had been thrust into a perilous existence.

Chapter 8
Miriam's Exodus

Miriam was a Syrian Christian whose journey to New York City had been nothing short of a nightmare. Life in Syria was difficult enough for a woman, but for a Christian woman—especially in recent years—it became downright perilous. Miriam had lived in Homs, once a productive and stable city before the Syrian Civil War. Under the iron rule of the al-Assad regime, Homs's sizable Christian minority had been able to function with minimal interference.

Before the war, Miriam worked as a daycare provider for children of the city's professional class and established merchants. Her father, Adin, enjoyed success as an investment manager and financial advisor, while her mother, Sophia, was a licensed nurse. Miriam herself served as a paraprofessional, working in an environment where English was widely used as a second language—a skill that would prove invaluable later.

However, with the rise of Islamist insurgents during the civil war, simply being Christian in Syria became exceptionally dangerous, and the added reality of being a woman made it even worse. The legitimate fear of rape or murder weighed heavily on Miriam every day, growing in intensity as insurgent activity flared.

Homs had traditionally been an Alawite stronghold, favored by the ruling al-Assad family, whose lineage also hails from the Alawite sect of Shia Islam. As Syria's political situation erupted, Homs became a flashpoint of dissent, leading to devastating clashes. Protection for minorities—both Alawite Muslims and Christians—soon waned, and survival became precarious for all.

Sunni fundamentalist radicals labeled Alawites as dissenters and infidels. Driven by religious and ethnic zeal, they turned minority groups against one another, promising protection and freedom in exchange for information. This vicious cycle of betrayal led to oppression on all sides. Infidels or apostates were beaten, robbed, raped, enslaved, or outright executed, depending on which faction happened to be in control.

When Islamist insurgents temporarily seized large parts of Homs, brutal combat raged in and around the city for weeks, followed by a short lull in which insurgents roamed the streets, enforcing their own brutal brand of Sharia "justice." Anyone suspected of being an infidel risked assault, robbery, rape, or execution.

During the ebb and flow of combat, Miriam's family—the Bednars—feared for their lives, as did their neighbors. Alawite militias and Jihadist insurgents committed equal atrocities, exacting revenge on one another while Christian families like Miriam's remained caught in the middle with no significant allies. During the so-called Homs Massacres, the death toll climbed from hundreds to possibly thousands.

Eventually, the Bednars were able to find temporary refuge with relatives in a nearby suburb. After a few months, Syrian government forces and allied militias retook Homs, but reprisals against anyone suspected of aiding the insurgents soon followed, bringing more terror. It felt to many as though the people of Homs were damned, no matter who held power.

Chapter 9
The Bednars' Journey

After a few weeks of domestic terror, Syrian-allied militias threatened to abandon the fight, and international relief organizations exerted enough pressure on Syrian authorities that some sense of normalcy was restored to Homs. During the unrest, the Bednars realized that fleeing the country was rapidly becoming their only option for survival. Such flight, though, brought its own challenges. While the Bednars were financially capable of fleeing, it would cost them nearly all they had. As political refugees, they were not genuinely welcome in the places they traveled and were vulnerable to danger.

For Syrian Christians, flying out of the country during a time of national crisis was nearly impossible. However, flying from nearby Cyprus was more feasible. Being somewhat affluent, the parents and Miriam managed to arrange a somewhat haphazard escape from the chaos engulfing Syria. Miriam, then 24, along with her parents, her sister Sofia, who was 5 years younger, and her younger brother Ali, aged 14, were able to leave.

In December 2013 and the following January, the Syrian conflict devolved into a multifaceted free-for-all. The mostly Sunni Muslim Free Syrian Army was the initial opposition force to challenge the Bashar al-Assad regime effectively. The result was a dispersed, distracted, and damaged Syrian military. Into the void stepped additional combatants—the Army of Mujahedeen, and the Arab group, Islamic State of Iraq and Syria (ISIS). Subsequently, the al-Nusra Front, the Saudi-supported Green Battalion, and then Iranian-supported Shia Islamist Hezbollah joined the fray. As these forces clashed with each other as well as the Syrian military, the Bednars slipped away.

The timing of their departure was fortunate. First, the turmoil and chaos of the civil war had consumed the attention and function of the entire Syrian civilian bureaucracy, making escape easier. Also, Hungary and other European nations were not yet as vigilant in protecting against the influx of Syrian refugees. The Bednars' escape came at a crucial moment, positioning them at the forefront of what would soon become a seemingly endless flow of refugees from the Middle East.

Through contacts within and various connections the family had developed beyond their local Christian community, the Bednars were able to piece together a fragmented journey to what they hoped and prayed would be freedom and security.

Because flying directly out of Syria was complicated and uncertain, they chose to leave by sea. It is 96 miles from Homs to Tartus on the Mediterranean shore. There, they and several other Christian refugees fleeing Homs managed to hire a small fishing boat for escape. It was their first, but not their last, episode of vulnerability and victimization. The boat's owner/operator was somewhat Muslim and not particularly sympathetic toward Christians. His primary devotion, however, was to money rather than any particular deity. He and two deckhands operated the 36-foot Mediterranean fishing boat.

His first act of chicanery with the Bednars was to double the price he initially agreed to. He knew, as did the Bednars, that they needed to leave Syria immediately, and they were ready to pay whatever cost necessary at that moment.

As the small, old boat made its slow journey from Tartus to Cyprus, heavy seas challenged the frail craft and its largely inexperienced crew. At no time during the brief sea trip was the vessel in immediate danger of foundering. However, they had just over 231 miles of open sea to contend with in a vessel that could barely maintain 12 knots per hour, making the trip approximately 21 hours long.

Given the shoddy crew on hand and the second-rate condition of the small craft, safety was not assured. The danger seemed very real to the passengers, and even occasionally to the crew.

The next act of double-cross by the Muslim boat gang was robbery at sea, once their victims were aboard and trapped. Everyone aboard, both passengers and crew, emanated an aura of foreboding. It seemed as if the potential victims sensed imminent danger, and the potential perpetrators knew there was some nasty business ahead.

Mr. Bednar, being a money manager, not only understood the advantages of using traveler's checks, he was able to arrange for the deposit and payment of money ahead of schedule at various planned stops along their route. Despite these precautions, they were indeed robbed of whatever they had with them on the boat.

The captain and crew beat and abused their victims. They engaged in amateur, unsuccessful attempts at torture to force the Bednars to reveal the location of and access to more money. In botched attempts to inflict enough sustained suffering, both of Miriam's parents sustained painful hand and finger injuries. Adin suffered a broken thumb, and Ali had a sprained wrist and a seriously bruised foot from being stomped.

Although rape was threatened as a tactic, none of the pirates were willing to risk having to answer for that crime, as punishments in the area could be quite severe.

The Bednars survived, dumped on the Cyprus shore, beaten, robbed, and dismayed. However, because Mr. Bednar was an astute and accurate planner, they were not as destitute and defeated as most other Syrian refugees in flight.

Cypriot customs officials had a long history of not being overly concerned with who was leaving Cyprus, so long as the well-established tradition of patronage was observed. $150 US cash got the Bednars through and out of Larnaca International Airport on a flight to Hungary without delay.

Mr. Bednar had established, through several well-traveled and well-trusted contacts, that undocumented entry into Hungary was not unheard of, but it would take significantly more than $150. Therefore, when asked by a Hungarian customs inspector for his visa, Miriam's father replied, "Ah, well, yes...I have this..." and handed over another kind of Visa—a VISA traveler's check in the amount of $1,500 US, made out to cash. This sufficed for entry.

Having fled Syria and Cyprus, the Bednar family eventually made their way to the European mainland, where they fell into the clutches of a group of opportunist con artists in Hungary. They were a gypsy clan, a family born of years of experience wandering Europe and engaging in a variety of felonious larceny to get by. This particular band of opportunists was focused on taking advantage of whatever new wave of refugees stumbled across their path. Most recently, these were the refugees fleeing the latest unrest in the Middle East. The gang of Hungarian gypsies posed as sympathetic Christians to the Bednars, offering safe haven and assistance in flight. Instead, they kidnapped their victims and inflicted misery and suffering.

These gypsies used the Catholic Church in Hungary as a phony front for their criminal activities. They also took advantage of the opportunity the local parish provided in securing new victims. The local church had undertaken the mission of providing assistance to the latest influx of refugees fleeing across Europe. The church provided aid, particularly but not exclusively, to Christian Middle Eastern refugees like the Bednars. Unknown, but not unsuspected by the church and Hungarian authorities, Europe was on the verge of the largest and most severe refugee crisis since World War II.

Through the church, the gypsy felons had volunteered their home and "assistance" to refugees in flight. Listed as concerned and caring "Catholic volunteers," the gypsy clan received the distraught Bednars into their home. The vagabonds were actually squatters in an abandoned late 19th-century countryside limestone hovel they had somewhat restored. The first night of the Bednars' stay was a completely phony, staged event, designed only to instill a false sense of security and hope for the refugees.

The next few nights and days, however, revealed the criminals' real intent. The intent was the imposition of degradation, suffering, and ultimately, larceny. On the next day, the Bednars were given a meager and cold breakfast, as well as a meager and cold welcome. Lunch brought some warming, both in the food and reception. This deception was intended to confuse and again inspire false hope. And it worked.

During this lunch, the hosts discussed the refugees' resources. Not for the advantage of the hosts, they readily assured the Bednars, but more as a means of "pooling resources" to better provide for all. Adin Bednar agreed that this was reasonable, and agreed to share some of the family's meager purse. This was exactly what the conspirators hoped for; the disclosure that there was indeed some money to be had. This led to several days of torture and humiliation for the refugee family. The gypsy gang proceeded to beat and rob their victims.

* * *

Each of the Bednars endured individual and collective torture and beatings. The tormentors' goal was not only to assert temporary dominance and derive amusement but also to extract information about any hidden assets. Adin was subjected to severe physical and sexual abuse. Tragically, as was routinely inflicted by the captors, the women were also sexually assaulted.

After having subjected the Bednar women to rape, the criminals briefly considered murder but decided against it due to the cumbersome effort required to dispose of bodies. They reasoned it was easier to let them live, potentially to recount their ordeal to disinterested Hungarian authorities. After enduring days of torture and frightful nights, the captors bound and gagged the Bednars, drove them 30 miles deeper into the Hungarian countryside in their 18-year-old family sedan, and abandoned them.

The next day, despite being beaten, bound, raped, and robbed again, the Bednars were alive. They spent the morning trying to find the least painful positions, praying, and gradually coming to terms with their survival. As the day progressed, it became clear that they had to act quickly to ensure they remained alive.

Fourteen-year-old Ali was the first to take action. As Miriam regained consciousness to the sound of Ali's crying, she soothed her brother and beckoned him closer. Despite being bound, Ali managed to wriggle over to Miriam, who noticed that the rope around his wrist was loosely tied. With some effort and Miriam's guidance, Ali freed his hands.

Once free from their bonds, the Bednars walked several miles back to the narrow path leading to a tree-lined side road, retracing part of the route their captors had taken. After walking another two miles, a car with a middle-aged couple and their two children slowed down as it passed them. The couple needed a few moments to process the sight before braking to take a closer look.

As dusk settled over the eastern Hungarian countryside in late March, the light faded, making the family's plight even more visible to the passing couple. The driver, realizing the severity of the situation, pulled over to offer help.

Understandably wary from past betrayals, Adin instructed the women to hide in the roadside brush while he and Ali stood watch.

When the stranger approached and asked if they were alright, a dazed Adin managed to say, "The Police. Send the Police, we will wait for the Police." The driver, now cautious but understanding, offered to drive them to the nearest hospital instead, assuring them that the hospital staff would contact the authorities.

Gratefully, the Bednars accepted the ride. Upon arrival at the hospital, the staff provided the necessary emergency medical care and contacted the police and the International Red Cross on their behalf.

Chapter 10
Escape to Canada

The Bednars, now broke and battered but still clinging to some hope, were able to leverage their status as victimized Christian refugees to access governmental and social assistance in Hungary. Eventually, they secured passage to Canada, arriving as persecuted Syrian Christian Civil War refugees seeking religious and political asylum. With various forms of support, they began working to rebuild their lives.

Their escape from Syria's deadly chaos came at great pain and suffering, yet certain factors worked in their favor. One key advantage was their Christian faith. As active members of a Syrian Christian church community with connections to similar churches in the West, they were aided by American and Canadian citizens who vouched for them and pledged support. At a time when many Syrian refugees were viewed with suspicion, the Bednars had credible Western sponsors willing to facilitate their resettlement.

The family ultimately stayed as guests of a Christian pastor's family in Canada. Navigating the complexities of international refugee and immigration policy, they needed either temporary Canadian citizenship or resettlement elsewhere. Concurrently, the Bednars had filed for refugee status in the United States—a long, arduous process. In due course, Miriam, with the necessary support, found refuge in New York, while her parents and younger siblings remained in Canada.

Chapter 11
Fasil al-Marsi's American Mission

Another Middle Eastern 'visitor,' recently from Syria and by way of Europe, had made his way to the U.S. through a circuitous route. The purpose of his stay in America, however, was violent revenge. This mission of revenge would soon involve James and other 'Vessels' across the United States.

Fasil al-Marsi was one of the cave dwellers in the hollows of Hell; he was a Jihadi bomb-maker. Al-Marsi bore scars that testified to his dedication to The Cause, including the loss of three fingers on his left hand. Such injuries were not uncommon in the dangerous practice of al-Malaki's Holy Trade.

His commitment to The Cause fluctuated between unwavering and casually indifferent, for al-Marsi was a genuine psychopath. From as early as 7 or 8 years old, he mostly remembered violent arguments and fights, including brutal assaults among family, neighbors, and countrymen, over Islam and politics. It was a mixed bag: some Muslims were right, others wrong; the government was either just and fair or oppressive and sacrilegious; his father was right, and his mother's family were demons.

He found cruel amusement in belittling and attacking young girls, a behavior largely ignored in his upbringing. He was also fascinated by torturing and killing cats and small animals. By the age of 13, Fasil had embraced the belief that might makes right, and that those capable of destroying anyone in their path were the victors.

He spent most of his adolescence and early adulthood devoted to creating instruments of mass death and destruction. Starting with simple explosives, he progressed to shrapnel and nail bombs, and eventually to crude chemical weapons.

Al-Marsi first found allies in his anarchistic tendencies in his native Saudi Arabia. There, he connected with fledgling al-Qaeda members and contemporaries of Osama bin Laden. Osama, the wealthy son of an extremely wealthy father favored by the Saudi Royal Family, and his group of Islamist terrorists practiced their early 'exercises' in various countries, including Syria, Pakistan, Afghanistan, and Sudan. Al-Marsi frequently joined these expeditions.

Eventually, bin Laden caused enough trouble for his family and political pressure on the Saudi Royal Family that he was compelled to join the Islamic Holy War against the Soviet Union in Afghanistan. Al-Marsi, too, found it advisable to leave home, joining his comrades in Afghanistan.

The Saudi Royal Family, while tolerating a fair amount of political dissent as long as it did not trouble the monarchy, found it difficult to banish Muslim clerics and their followers as long as they professed adherence to the faith. However, when one's companions scatter and one continues to be viewed as a problem, life in Saudi Arabia can become unbearable. Thus, when those with influence suggest it is time to leave, it is wise not to delay. This is how al-Marsi came to join bin Laden in Afghanistan.

After the defeat of the Soviets by al-Qaeda and the newly established religious police, the Taliban, bin Laden and his zealots briefly enjoyed a Jihadi paradise. This period gave rise to terror projects like the 9/11 attacks in the U.S., the 7/7 bombings in Great Britain, and subsequent railroad attacks in Spain.

The profound hatred fueling such atrocities often stems from a pathologic obsession seen in figures like Hitler and the Nazis, Charles Manson, and the Taliban. Firmly entrenched resentment is molded into a destructive force. Crippled by this poisonous obsession, otherwise talented and energetic individuals stew for years in simmering hatred, which occasionally boils over in violent outbursts.

Violence is, of course, a key component of this destructive force. Not only as the obvious end product of terrorist activity but also at the core of a terrorist's existence. They grow up in environments where force rules, without positive role models or heroes to emulate. Naturally, a disturbed childhood is common among these individuals, and those who have been hurt often hurt others. Violence is a social infection: those infected by it spread it to those around them. In New York City on November 11th, such destruction was on display once again.

Chapter 12
The Deep Roots of Sectarian Conflict

The fuel for such hatred, centuries of deep-seated, seething resentment and persecution on each side against the other, remains potent. "You have done us wrong, and there shall be no peace!" echoes as the ancient war cry. Stories are passed from one generation to the next about the grave injustices inflicted by 'the enemy'—the opposing group—upon the innocent and peace-loving members of the present family group. These legends are loaded with dramatic flair and are often anti-Semitic, though not exclusively. The tales that are, however, are marked by dark and violent tones.

This pervasive feuding is not limited to Arabs and Jews. In the recounting of fundamentalist Islamic legends, tales of oppression and injustice are told, illustrating the struggles of one Muslim group to survive the tyranny of another, typically describing Sunni versus Shia infighting.

A common theme among all combatants is the fervent belief that their side is executing God's will. Each group, whether it be Shiite versus Sunni, Arab versus Jew, or al-Qaeda/ISIS versus everyone, believes that God is on their side, or that they are on God's side, while the others are not. Osama bin Laden and his al-Qaeda followers believed they were doing "God's will" by crashing passenger airliners into office buildings, proclaiming, "God loves us but hates you, and wants us to kill you."

A centuries-old rivalry, fueled by years of violence and injustice between Sunni and Shia Arabs, has once again erupted into open warfare. The latest conditions in the Middle East have brought this age-old conflict front and center. This resurgence, as always, has been facilitated by war, with warring Arab factions seizing weapons, money, land, and hearts and minds.

The Soviet invasion and attempted occupation of Afghanistan, culminating in their defeat, destabilized the region—hardly a nation—enabling the rise of the Taliban and al-Qaeda. This situation was ironically exacerbated by the armed rivalry between the Soviet Union and the United States and its allies, with the U.S. inadvertently helping to fund and arm Osama bin Laden, al-Qaeda, and Taliban fighters.

Mass destabilization in the aftermath of the U.S. invasion and occupation of Iraq, coupled with widespread infighting among warring Muslim sects there, set the stage for a devastating insurgency. One of the most disheartening aspects of this conflict was that U.S. forces frequently discovered that the combatants they captured were well-armed with U.S. weapons, which the insurgents had either taken from retreating Iraqi forces or procured from other sources.

Chapter 13
The Global Footprint of Al-Qaeda

Muhammad and his 'friends' were followers of an offshoot group of a shadow al-Qaeda band of terrorists—the al-Nusra Front, which itself derived from the group al-Qaeda in Iraq (AQI). AQI is a well-known 'shadow' or 'follower' group of the band of terrorists in the Afghan-Pakistan region, originally operated by Osama bin Laden and his group: the maniacs responsible for 9/11.

This labyrinth of 'shadows' and 'followers' is typical of the shifting alliances and loyalties that proliferate in the radicalized Arab world. It was this shadowy and loosely affiliated terrorist network that eventually recruited James Waters, Scott Warren, and the other 'Vessels.'

Following the 9/11 attacks in the U.S., and subsequent attacks in London and Madrid, al-Qaeda was forced to flee and splinter in the Tora Bora region of the Afghan-Pakistan border. We later learned that Osama bin Laden himself was secretly moved to Pakistan for safekeeping after a series of epic failures in U.S. intelligence, military, and diplomatic decisions.

In December 2001, U.S.-led ground forces pursued bin Laden and his followers into the high hills of the mountain region near the Pakistan border. After a persistent military campaign, the terrorist leader was cornered.

Operational intelligence at Tora Bora could not accurately estimate the number of enemy combatants, with figures ranging from 400 to 4,000. Nor could their determination to fight be predicted. A senior intelligence official informed military officers, "They may fight to the death, or perhaps, flee." This uncertainty led to dramatic indecision, divisiveness, and horrendously poor choices.

Then, local Afghan mountain tribesmen, who had been assisting U.S. forces and appeared genuinely sympathetic, engaged in high-stakes subterfuge. It was later determined that these tribesmen were indeed sympathetic to the cause of eliminating bin Laden and his al-Qaeda loyalists. However, the support arrangement unexpectedly flipped, with some suggestions of Pakistani involvement in aiding bin Laden.

The Afghan tribal leaders began to hint to their U.S. 'bosses' that a trap was being set for the Westerners. They advised that the only way to avoid the trap and a diabolical ambush was to let the Afghans lead the operation and conduct the pursuit and capture of bin Laden, with the U.S. playing a substantial but background support role.

The U.S. administration at the time, tough-talking but increasingly cautious in Afghanistan and having diverted their attention to Iraq (for reasons still unclear), enthusiastically endorsed the new plan.

The rest is now history: bin Laden escaped into Pakistan, finding refuge just a few miles from a Pakistani military/intelligence facility, until he was finally caught years later by U.S. Navy SEAL Team 6. According to a Pakistani official, the United States had direct evidence that Inter-Services Intelligence (ISI) chief, Lt. Gen. Ahmad Shuja Pasha, knew of bin Laden's presence in Abbottabad, Pakistan.

Chapter 14
Al-Nusra's March to the West

After the eventual dispersal of al-Qaeda at Tora Bora, al-Marsi joined Jihadi 'Warriors' to participate in the conflict in Iraq. Contrary to the rosy picture painted by the George W. Bush Administration, post-U.S. invasion Iraq was far from a stable, free, and democratic nation. Despite Bush displaying 'Mission Accomplished' banners, Iraq was the apocalyptic mess many had predicted. Into the resulting power vacuum surged Sunni, Shia, al-Qaeda, Iranian, and Syrian warriors, with Fasil al-Marsi eventually among them.

The success of the Iraqi insurgency for the al-Nusra Front 'Warriors' fluctuated—there were good times and others not so much. In the period leading up to the U.S. 'Troop Surge', times were 'good'— Jihadist insurgents enjoyed causing mayhem and massacring various opponents. However, during the U.S. 'Troop Surge', the situation changed dramatically, and al-Marsi and his comrades were very nearly killed or captured.

Eventually, Allah seemed to shine upon them, allowing them to escape to enclaves in the north and west of Iraq near the Syrian border, where various insurgent groups gathered to regroup and wait out the latest U.S./Allied and Iraqi offensive. It was here, at the Syrian border with Iraq, that the al-Nusra cell that eventually made its way to New York coalesced and became combat partners.

Some very poignant circumstances came into play at this time. Although alive and fairly intact, al-Nusra and other combatants in Iraq were scattered and in retreat from battle. As their fortunes would have it, while conditions in Iraq for Jihadi warriors seemed to stabilize in favor of their enemies, the chaos in neighboring Syria continued to deteriorate stability there.

Interested parties in Russia, notably the Russian regime, watched the Syrian debacle with great interest. Bashar al-Assad was always a staunch ally and customer of the Russian regime. Vladimir Putin and his marauding gang of thieves, needing some diversion from escalating scrutiny of Russian affairs, found that instability in Syria meant not only diversion but also greater reliance upon Russian support for a Syrian regime facing increasing isolation from other world players. Putin and the gang were not above engaging in world-class treachery to capitalize on an unfolding international or intranational crisis.

These miscreants had no hesitation in immersing themselves in the instability of the area. Putin and his cronies had amassed unfathomable wealth from Russian coffers, which they spent freely through a variety of networks of nefarious troublemakers. Word reached the holed-up combatant groups in the Syrian-Iraq border regions that material and financial support was available to any 'Warriors' willing to extend their operations into the Syrian Civil War. The al-Nusra Group enthusiastically joined the fight and began to reap the rewards for their participation.

They were supported in this effort morally and psychologically by other Jihadist madmen, and financially and physically by governments and organizations committed to the proliferation of mayhem in the arena. At one point, al-Marsi's way through life was

57

paid for by those dedicated to Bashar's removal from power. Quite ironically, his way these days was sponsored by those secretly backing the Syrian Bashar al-Assad regime.

Born on September 11, 1965, Bashar Hafez al-Assad, the second son of the late Syrian President Hafez al-Assad and his wife, Anisa, rose to power through the Syrian military and the minority Alawite political party in 1970. Bashar was content to let his father and brother handle political matters in Syria, pursuing a medical career until the death of his brother Bassel in a car accident in 1994 led to his withdrawal from medical studies in England. Groomed by his father Hafez for leadership, Bashar ascended to the Syrian presidency upon his father's death in June 2000, first appointed and later 'elected' president in an uncontested vote, winning a stunning 95% majority.

Like his father, Bashar ruled with tight control and monitoring of any political opposition. Most analysts contend that Bashar continued his father's foreign policy, providing direct support to militant groups such as Hamas, Hezbollah, and Islamic Jihad, though Syria officially denied this and Bashar was hardly enthusiastic about their cause.

In recent days, opposition, largely from al-Marsi's employers, were on the verge of completely overrunning Syria. Among the list of 'The Hated' by the bomb-makers' masters were not only the current combatants in Syria but also Israel and its steadfast ally America, including all of America and everyone in it.

After a while, combat conditions in Syria, as in Iraq, seemed to have reached and passed their peak of frenzy. By now, Muhammad, al-

Malachi, Ahmed, Mehmet, and their al-Nusra allied group of combatants were mired down once again. Although faithful and enthusiastic to 'The Cause', they'd grown somewhat weary of years of battlefield cat-and-mouse. When their 'managers' asked if they would be interested in something more international in scope and sophisticated work to further 'The War', their response and subsequent participation culminated in their activity in the New York City Transit System. It was this activity that brought al-Marsi's bombs to New York City, just a few feet away from Miriam Bednar. As she sat across from a suicide bomber, millions of refugees had fled Syria, nearly a hundred thousand were stranded at camps at the Turkish border. It seemed that no matter how far she fled or what she endured along the way, she could not escape the insane violence of Syrian Jihad.

Chapter 15
The Indoctrination of James Waters

For James Waters, the journey from Brooklyn to London and then points east was a sojourn not just physically, but spiritually as well. After participating in perhaps a dozen all-night Islamic marathons in Brooklyn, James became convinced by Muhammed and others that further exploration and development of his spiritual quest was necessary. Though somewhat distorted, this was an ideal nonetheless.

In London, James Waters met several Western converts to radically fundamental Muslim extremism. Under Muhammed's frequent instigation, these peers shared feelings of displacement and disillusionment with life. Through these discussions, each grew more convinced that they were finally part of something truly meaningful.

Hours at the mosque were followed by intense lectures and discussions about the necessity and principles of Muslim extremism and radical action. Sleep deprivation became the norm, and nutrition was often minimal. In such a condition, disorientation and confusion were constant, consistently supplanted by hours-long instruction in radical Muslim fanaticism. It was under this mysterious spell that James, disheartened and seeking, strayed deep into the clutches of Muhammed, Mehmet, and other Muslim extremists.

U.S. Department of Defense efforts to contain Jihadi terror groups operating in the Middle East yielded mixed, mostly ineffective results. While the occasional dramatic airstrike did bring death and destruction to opponents, it did little to substantially or long-term interrupt terrorist activities. Although substantial gains were made in

Iraq, Jihadists enjoyed significant success in Syria. This failure to disrupt operations on the ground resulted in Jihadi terrorist recruitment, training, and operational success, providing opportunities for people like Muhammed and his group to recruit and train individuals like James.

The al-Nusra Front, distinct from ISIS (the Islamic State in Iraq and Syria), consisted of Islamist extremists, treated as such by both friends and foes. While ISIS made dramatic gains in territory, power, and infamous prestige, their Arab brethren felt compelled to consider their own interests. The Arabian princes reacted with their centuries-old philosophy: how can we benefit from this disturbing chain of events?

In their customary manner, they decided to hedge their bets. They quietly funneled vast amounts of cash into the coffers of these nefarious interlopers while publicly expressing righteous indignation. The al-Nusra Front benefited from this cash flow. Simultaneously, the oil-rich royalty physically and financially supported Western military opposition against the Jihadi insurgents, thereby sponsoring both sides of the conflict. Thus, they could claim support for whomever held the upper hand in the turmoil. This was the same behavior that forced New York City Mayor Rudolph Giuliani to return a 'generous donation' from the Saudi Royal Family following the 9/11 attacks in 2001.

By the time of the 11/11 attacks, certain members of the U.S. Congress had proposed legislation to compel the release of 28 redacted pages from the 9/11 Commission Report. These 'classified' pages reportedly contained information regarding the Saudi Royal Family's knowledge of, and/or possible complicity in, that monstrous event. The Saudis posed vehement and enthusiastic opposition to the American legislation, causing the Congressional effort to stall.

Chapter 16
Preparing for the 11/11 Mission

Following repeated emphatic lectures and spirited discussions about Islam as the One True Way of Peace and Fulfillment in such a disturbed and unjust world, the talk, when Muhammad thought it was time, turned to Jihad. Reinforcement and rationalization of that profound feeling of estrangement from the world and its ways, followed by an ego-building sense of special purpose, led James Waters and the other fledgling 'Vessels' to the logical conclusion that their special purpose was, in fact, a calling to Jihad.

Muhammad was the overall leader of the monstrous plot for the 11/11 attack on New York City. He was not only the Mission Commander but also the Spiritual Director. Having preached at madrassas in Afghanistan and Pakistan, he had earned the right to bear the rank of Imam in the group.

"My friends," he would address his recruits, "my Western brothers. Allah has led you to us for a special purpose. You yourselves have felt a constant, nagging yearning for something else, something of tremendous importance in your lives. This is your call to Jihad. This is your summons from Almighty Allah, to break free from the shackles of some meaningless existence, and join us in bringing His justice to the dreadful, greedy, capitalist, imperialist masters of the evil West. You know you have been called by God to bring about dramatic change."

Further development of this particular squad of 'Martyrs' consisted of constant indoctrination and support of these feelings of uniqueness and yearning for True Justice.

The reality of the situation, though, could be reduced to a more basic premise. The Jihadists have been described by various security officials as essentially a global gang, preying upon angry, isolated youth and providing an identity for self-seeking men and women in search of a mission in life. Terrorist suicide attacks, cloaked as 'Jihadist Martyrdom,' provided such a mission.

In an interview published in an online magazine, a senior ISIS operative identified as Boubaker al-Hakim, known as the godfather of French Jihadists, advised his followers to abandon the symbolism of attacking smaller, symbolic targets such as the attack on the Jewish Museum in Brussels: "My advice is to stop looking for specific targets. Hit everyone and everything." This credo found enthusiastic adherence from the likes of Muhammad and his al-Nusra group bound for New York.

At the core of any act of suicide is a fundamental need for escape, flight. Fleeing the scene of one's life justifies any irrational act. Whether he could accept it or not, James was, as were the other 'Vessels' on some level, in complete denial and protest of the circumstances of his being. Deemed for centuries as the ultimate act of selfishness and defiance, suicide is the most extreme definition of protest of one's existence.

At a place very deep in the core of James' persona was this sense of abandonment by his father, and subsequent domination by his mother. That the paternal abandonment had not much at all to do with James personally, or that the maternal domination was frequently welcomed and occasionally even invited, did little to squelch the deeply-rooted resentment and defiance James experienced. The absence of a 'Hero,' of an influential role model, exacerbated his feelings of resentment and abandonment. Ultimately, he would take out that feeling of abandonment and betrayal on everyone he could reach.

The next phase of 'fulfillment' for 'The Vessels' consisted of Commando Training in Pakistan. James informed family and friends at the time that he was taking some time off from school for sightseeing and exploration in Europe. James made a purposefully weak offer for his girlfriend Joann to join him, saying all the while that plans were in place and arrangements already made.

He was also decidedly vague with his mother about any particular details. This, in turn, further fueled Carol's recent and persistently increasing sense of estrangement from James. Carol questioned him about specific details of his European trip – When and where would he be, she asked? And with whom, exactly? "Mom, please..." James would moan in exaggerated and aggrieved protest, "You're treating me like a child. I'm a grown man. I'll be in touch. All will be well, I promise."

A mother's love and maternal intuition know no bounds. Her instinctual reaction amplified her feelings of alarm at the recent dramatic changes in his persona.

Throughout his young life, Carol had been James' mentor. She had always provided a person and place in whom James found solace. Even during his turbulent and defiant teens, she'd somehow been able to let 'her boy' go through whatever was going on at the moment, and then return to Earth. She also, quite naturally, instilled in her son a sense of justice. Nothing though, to the extremes it was now running. Lately, she felt him slipping away, and it was extremely disturbing.

In Pakistan, physical, spiritual, and emotional conditioning were the order of the day for several weeks. This included martial arts discipline, practice, and combat. There followed intensive weapons training, both with small arms and automatic rifles. Finally, the handling and deployment of explosives. All the while, the ranting of jihad and self-sacrifice for the Greater Good continued, over and over.

And so it was, this day too. In James's mind, jihad and justice, over and over. Indoctrination, as intended, at work. James knew that Union Square Station was also a target; he'd assumed that the mission there would take place either after or during his own mission.

Recent spikes in coded telecommunications among suspect senders and recipients had led the National Security Agency and the Department of Homeland Security to alert the 'usual' priority targets of 'increased chatter' on monitored networks. The most notorious occasion of such 'chatter' was 9/11/01. Unfortunately, at the time, that increase was observed, noted, and fretted about at the highest levels of government. Little else was done in the way of an actual response to the alarm.

In the time since, there came the creation of more elaborate and intricate monitoring of, and responding to, such 'spikes.' Thus, from the massive networks of telecommunications 'observation' apparatus of the National Security Agency to the many tentacles of response of the Department of Homeland Security, the NYPD was notified and on 'very-high alert.'

The NYPD, in turn, deciphered and prioritized the chatter in their own particular mode; translated to the NYPD's needs, and then sent out along appropriate channels and the chain of command as needed. Among the various 'customers' of NSA/DHS/NYPD intel were the FDNY and NYC Transit PD. As the horror of the 11/11 attacks neared, the New York City Police Department, and its various counter-terror partner agencies and information customers, were alerted that something, no particular and specific information, but something, was in the works.

Chapter 17
A Morning of Uncertainty in NYC Transit

While the Rail Transit Operations served as the 'guts' of the system, the brains were located at MTA Headquarters. The RTO Trainmaster had the authority to halt all subway traffic into and out of Manhattan, but such a decision required immediate justification via the intercom system to the MTA Subway Department at Transit Headquarters.

The RTO Supervisor was informed by the Transit Police Liaison that a suspected 'attacker' had been shot and killed at Union Square, and that the NYPD had ordered the complete evacuation of the station. Additionally, the Bomb Squad was called in due to a 'suspicious situation'. Initially, his first instinct was to 'shut it all down.'

However, after taking a deep breath, he opted to 'split the difference': he ordered the shutdown of all train traffic into Manhattan from south of 14th Street to just north of 42nd Street. This directive required all trains at or approaching stations within the affected area to discharge all passengers at the first available station, check each car to ensure it was empty, and then proceed 'light' to the next station or designated 'lay-up' area. This massive operation involved over 100 trains, each carrying approximately 1000 passengers.

This railroad decision, like all decisions, had its pros and cons. It allowed the majority of Manhattan-bound commuters from Brooklyn, Long Island, and the Rockaways in Queens to travel into lower Manhattan, which is the destination for most inter-borough commuters during the morning rush hour. While this led to substantial delays as things began to back up, it enabled a significant portion of passengers to reach downtown Manhattan. However, the decision had drawbacks; many commuters from the Bronx, uptown Manhattan, and the city's northern and western suburbs were unable to reach downtown by subway. Consequently, a huge fleet of shuttle buses had to be organized and dispatched to transport these commuters below 14th Street.

As soon as the order was issued, the Subway Department VP was on the horn to the Control Center, expressing his concerns: "Yeah, this Union Square thing... I think we may have to shut it all down," he remarked at the moment. He then called the mayor. Meanwhile, the uptown local that James was on received the instructions as it pulled into his destination—Grand Central Station.

Chapter 18
Moment of Truth

It was here. This was it—the *NOW*. James wasn't entirely certain he believed in the eternal paradise, one with Allah and the Prophet, as Muhammad and the others had constantly preached and ranted. However, he was certain that he believed in the pervasive injustice and greed of the world, a reality that tortured him. Whether it was his conscience or his soul troubling him, he didn't care. All he knew was that he couldn't tolerate the world as it was, and he could, in fact, lash out at it. And now, it was here; it was on, and he was in the moment, aware, focused, and ready.

Muhammad's instructions were explicit, constant, and consistent: "Pray to the One True God, Allah, for His grace and might to do what comes next. When the train pulls into Grand Central, be at the door. Be first. When the doors open, take one quick step onto the platform and stop. Press the button on the detonator. Paradise." Everyone within 20 to 30 feet, either on the train or on the platform, would be killed or critically maimed. Those up to 40 feet away would be seriously injured. Mayhem and angst; well-deserved and well-delivered.

And it was here and now. James positioned himself first at the nearest door as the train rolled to a quick stop. He was vaguely aware of the conductor's voice announcing that this was the last stop on this train—James nearly smiled at the irony. The announcement that "This train is now out of service..." alerted him that this was not usual, that something was happening. James felt even more emboldened that things were unfolding and that he was a part of it. Paradise or not, he had a job to do, and he was about to do it.

The train stopped. The doors opened. He was moving forward. He felt as if he was floating... The button was in his hand. He was momentarily distracted by a woman arguing with a police officer about 15 feet to his right. Startled, his mind began playing tricks on him because for a split second, he could swear the woman was his mother.

Chapter 19
The Clues Before a Crisis

Carol Waters had been worried about her son, James, for weeks leading up to the encounter at Grand Central. The last of James' family and friends to hear from him was his girlfriend, Joann. Their relationship had cooled recently, transitioning from intense and passionate to increasingly distant as James withdrew into himself and his concerns. In fact, he had begun to feel guilty and ashamed for what he perceived as 'selfish' indulgence with Joann amid all the tragic injustice around him.

After avoiding Joann for nearly two weeks, he received a voicemail from her saying his mom had called. When he last spoke to Joann, his message carried a mysterious tone, tinged, she thought, with a hint of finality. "So, yeah... I'm going in... and that's it." Lately, James had withdrawn from and eventually abandoned their once intense and enmeshed relationship. Before his encounter with the Jihadi, James had plunged into a dramatically intoxicating involvement with Joann. Typical of James' complexity, he soon developed strong feelings of regret and shame for his unrestrained self-indulgence, which led to his cryptic message on Joann's voicemail.

Because James had mentioned work, Joann initially thought that's what he meant: He was going into work, and 'that would be it.' Quitting, perhaps? The more she thought about it, and after listening to the message again, something intuitive—his hesitation and the subtle emphasis on those final words—caused her to wonder.

So when Carol Waters called again, anxious for any clue, Joann felt compelled to repeat the message. She decided to let Carol interpret it as she might. Immediately, Joann regretted her decision. Carol latched onto the phrase immediately and repeated it, "That's it. What's that supposed to mean? How did he sound?"

Joann was caught between not wanting to alarm Carol and not withholding any potentially relevant information. She chose her words carefully. "He sounded," she began, "sort of distant, you know, not quite himself," was the most diplomatic way she could explain. "Well, he must be going into work then," Carol replied, seeking some sort of confirmation from Joann. "Well, I guess..." Joann responded, letting it rest.

"Joann, I'm sorry to bother you so... I'm worried. I think perhaps I'll go up to his job and see if he's there, or if they know anything." With that, Carol hung up and headed to Grand Central Station. It was the train stop closest to where James worked, and the route he had previously described to her.

James had grown up the second of two children, his mother's only son. He had clung close to his mother throughout his childhood, and she to him. James' father was a heavy drinker and smoker. Although often a good earner and provider, James Sr. could be quite immature and irresponsible, something of an absentee father and husband.

Growing up, whenever James' dad arrived home drunk, his moodiness made the atmosphere unnerving, not only for Carol but also for the children, particularly sensitive young James. When James Sr., drunk and rowdy, raised his voice or his hands, Carol became quiet and compliant. James subconsciously learned that hostility and noise could win battles. It was not a trait James often displayed, but it was there.

James' father died of cirrhosis when he was 46; James was just 14 at the time, and Carol was 41. Quite naturally, and quite unconsciously, James quickly developed an innate sense of abandonment and persecution.

The close bond between James and his mother naturally progressed and intensified in the time following his father's death. As James came of age, Carol was his mother, surrogate father, and friend. And she alone was the only person on earth who could give James a moment's pause in his mission that day at Grand Central.

Chapter 20
Countdown to Catastrophe

Having been notified that the D.O.A. terrorist at Union Square was wearing a bulky overcoat over an explosive-laden 'Suicide Vest,' all officers on patrol were alerted to pay 'Special Attention' to any suspects dressed in similar fashion. Given the chilly New York City November morning, officers had their work cut out for them. However, most seasoned police officers know that suspects usually appear 'suspicious,' and non-suspects usually do not. Police surveillance and observation is an art born of instinct and experience.

As soon as James Waters stepped onto the platform, he appeared startled upon seeing an uncooperative and upset woman arguing with an officer. His ill-fitting, bulky overcoat drew immediate 'Special Attention' from the Counter-Terror cops on the platform.

A red laser dot appeared on James's forehead, millimeters above his nose. Officer Rob Jones was less than one second from squeezing the trigger. The only thing that caused a second's hesitation was a pathetic plea that interrupted his focus. Carol Waters, whom he had just met as she refused instructions to leave the platform—mentioning something about her son....

"James! God, please raise your hands!" Carol spotted her son as he stepped from the train, then saw the tiny red dot on his face. At that moment, an explosion occurred.

To those in Grand Central Station, it arrived as a vague, low rumble of distant thunder. To many at 8th Avenue and 42nd Street, six blocks west, it announced their last day on earth. The carnage was tremendous and ungodly.

At the MTA Rail Transit Operations Center, Rail Transit Operations Director Randy Black and those working around him knew something very wrong was happening at the Port Authority Train Station. All electronic and voice communication from there ceased at once as all the computer screens and other electronic monitors for the station suddenly went dark. "Somebody get 42nd and 8th on the horn now!" he bellowed. But there was no communication to be had with any rail operations staff there for some time to come.

The first news that reached 'Operations' came from the Transit PD Network. "Boss, there's been an explosion..." one of the startled operators informed him, her voice trailing off.

Chapter 21
James's Path to Jihad

James had begun to grow out of his intense closeness to Carol as he entered college but quickly became quite attached to his girlfriend, Joann. James was already inclined to maternal, and nearly maternal, care, and this trait carried into his newest significant relationship. Joann and James were a perfect match. James had a profound need for motherly care and attention, while Joann yearned for a man to take care of and nurture into an attentive and compliant partner.

Needing and meeting each other in a variety of ways and on multiple levels, their initial attraction took on a mutually dramatic sense of urgency and intensity. This feeling, for each of them, translated into a mysterious and compelling romantic desire. Although Joann was not a particularly sexually active woman, James was in her bed after their second date—an encounter very much out of character for her, but her yearning for James was powerful and unyielding.

For a college freshman—young, attractive, bright, and single— James wasn't much of a ladies' man. He'd had only two committed romantic relationships in high school and a somewhat limited love life considering his looks and personality. His experience with romantic love consisted of two intense but brief relationships and a few hit-and-miss encounters.

When James's intense need for female attention and energy collided with Joann's internal desire to give herself completely to a man who craved her, the result was spectacular. Each was certain at that moment of consummation that this was it.

As James continued to mature, he developed a heightened sensitivity to unfairness and injustice, partly disturbed by this uncomfortable sense, mostly subconsciously but increasingly consciously. This sense intensified as he studied social justice and human services issues at NYU.

As James became more passionate about and attentive to his studies, and his observations and conclusions of a largely unjust world, he became more distant and introverted. Almost imperceptibly, James identified with those who felt persecuted by society. He was prime material for the likes of Muhammad and his gang when they crossed paths.

To most contemporary Westerners, the 9/11/01 attacks against the U.S. are considered the touchstone of modern terrorism. In James's view, Osama bin Laden could righteously justify al-Qaeda's jihad against the U.S. and the West, at least in their own minds, and therefore the 9/11 attacks. Although James could comprehend such radical vengeance, he dared not express such musings aloud. This was one of James's deep and unsettling secrets. And then he met Muhammad.

Over time, Muhammad and his cohorts had become rather sensitive to and responsive to whichever prospects they encountered. A tried and proven successful gauge of possible acceptance of their own radical notions was to throw them out for reaction. Naturally, one did not initiate such a discussion by saying, "Osama bin Laden and al-Qaeda were justified…" But, as conversation about persecution and marginalization unfolded, a segue into, and then an ideological advance from there, about extremist reaction, became a reliable tool to gauge response.

Eight or nine times out of ten, the reaction was quite predictable and expected. Every now and again, though, listeners did not revolt or flee. They listened. James was one of those who listened. And he listened to these ideas more than once. After the third time he nodded quietly as Muhammad spoke, Muhammad knew they had to meet and speak some more.

Another tried and true tactic for Muhammad and friends was the lore of the 'Chechen Rebellion.' According to Vladimir Putin and his Russian cronies, the Muslims of Chechnya were responsible for everything from the bombing of apartment buildings in Russian cities in 1999 to the downing of civilian airliners.

According to the jihadi version, peaceful Muslims were just standing around Chechnya, minding their own business when the Russians invaded. The truth likely lies somewhere in the middle: Chechen Muslims had nothing to do with blown-up apartment buildings or civilian airliners, but they were hardly "just minding their own business" either. Chechen Muslims were stirring up trouble, and Putin and his band of Russian thieves needed a distraction from their own treachery.

Thus, Muhammad and other jihadis told the tale of how Putin and his gang of criminal conspirators, about to be publicly exposed for the theft of billions from the Russian economy, suddenly decided that Russia needed to invade Chechnya and eradicate the "Muslim uprising." The fact that there was indeed a measure of truth to the story was a strong selling point for the jihadi. Those inclined to and alert for yet another tale of greed and injustice proved to be enthusiastic students. After a while, James was among them.

Chapter 22
A Suburban Boy's
Journey to Jihad

Tommy Woods was 24 years old, stood 5'10", and weighed a moderate 193 lbs. He had blonde hair, green eyes, and was white. He was a handsome young man in a quiet, unassuming way. Tommy was fiercely loyal to his conviction that the world, the people in it, and the overall way of things were severely unjust and needed to be rocked from their decadent and indifferent axis. Tommy was a jihadist's dream.

Tom had grown up, or at least gotten older, in a suburban Massachusetts town east of Boston. He was the only child of an overprotective, domineering mother and a largely unenthusiastic father. Alternatingly smothered with attention, direction, and affection from his mother, and receiving treatment from his father ranging from casual disregard to a heavy hand and a berating tone, he grew up mostly anxious and confused. Tommy Woods, like most young adolescent boys, sought his father's approval, or at least some patience and understanding. Tom Sr. came up short on all of this.

The overall result for Tommy was a perpetual sense of confusion and frustration. This quite predictably led to a profound air of persecution and malcontent as he developed from a disturbed adolescent into a maladjusted and malicious young man. All of this was near, but not at, the surface of Tommy's persona.

As a defiant teen, Tommy gravitated toward the 'Bad Boys,' soon landing in the kind of juvenile trouble that bad boys often find themselves in. This fueled the simmering fire between Tom and his father, and their encounters escalated in tone and tenor.

When Tommy's behavior or attitude failed to meet his father's expectations, trouble ensued. "Why, for God's sake," his father would dramatically moan with a pained expression, "don't you just do what your mother and I ask? What the hell is wrong with you anyway?" Thus, Tommy ingrained that he was a profound disappointment to his parents, and that there was something inexplicably 'wrong' with him.

By the time he was 16, he had become a maladjusted and emphatically oppositional drifter. Being 16 and defiant, whenever his dad launched into the "What the hell is wrong with you..." speech, his unspoken reaction was, "I hate your guts, why don't you just leave me the hell alone?"

One day, as Tommy neared 17, the previously unspoken thought came out. An intense, brief shoving and swinging match ensued, and Tommy was out and on his own.

A few short years later, when this maladjusted malcontent fell into the company of Muhammad and his band of thugs, the result was not all that surprising. Tommy was ripe for the tending and promotion of his discontent provided by the gathering marauders.

Tommy then embarked on a dramatic and moving adventure along with James and the others. During this time, they were praised as 'Specially Blessed Warriors' and pronounced 'Spearheads' and 'Vanguards' of an 'Enhanced, Deadly Campaign' against the 'Infidels and Pagan Non-believers of the Eternally Damned West.' This was exactly the profound and dramatic description Tommy yearned for—

he was not as his father told him, bad and wrong. He was 'Special', 'Blessed', 'Vanguard'…

There was some sort of blurred line between Muhammad's al-Nusra compatriots and ISIS, and for that matter, some of the murderers of al-Qaeda. They had spent time conducting missions for each of these jihadist groups. Whether one or the other, they remained, for all intents and purposes, violent Sunni extremists.

Muhammad urged his recruits, the Noble Lone Wolves of our deadly Wolfpack: "This, my friends, is a game-changer! I swear to you, my brothers, we are on the verge of a new and deadly campaign which will pound the Infidels into a state of profound suffering and confusion. At a time and place of our choosing, we make our statement to the infidel West: No longer shall you and the Jews dictate to us where, when, and how we should live. The Infidels say to us that there is no place we can run and hide from them… We say to them – there is no time or place for you to hide! We shall come for you repeatedly and often!"

Muhammad further encouraged and praised his new Western terror recruits, "I promise you, my friends, your place in Paradise with Allah and the Prophet is assured. You are at the absolute sword tip of a new and superior campaign of retribution against all who oppose us!" Muhammad paused for the effect of his words to resonate, then pressed on, "You are, I'm sure, aware of the Mumbai attacks. I declare to you now – that model was just a forerunner of a continuing and escalating war… and because of the mission you now undertake, the West will soon have a first-hand taste of the relentless energy of our jihad!"

It was this urging that led ultimately to Tommy's presence on the 'A' Train that day. When the 'A' Train pulled into the Port Authority Bus Terminal Station at 42nd Street, the Vessel of Supreme Justice assigned to it stepped onto the platform and detonated his 'Special Vest'.

At first, a blinding flash filled the immediate area for 15 yards around the spot where Tommy once stood, his body now shredded and flying through the air. For maximum effect, his pre-planned arrival was timed to coincide with the 42nd Street Station when the Express 'A' Train met there with a Local 'C' Train. Over 30 passengers nearest to the suicide bomber were immediately incinerated. Their burning bodies were tossed about like stuffed dolls in all directions. Scores of other passengers both on trains and on the platform in the vicinity of the explosion were either horribly burned or savagely maimed by the force of the blast. Many victims were some gruesome combination of the two. Nearby, those who weren't incinerated and shattered began to choke to death on the toxic plume that emanated from that blast zone.

The Port Authority operates the nation's largest bus terminal, which also ranks as the busiest in the world. Every day, over 7,200 buses arrive and depart, with roughly 200,000 people passing through. During the weekday morning rush hour, the building hosts over 40,000 individuals. The terminal comprises three upper levels, a main (street) level, and two lower levels. The first lower level houses the subway, while the second features bus arrival and departure gates. The main level includes various facilities such as a bank, a post office, nine food outlets including Starbucks and Au Bon Pain, and five retail shops, including Duane Reade and General Nutrition Center.

In a catastrophic instant, a platform and trains were engulfed in fire and smoke following a massive explosion. The blast, fueled by TATP and magnesium, dispersed blood, bodies, and limbs, creating a horrific scene reminiscent of hell. The magnesium ignited, consuming the surrounding oxygen and releasing hydrogen cyanide, which formed a deadly cloud.

The impact caused an immediate blackout on the platform and railway, plunging the area into darkness. It took several minutes for emergency lights to activate, adding to the chaos and horror. As auxiliary lighting gradually returned, the air was filled with screams and moans from survivors and the injured, amid ongoing fires.

The explosion resulted in immediate fatalities, with many others succumbing to asphyxiation from the toxic gases and lack of oxygen. The situation worsened as the injured were moved within the terminal, spreading the impact of the attack.

Debris and toxic gases were propelled upward to the main level by the force of the blast, causing widespread panic. Many survivors rushed to the exits, while outside, the streets between 8th and 9th Avenues from 42nd to 43rd Streets were overwhelmed by escaping crowds, smoke, and confusion.

Victims displayed varying degrees of injury—from those in cardiac arrest to others suffering severe burns or beginning to experience the effects of cyanide poisoning. Emergency responders, including NYPD officers, FDNY firefighters, medics, transit workers, and courageous civilians, rushed to aid the victims. However, the initial wave of rescuers quickly became overwhelmed and, in some cases, incapacitated by the conditions.

Before long, specialized Haz-Mat equipped Units of the FDNY, NYPD, and the Port Authority Police Department began to identify the presence of highly-toxic gasses in the atmosphere near the detonation point of the terrorist explosion.

One of the most distressing immediate after-effects of the poison bombs was the secondary contamination of rescuers. The first FDNY units to respond at the Port Authority Terminal were the Special Operations Company; Rescue 1, Engine Company 34, and Ladder Company 21. Members of Rescue Company 1, extensively trained and well-drilled, took the necessary extra minutes to don special chemical-protective clothing (CPC) before entering the chaotic scene at the Port Authority Building. Meanwhile, Engine 34 and Ladder 21 crew members, equipped with standard self-contained breathing apparatus (SCBA), quickly entered the building to investigate and rescue victims.

Unfortunately, the hazardous nature of the explosion meant that only emergency personnel with specialized Haz-Mat detection and protection gear could safely conduct rescues, significantly reducing the number of available rescuers. Sending unprotected rescuers into contaminated areas resulted in additional victims among the rescuers themselves.

The SCBA provided sufficient protection for FDNY members to assist and evacuate some victims from the building. However, once outside, these members began showing signs of contamination and required decontamination, evaluation, and treatment for symptoms.

Many initial responders, who carried casualties from the inferno below 42nd Street, soon found themselves gasping for air, with their eyes and noses irritated and streaming from the toxic cyanide cloud. This prevented them from further assisting victims and turned them into casualties needing help. Fortunately, Ladder 21 had responded with its '2nd Piece' (unit), which carried additional CPC. Arriving companies quickly realized the on-scene firefighters were being overwhelmed by the toxic environment, donned the protective gear from Ladder 21, and continued rescue operations.

The NYPD and FDNY soon took command of the terrorist disaster scene, limiting the number of rescuers to prevent further exposure to toxic fallout and the risk of secondary explosions. This precaution made an already perilous situation even more hazardous and complex. Shortly after their arrival, a Fire Department Chief transmitted the Signal 10-80, declaring a mass-casualty and hazardous materials incident, which activated new protocols for managing and responding to the disaster.

The FDNY and FDNY/EMS have detailed protocols for managing mass casualty and hazardous materials incidents, which require a minimum response of specific types and numbers of emergency units. At the highest level of FDNY response—the Specialist I Level—Hazardous Material Unit #1 and Haz-Mat Battalion Chiefs are involved, who possess over 600 hours of professional training and carry advanced instrumentation.

Additionally, FDNY maintains an on-call standby Haz-Mat unit and specially designated Squad Units staffed by Specialist-Level Haz-Mat Technicians. Furthermore, 39 EMS Haz-Tac Ambulances are available for response.

Chapter 23
The FDNY's Battle
Against Time

On this astonishing morning, the New York City Fire Department Operations Center at MetroTech Plaza in Downtown Brooklyn was teetering precariously on the brink of mayhem. Normally assigned units, along with city-wide special units such as Rescue Trucks, Collapse Trucks, Technical Rescue Support Trucks, Squad Companies, and Haz-Mat, Special Operations Support, and Logistics Trucks were being assigned to and then diverted to various locations as the day's harrowing events unfolded. The FDNY Headquarters building on Flatbush Avenue, in the shadow of the Manhattan Bridge, was bustling with activity.

Post-9/11 FD operations had been revamped after the tremendous tragedy that befell the department that day. Three hundred forty-three brave and dedicated New York City firefighters perished, including nearly all top-level command staff. Those left to carry the department into the new century were compelled to ensure that nothing close to that epic loss would be inflicted upon the FDNY again. Therefore, the department command staff had not only the response of field units to consider post-9/11; they also had to decide how to deploy and protect the department's top commanders.

A tragic lesson learned on 9/11 was the response and management of mega-disasters. While no one could have imagined those towers coming down, in hindsight, it was clear that it was at least imprudent for most of the senior command staff of the department to be on-scene and exposed at the site of a colossal disaster. It was an event that was extremely beyond control and was still escalating.

Emergency managers later cited the incident as an episode of improper on-scene management: almost all the department's special units were on the scene. Because of the unprecedented destruction, the members of these units nearly all perished or suffered serious injuries, and all their special equipment and apparatus were destroyed.

John Reardon, the 62-year-old Chief of Department of the FDNY, had more time in the department than 60-year-old Commissioner Dave DeVito. Following his retirement, DeVito was returned to the FDNY as commissioner by the newly-elected mayor. One of the first moves DeVito made was to promote his long-time colleague Reardon to Chief of Department.

Both men had risen through the ranks together as firefighters, company officers, and then company COs, battalion chiefs, division chiefs, and then up into command staff. After DeVito retired, and a new mayor was elected, most City Hall and Fire Department insiders knew it was almost a coin toss between DeVito and Reardon for commissioner. Unfortunately for Reardon, he had a history of being active for a political party other than the new mayor's. Dave DeVito was in. But, he quickly brought his old pal 'up the chain'.

In large enterprises of all types, each organization maintains a set of protocols; policies & procedures. Just as McDonald's and Burger King have very specific directions for how their French fries are to be cooked and packaged, and General Motors has specific instructions on how many employees work each shift and who is in charge, so too does the Fire Department of the City of New York have a set of policies & procedures; protocols for its operations.

Of course, providing life-saving and fire protection services for the world's commercial and cultural capital amidst mass destruction can be somewhat more involved and consequential than producing cars or hamburgers, but FDNY had protocols and P&P to follow as well. Notably, that a certain amount of unpredictability is inherent in terrorist mass destruction, therefore significant flexibility is allowed for. However, FDNY commanders are expected to adhere to pre-designed plans as much as possible.

In a post-9/11 report, FDNY Command looked back on the substantial progress it had made in terrorism and disaster preparedness. At the same time, the report noted, "Leadership looked forward, anticipating the organizational changes necessary for the FDNY to continue executing its role as New York City's lead life-safety agency across a wide spectrum of responses."

"The Department thus had refocused its efforts to better align itself with today's, and tomorrow's challenges in the ever-changing world of counterterrorism (CT) and risk management."

It had been decided then that, for example, Brooklyn's Squad Co. 1, FDNY's model squad company, should not be assigned to the same terrorist attack site as Manhattan's Rescue Co. 1, the city's premier rescue company. There was also improved cooperation between the NYPD and FDNY, as well as Homeland Security, including intelligence and operational logistics.

Both Commissioner Dave DeVito and his personally-selected

Chief of Department John Reardon had superior knowledge and understanding of FDNY protocol compared to most others in the department, though no one person knew everything there was to know. The two men had to work together, along with their command staff, to try and maintain policy as much as possible, in the face of unprecedented horror.

Both commanders understood that current operational policy is that as the department refines and clarifies its role in Homeland Security, the FDNY must constantly re-evaluate its goals.

Commissioner DeVito and Chief of Department Reardon knew that the ungodly task at hand was to manage effective response to the unfolding disasters, and at the same time, adhere as much as possible to department policy & procedure.

"John," Commissioner Dave DeVito addressed his friend and Chief of Department, "we've got a massive array of city-wide special units available..." Reardon nodded in knowing agreement. "We also have," DeVito continued, "attacks at multiple sites across Manhattan that continue to escalate. As much as we understand at the moment, we have no way of knowing how big this thing is going to get. I know you want to be out in the field directing the action. But, the 'big job' is right here."

"What if..." the Commissioner went on, "there's an incident at JFK or LaGuardia? What if there's an explosion at the Atlantic Avenue Terminal?" DeVito was thinking of the expansive Long Island Rail Road Terminal in Brooklyn that connected thousands of LIRR commuters with the New York City Subway System. "What if," the

Commissioner continued, "God forbid, a bomb that was planted here at Headquarters or parked around the corner goes off? We have to be prepared for anything."

At the same moment as the conversation at FDNY HQ, scores of victims who, just minutes earlier, were part of the New York City transit's morning rush, lay dead on the platforms and trains. Dozens more were in varying stages of dying within the Port Authority Terminal and the surrounding city streets. Those who survived long enough were the casualties rescued and treated by New York City's Haz-Mat Response Units.

The Fire Department's 'Haz-Mat Unit 1' is intentionally located outside Manhattan, probably the number one international terror target. However, its quarters are strategically placed within easy reach of Manhattan, near the Queens-Midtown Tunnel. The other Specialist I Units, including Squad Companies, are distributed across the five boroughs.

As a 'working fire' in any New York City neighborhood significantly impacts the demand for FDNY protection for that neighborhood and the rest of the city, so too does the transmission of the Code 10-80. Very quickly, Fire Department units from residential neighborhood firehouses across the outer boroughs were called to respond to the unfolding catastrophe in Manhattan.

The next level of Fire Department response includes 10 Haz-Mat Tech II Units, neighborhood Engine Companies strategically located throughout the city. Engine Company 250 in Brooklyn, typical of such specifically designated Engine Companies, is situated in the relatively quiet residential area of Kensington, bordering the Borough Park community. Although most of the company's time is spent attending to routine medical calls, motor vehicle accidents, kitchen mishaps, and small trash fires, with the occasional multi-alarm inferno, Engine 250's strategic location on Foster Avenue near the Prospect and Gowanus Expressways allows for quick access throughout Brooklyn and into Manhattan. Members of Two-Five-Oh are all trained as Haz-Mat Tech Firefighters and are available for deployment in citywide emergencies. Accordingly, much of the downtime for 250's crew is spent on training, drilling, and special equipment maintenance, preparing for Haz-Mat disasters such as the 11/11 attacks. Just two minutes after leaving their quarters in response to the alarm, Engine 250 was on the Gowanus Expressway, headed to the Port Authority blast via the Brooklyn-Queens Expressway. Similarly, Engine Company 274 in Queens left its neighborhood in Flushing to respond to Midtown Manhattan.

Engine 274 rolled out of quarters down the street from Murray Hill Park and onto Northern Blvd for the ride to the Whitestone Expressway. In just a few minutes, they were on the Grand Central Parkway, then the Brooklyn Queens Expressway, and shortly after, through the Queens-Midtown Tunnel, arriving in Midtown Manhattan.

Available at the next level down of Haz-Mat response are 25 Haz-Mat Tech II Units - Decontamination Engine Companies, and 29 Chemical Protective Clothing Ladder Companies, which can operate in hazardous environments. At the basic level, all fire and EMS personnel are trained in Haz-Mat/WMD operations.

As the scope of carnage, dying, and misery became clear to the arriving rescuers, NYPD, EMS, and FDNY began to escalate their emergency response to the horrific disaster. Upon arrival, the Chief of FDNY Battalion 8 elevated the incident to a 10-80 Code 3.

A 10-80 Code 3 is used for incidents involving five or more victims and requires Haz-Mat resources for possible rescue, mitigation, and decontamination. Numerous different units are assigned under a 10-80 Code 3, placing significant city-wide demand on the department. This includes the initial assignment of a 10-80 Code, with various Special Operations Command Units: the Safety Battalion Chief, Rescue Battalion Chief, three additional Battalion Chiefs, a Field Communications Unit, one additional Haz-Mat Tech Unit, Decon Support Unit, Tactical Support Unit, three Chemical Protective Clothing Units (CPC Unit), and also responding are a Rehab and Care (RAC) Unit, Medical Director, and a Public Information Officer. For a Code 3 Response: an FDNY Command Staff Chief, one additional Division Deputy Chief, Decon Shower Unit, one additional RAC Unit, and Mask Service Unit are involved.

EMS also has a specifically required 10-80 response - one additional Haz-Mat Tactical Ambulance, a Basic Life Support Ambulance, and an additional Advanced Life Support Ambulance. A 10-80 Code 3 requires an EMS Deputy Chief, three additional Haz-Tac Ambulances, three Basic Life Support Ambulances (CPR-Defib.), and three Advanced Life Support (I.V./Paramedic)

Ambulances, significantly impacting New York City Emergency Medical Services.

After the initial assessment of a Mass Casualty Haz-Mat Incident at the Port Authority, a 10-80 Code 4 was transmitted - a mass decontamination response to decontaminate a large number of victims as quickly as possible. A 10-80 Code 4 results in the dispatch of a 10-80 Code 3 plus the Mass Decon Task Force (MDTF). Additional EMS Units are also assigned.

The MDTF includes one Battalion Chief, two Engines, one CPC Tower Ladder, one Haz-Mat Tactical Ambulance, two Special Ops Command-Support Ladder Trucks or Haz-Tech Units to monitor victims to determine the need for additional Technical Decon. The poisonous terrorist explosion and fire at the Port Authority Terminal had its intended effect on the city by involving all available Haz-Mat Decon resources.

NYC Fire Department Special Operations Orders require that for every 250 victims, an additional MDTF be called. At the Port Authority attack, the initial on-scene FDNY mobilization was for 10-80, then 10-80 Code 4, requiring the response of one Mass Decon Task Force, which was soon followed by the order for a second MDTF.

As Fire Commissioner, it was Dave DeVito's job to ensure that all these additional resources were available to the department for this disaster, and if not, what needed to be done about it, including locating and mobilizing additional equipment and personnel. As Chief of Department, it was John Reardon's job to properly assign the appropriate resources – managed chaos.

Just moments after New York City Emergency Services units arrived at the Port Authority attack, it was determined that there were at least 45 victims DOA. Within a few more minutes into the Rescue and Recovery Operation, that number was revised to 60, with another 20 or more in extreme critical condition and 'likely to die.' Within the first hour of Rescue Operations, authorities had classified 66 victims as Dead on Arrival at the scene of the attack.

Another 21 were pronounced Dead on Arrival at area emergency rooms, and 16 more victims expired within an hour of arrival and emergency treatment at local hospitals. In total, 104 people were dead in the immediate aftermath of the attack. A few more would die in the coming days from the complex injuries and illnesses brought about by the toxic bombs.

Additionally, several more would succumb during the ensuing weeks and months, and an untold number would experience chronic illness and premature death in the months and years to follow. Over 500 survivors were rescued on-scene in the train station and bus terminal by the FDNY, FDNY/EMS, NYPD, Port Authority of NY/NJ Police Dept., FBI, ATF, DHS, NYC Transit and Port Authority employees, and brave, concerned citizens. Overall, thousands more were successfully evacuated from the massive transportation complex.

On any given day, New York has approximately 60 hospital emergency rooms operating in the five boroughs that comprise the city. On average, there are about 10 available ER beds, approximately 600 emergency beds available in the immediate metropolitan area.

Naturally, critical ER patients are going to be transported to hospitals in close proximity to the scene of an incident.

Nearby hospitals become overcrowded and strained to provide emergency medical treatment to a sudden dramatic influx of critical care patients. When possible, stabilized patients can be transported to other area hospitals. This again places additional demand on EMS units for transport.

Also, in preparedness for disaster, the New York City Emergency Medical System has several mobile emergency room vehicles and mass casualty treatment units which can stabilize about 10 patients each for a brief stay. On the day of the horrific 11/11 attacks, the entire system was strained to the max.

Chapter 24
New York's Finest in
the Face of Chaos

Both on-scene at the Port Authority and back at FDNY Headquarters at MetroTech Center in Downtown Brooklyn, the command staff considered mobilizing a third Decon Task Force for the incident. However, subsequent events shifted their plans. On this day of unprecedented disaster, FDNY and EMS, like all other emergency response agencies, were compelled to creatively mix and match resources to try and meet the minimum standards of service. The day's multiple-site incidents required FDNY to operate its Tiered Response Plan, enabling the deployment of various specialized units to simultaneous disaster operations.

FDNY has two Field Communication Units to coordinate emergency responses to, as well as on-scene operations at, disaster sites. There are also two less advanced and complex communications units called Mobile Command Units, and several city-wide response engine companies especially equipped for on-scene/emergency communications. Additionally, there is an on-duty Field Mask Service Unit (MSU1) and two on-call Mask Service Units (MSU2, MSU3). These trucks carry extra air bottles for rescuers, as well as equipment to decontaminate and replenish empty bottles.

Thanks to the dedicated persistence, discipline, and imagination of Commissioner DeVito, Chief Reardon, and all FDNY command staff, all Field Comm. and Mobile Command Units, a specially-equipped Command Tactical Unit with remote broadcast capability, as well as every Haz-Mat, Mask Service, Rescue, and Squad Company of the immense FDNY, would be utilized.

Just a few minutes into the Union Square operation, word began to spread across all networks of the emergency services operating there that there had been a massive explosion at the Port Authority Bus Terminal and something about a standoff situation on the Lexington Ave Subway at Grand Central Station. Very quickly, the events of 11/11 seemed hauntingly similar to those of 9/11.

At the Rail Transit Office, Battalion Chief Watson and NYPD Lt. Palmer heard nearly simultaneous reports from both MTA and Fire and PD Units about the Port Authority Terminal Explosion. In unison, both muttered "God damn it" in an exasperated sigh. Now, these men were engaged in the nearly impossible task of communicating with MTA sources and field supervisors to direct the nearest emergency units to the morning's escalating disasters.

As soon as the news registered, each was on the horn to their respective commanders at FD MetroTech HQ in Brooklyn, and One Police Plaza in Downtown Manhattan: "Yeah, Chief," Watson spoke to John Reardon – "we've got the Port Authority explosion now... we're probably gonna need an MDTF there..." At the same time, Lt. Palmer was on the radio-phone to the City-Wide Communications Coordinator at Police Plaza – "Redirect any ESU Units not already on-scene, to the Port Authority Building at 42nd & 8th... Activate the Reserve Squad at Floyd Bennett to stand by at the Brooklyn side of the Brooklyn Bridge and await further orders."

By this point in the morning's events, the Emergency Services

Division of the NYPD was stretched very near its limits. When people need emergency help in New York, they call the police. When the police need help, they call Emergency Service. The Emergency Services Division's first line responders are called Squads. Each Squad usually consists of one heavy-duty rescue unit known as a Truck, and two or three smaller, specially equipped light trucks called Cars.

Individually, the vehicles are referred to as an Emergency Service Unit, giving the division its NYPD nickname, ESU. The ESU makes up what other police departments in the U.S. call SWAT (Special Weapons And Tactics). There are ten Emergency Service Squads normally on-duty each day for the NYPD.

Given the extra amount of "chatter" Homeland Security and the NYPD's Intelligence Division had been receiving lately, and the devastating precedent such chatter had set, the entire NYPD, but especially the Emergency Services Division, was on high alert. An additional ESU Squad was on stand-by at Floyd Bennett Field in Brooklyn. All off-duty ESU personnel were instructed to be prepared for possible extra-duty assignment. Moments after the Port Authority explosion, off-duty ESU officers began to be called in.

The ESU Squads are assigned throughout the city to Radio Motor Patrol Duty across the city's police precincts, with each squad covering three or four precincts, though they are all available city-wide to respond to any major emergency. This day's multiple major emergencies had Emergency Service Units responding from as far away as the northeast corner of the Bronx at Pelham Bay, and the west shore area of the Staten Island/New Jersey border, into Midtown Manhattan.

Chapter 25
Manhattan's Morning Mayhem

At Union Square Station, a total evacuation was in progress when on-scene emergency units were informed of the mass-casualty Haz-Mat situation unfolding at 42nd & 8th. This necessitated a new operational plan at Union Square. The toxic explosion at the Port Authority attack led to both Union Square and Grand Central being designated as Haz-Mat and potential mass-casualty incidents. A Signal 10-80 was transmitted for each event, requiring FDNY, FDNY EMS, NYPD, and other agencies to adjust their emergency responses while striving to maintain minimum response standards.

Overhead, motor vehicle and pedestrian traffic was diverted away from the streets surrounding Union Square. Broadway and Park Ave South, from 13th Street north to 17th Street, were closed, and the complicated process of evacuating all businesses and residences began, orchestrated by the NYPD. Similarly, 14th, 15th, 16th, and 17th Streets from west of 3rd Avenue to east of 5th Avenue also needed to be vacated. This was all while dealing with the delicate situation downstairs involving a deceased terrorist and an unexploded suicide vest.

Moments after the suicide attacker at Union Square was neutralized by NY Transit PD, James Waters arrived at Grand Central Station. An evacuation of a very similar nature but on a significantly larger scale was soon needed for the Grand Central area.

Grand Central Station, primarily located at E. 42nd St. and Park Ave, actually spans several city blocks, mostly bounded by E. 41st

St. to the south, E. 46th St. to the north, Madison Avenue to the west, and Lexington Avenue to the east.

This led to a 16-square-block street closure and evacuation in the heart of Midtown Manhattan, occurring just moments after about 15 blocks were closed at Union Square. This traffic disruption during the height of the morning rush hour resulted in unparalleled gridlock across Manhattan. Moreover, it was subsequently decided that all traffic—vehicle, transit, and pedestrian—into Manhattan should cease.

Just over one minute after the explosion at the Port Authority Bus Terminal Subway Station, an IRT #2 train pulled into the Times Square Station, located two blocks north and two blocks west of the Port Authority. The two stations are connected by a series of stairways and passageways.

The blast from the Port Authority station was loud but muffled at Times Square Station. Smoke had just begun to vent into the station as those fleeing the blast at the Port Authority began to arrive. Before transit officials could manage the situation and warn other trains about the explosion, the #2 train had already arrived and opened its doors.

Chapter 26
Times Square Standoff

The Times Square Station at West 46th Street is bounded by Broadway, West 47th Street, and 7th Avenue. It is actually a four-station complex, serving three IRT (Inter-Borough Rapid Transit) lines and one BMT (Brooklyn-Manhattan Transit) line. The stations are interconnected by an extensive common mezzanine and a series of stairways and passageways linking the various underground transit lines. There is also a passenger corridor of approximately two and a half city blocks connecting to the Port Authority Station on the IND (Independent) 8th Avenue Line. The names of these lines date back to a century ago, when the city was served by three different subway train companies.

Because of the stations' proximity—but still distinct separation—the explosion at the 42nd Street Bus Terminal had only a marginal effect on the Times Square Station. Exiting the No. 2 Train, Dennis Harding immediately sensed the confusion among passengers, as well as the odor and faint mist of smoke drifting onto the platform. Dennis was there on a mission. He was one of The Vessels, wearing his own "Special Vest" to deliver what they called "Supreme Justice."

Human nature led most of the Counter-Terrorist Police Officers on patrol at the Times Square Station to break their usual vigilance and turn toward the muffled explosion from the Port Authority Terminal. When the IRT 2 Train rolled in, some officers glanced at it briefly, then refocused on the sounds of screaming passengers fleeing from Port Authority into Times Square. A faint fog of smoke, the odor of explosives, and grim human wreckage began to drift in.

Transit Officer Tara Wallace, a 24-year-old, somewhat petite African American with just under three years on the job, and new to Counter-Terror Operations, was among those officers. She, too, had looked away from her designated patrol area toward the mezzanine that led to the Bus Terminal passageway. Like her colleagues, she barely registered the arriving No. 2 Train before resuming her watch on the mezzanine stairway. But something deep inside made her look back at the disembarking passengers. The sergeant in charge also glanced back and then directed the other officers to manage the influx of passengers.

By then, Officer Wallace had already started moving in that direction, scanning the arrivals. One passenger in particular—though she couldn't say why—grabbed her attention: Dennis Harding. She became laser-focused on him. She noticed immediately that he seemed not fearful but possibly amused by the pandemonium. He wore a bulky, ill-fitting overcoat. She drew her weapon and trained it on him.

When Dennis Harding realized Wallace had drawn on him, he tried to command his hand and fingers to press the detonator button. To his horror, staring into the muzzle of Wallace's .45 Glock automatic pistol, he found he could not move a muscle.

In their indoctrination, the "Vessels of Justice" had been persuaded to consider their fate if they failed in their mission. "You know what happens to the likes of us," Muhammad had emphasized, indicating his Arab companions. "Our comrades and kin have been sent to Gitmo and hidden away in other prisons like Gitmo, enduring unimaginable horrors, never to be heard from again. They've been tortured and 'disappeared.' Westerners like you have met the same fate. You've seen news stories about people who left to join the fight and then disappeared. I promise you, before Allah, they have not simply disappeared—they've been made to disappear by Western intelligence organizations! Many have been killed, but many linger to this day, tortured and abused in hidden prisons!"

"And of course," he continued, "you've seen and heard about certain Westerners, and some of our own people, in American prisons and detention facilities. Let me assure you, they do not fare much better. They are abused, beaten, raped by inmates, then beaten and ignored by their guards. I promise you, my brothers, if you fail to detonate your vest, you will live to regret it for the rest of your days on this earth."

For emphasis, these sermons were repeated. "You, too," he would say, "will be waterboarded, chained, leashed, and paraded like dogs. You will be tortured, raped, abused, beaten, then starved and ignored."

After "the stick" came "the carrot." "When you detonate your vest, you will be immediately in Paradise with Allah and the Prophet. The Quran promises all martyrs of the Jihad 72 virgins at your complete, unending service. Our brother Osama bin Laden said of his warriors: 'These youths love death as you love life.'"

After three such sermons, Muhammad left the disoriented, bewildered "Vessels" to draw their own conclusions. What he completely ignored was the murder, rape, and pillage carried out by the "Jihadi Warriors"—against men, women, and children, Muslim and non-Muslim alike—in the captured villages and cities, all supposedly in God's name. In the perverted brand of extreme fundamentalist Islam embraced by the Jihadists, the Almighty Allah and the Prophet himself supposedly smiled upon the ravaging of "infidels."

During his wretched life, Dennis Harding had come to believe in almost nothing at all, beyond how to get himself through another day. Abandoned, abused, neglected, counseled, treated, incarcerated, and institutionalized, he emerged with the most basic philosophy: "Today is the day—find friends, survive."

He found common ground with Muhammad and his followers: "Today is the day. Seek fellowship. Destroy your enemies." Dennis agreed with the tone, tenor, mayhem, and terror. He was savagely angry, and Muhammad's teachings gave his anger focus, direction, and purpose. Still, a will to survive ultimately prevailed.

"Slowly—hands up!" commanded Officer Wallace. Instantly, the other patrol officers turned their attention to Harding. Within a split second, he was staring down multiple gun barrels. Whether or not he detonated his vest, he was a heartbeat away from death when he moved his arms. Summoning all his strength, he slowly raised them out to his sides.

Chapter 27
Emergency in the Tunnels

Now, the frenetic pace of emergency operations in New York City was mind-boggling. FDNY Transit Liaison Officer, 9th Battalion Chief Watson, was stationed at the RTO to coordinate the fire department and EMS response to the disaster. He walked into a scene of controlled mayhem. RTO operators were already initiating a system-wide shutdown and evacuation.

From the northeastern Bronx to Coney Island and Bay Ridge in Brooklyn, to the far reaches of eastern Queens and the border of Long Island, trains were halted in place, awaiting further instruction. Others were directed to the nearest station to discharge passengers, decisions left to the judgment of individual supervisory RTOs. This massive, unprecedented undertaking surpassed even the system evacuation that occurred on 9/11/01. Unlike the previous threat from above, this horrendous threat emanated from within the underground rail system itself. Transit operators considered the safety and logistics of evacuating crowded trains between stations, requiring thousands of commuters to move on foot through dark passageways and emergency exit stairs to the street. The evacuation plans also had to factor in disabled passengers.

FDNY Liaison Chief Watson consulted with transit operators to determine if FDNY and/or EMS assistance was needed at any point during these emergency evacuations, then identified and dispatched appropriate nearby units.

The Transit Bureau of the NYPD, at the forefront of the day's deadly events, was quickly supported by the ESU, Counter-Terrorist, Intelligence Units, Patrol, Tactical Patrol, and Highway, as well as Housing Bureau Units. The Special Operations Division, including Aviation and Harbor units, was also on counter-terrorist/special surveillance, and emergency transport status, patrolling and surveilling significant sites such as airports, railways, bridges, tunnels, stadiums, arenas, museums, and hotels by aerial and marine units.

From the Rockaway shorefront at the New York-Long Island southern border of Jamaica Bay and the Atlantic Ocean by JFK International Airport, some 30 miles north and west to the New York-New Jersey border of the Hudson River by the George Washington Bridge, and up to the Bronx County Line at Spuyten Duyvil. Then northeast out to Pelham Bay and the confluence of the East River and southwest end of the Long Island Sound and Riker's Island NY City Prison, across from La Guardia International. New York City Police Harbor Unit boats and Aviation Unit helicopters were on patrol and high alert.

They were also available and alert for sudden assignments to emergency medical evacuation, as well as emergency transport for VIPs or other strategically important personnel. This included possibly being tasked with the transport of emergency blood supply or other medically necessary supplies or personnel. This array of available emergency vessels included not only those of the NYPD and the Port Authority of New York & New Jersey but also the FDNY Marine Units and those of the United States Coast Guard – NY Harbor/Air.

At the RTO, Transit Operations Director Randy Black faced

some monumentally important decisions with only a few minutes to make them. He was already striving to make the right calls about a terrorist explosion at the Port Authority Station, a suspect armed with an explosive vest in police custody at Union Square, a standoff at Grand Central, and another suspect standoff at Times Square. Director Black and MTA Subway Operations Vice President Steven Hudson had agreed on a system-wide shutdown of the New York City Subway System.

It was up to FDNY 9th Battalion Chief Frank Watson to work with RTO staff to coordinate where and when trains would be laid up, and to initiate adequate fire department and EMS response. Central to the conversation was NYPD Lt. Steve Palmer, Operations Supervisor with the Police Department Special Operations Division.

Likewise, Special Operations Lt. Palmer faced the same set of tasks and assignments for the NYPD, in partnership with both transit and the FDNY.

Lt. Palmer, fit yet slightly overweight at 46, grew up athletic. Though his athletic days were mostly behind him, he still worked out regularly and ran when he had the time and energy. Lately, however, most of his time and energy were devoted to NYPD Special Operations. Palmer found himself in an intriguing state of being, loving and hating his work simultaneously. He loved doing it, yet hated that he had to. He often marveled that he completely enjoyed something he despised.

Battalion Chief Watson, working as the fire department/EMS coordinator with rail transit operations, needed to keep the FDNY fully apprised of whatever maneuvers the transit authority decided to make. At the same time, he was expected to keep transit fully current on FDNY/EMS availability to respond to any transit decision. To do this, he needed to maintain current and as complete contact as possible with both the FDNY and transit command staff.

It was subtly nerve-wracking and mind-bending work. The task seemed initially overwhelming, but as Chief Watson developed a routine, it became seemingly more tedious than anything else. However, the work involved a sort of subconscious awareness of who, in which task, was current on whatever information was needed to make an adequate decision. And, a constant undercurrent of which FDNY and EMS units were assigned where. It was subtly exhausting work.

And NYPD Lt. Palmer, just like FDNY Battalion Chief Watson, now had that constant underlying persistent theme running in his mind about who in his department knew what about what they now knew, who in this room had the information they needed about NYPD's availability to respond as needed, and which units were available where to respond to which assignments.

As more news came in about the expanding scope of the attack, the details of the railroad shutdown and evacuation needed to be adapted accordingly. And the news was not yet finished coming in.

Before the news of the Times Square standoff, they had agreed to have trains proceed to the next available station to discharge passengers. Once they received the news of Times Square Station, they decided to begin searching each individual train as they arrived in-station. This situation was tricky enough on its own. Each train would await the arrival of a sufficient NYPD patrol squad for a search. What then could or would transpire aboard each train in the meanwhile? Then came the news of Herald Square.

Chapter 28
The Internet's Role in Radicalization

The busiest subway stations in NYC are Times Square, Grand Central, and Herald Square at the intersection of 34th St., Broadway, and 6th Avenue. Seven different lines—the B, D, F, M, N, and R trains—all stop at Herald Square Station.

Tom Jennings was aboard a nearly fully loaded 'B' Train as it pulled into the 34th St. Station at Herald Sq. On board, there were almost 100 passengers per car on a 10-car train, totaling nearly 900 people. Jennings was certain that come what may, he was going to detonate his vest at some point. He was 28 years old, an unemployed 'freelance writer' and drifter, who would later be described as a 'self-radicalized' jihadist.

Jennings's home life growing up was a disaster. By the time Tom Jennings was 15 years old in suburban Wichita, Kansas, his father had deserted him and his mother, who later committed suicide. Jennings' parents, only by birth, were each addicted to booze and drugs and subsequently died from addiction. The same fate very nearly befell Jennings himself, save for a jailhouse conversion to fundamentalist Islam.

He eventually came to further develop his yearning for jihad via the Internet. As far as modern-day jihadists are concerned, after the Prophet, the Internet is probably the greatest thing to have ever come along.

Accessible from almost anywhere and easily used to transmit thousands of pages of propaganda, the Internet helps Islamist terrorists unify and motivate their zealous adherents almost anywhere on the planet. The most effective and secure way for terrorists to communicate and recruit new 'warriors' is by using encryption.

The latest technology has made encryption widely available, and its use across the World Wide Web is now prevalent. With it, Muhammad, Ahmed, and others could communicate easily not only with each other and their fellow cohorts but also with the likes of Tom Jennings and James Waters. Another form of communication among those who needed to remain completely obscure was internet 'gaming.' Many modern computer games used technology that made it possible for multiple 'players' to compete or conspire as 'teams' worldwide across the Internet. This anonymous technology was adapted by international terrorists such as al-Nusra, ISIS, and al-Qaeda to carry out not 'make-believe,' but very real missions of mass destruction.

All this is, of course, known to the CIA, NSA, and NRO (National Reconnaissance Office), which is responsible for the management and utilization of all U.S. reconnaissance satellites—the 'Spy in the Sky' agency. It is also understood by terrorists worldwide that the United States possesses this technical knowledge, equipment, and capability. Accordingly, whenever a 'mission' was entering its final stage of execution, all jihadi networks went 'dark.'

It has been noted in various spy circles that perhaps the 'quietest' day on all Middle East and sympathetic jihadi communication networks was 9/11/01. The most similar 'quiet' was the day before, on 9/10 of that year. The most 'noise' or 'chatter,' as it is called, when the most activity was observed across terrorist networks, was in the weeks and days leading up to that time. In response to the noise, the U.S. security apparatus did little more than hold 'priority' meetings comprised of fretting discussions but did nothing much else in response.

One U.S. security advisor later testified before Congress that he and his staff were 'running around with our hair on fire' trying to alert presidential staff, but no significant response ever came from the Oval Office.

On Twitter, the ISIS "Warning to the American People" campaign had been posted on Facebook, in YouTube videos, and on various extremist forums. Participants were encouraged to tweet using a hashtag in English or Arabic, although "tweeting in English is preferred." Participants were also encouraged to repost officially sanctioned tweets that appeared on the ISIS "Union Page" and use "photos of signs or designs with warnings to Americans" when possible.

In the time leading up to the 11/11 attacks in New York City, jihadists were urged in various arenas to utilize the 'modern technology of the Internet' to advance 'The Cause.' "Try to make it so that even if the idolatrous dogs intercept and decrypt your messages, the only information they will be able to find is your username and password," advised Islamic State's French-language magazine, Dar Al Islam.

On a variety of 'Islamist sites,' messages appeared compelling 'Muslim Internet Professionals' to spread news and information about the jihad via email, discussion groups, and websites. One electronic warning from the e-jihadis intoned: "If you fail to do this, and our site closes down before you have done this, we may hold you to account before Allah on the Day of Judgment."

Now, the ancient battle was once again being played out at the historic, cultural, and economic crossroads of the world, in New York City—a place derogatorily called by various anti-Semites as 'Jew-York.'

Chapter 29
Herald Square
in Flames

Tom Jennings was fervent in his complete disregard for America and American lives. He had decided that America was indeed "The Great Satan," and that most of the world's problems were caused by Jews and those who supported them. He had zero hesitation about blowing up what he called the "Jew-Landlord" properties at Herald Square. At the core of his discontent was a hatred for the profound disappointment of his own life. He had concluded, however, that "the Jews" were the source of his misery and thus the targets of his reprisal.

Jennings loathed the very notion of a place calling itself "The State of Israel" and was certain that without the United States of America, there would be no "State of Israel." He was adamant in his belief that "that place" was founded on stolen Palestinian land. Jennings was neither Israeli nor Palestinian—he was simply angry and hateful.

He admired and followed the terrorist zealot Anwar al-Awlaki, a U.S.-born Yemeni jihadist who was a notorious propagandist and hate-monger. Prior to his death in a U.S. drone strike in Yemen on September 30, 2011, Awlaki influenced a generation of extremists in the U.S. and abroad. One indication of Awlaki's widespread impact is the number of extremists and terrorists found in possession of his materials. Tamerlan and Dzhokhar Tsarnaev, the brothers responsible for the April 15, 2013 Boston Marathon bombings, were radicalized at least in part by his teachings.

In addition to the Boston bombings, Awlaki's influence appeared in other plots. Faisal Shahzad, sentenced to life in prison for his failed attempt to bomb Times Square in 2010, told investigators he had been influenced by Awlaki. Born in Pakistan, Shahzad gained U.S. citizenship in April 2009. He was arrested at John F. Kennedy International Airport on May 3, 2010, while trying to fly to Pakistan. Charged in a criminal complaint the following day, he was indicted by a federal jury in New York on June 17, 2010.

At his trial, Shahzad informed the sentencing judge he was "guilty, guilty, a hundred times over guilty" of conspiring to mass-murder Americans, arguing that U.S. military presence in Iraq and Afghanistan, along with drone strikes in Somalia, Yemen, and Pakistan, justified his actions. The presiding judge had no hesitation in sentencing Shahzad to 150 years in federal prison without parole.

After a dramatic and intense spiritual journey, traveling with his "Teachers" and training alongside other "Vessels of Supreme Justice," Tom Jennings now found himself on the "B" Train at Herald Square. Something was off. As the train pulled into the station, it came to a normal stop, but the doors did not open. Jennings immediately felt on edge. He sensed "the moment" was upon him. He was fully prepared.

An announcement came over the speaker: "Please pardon the delay as we are being held in-station due to an emergency in the station." Jennings knew exactly what kind of "emergency" it was and believed he was moments away from becoming "forever honored."

At each end of the stopped 10-car train—plus one of the

center cars—NYC Transit Police entered through single door panels they had "keyed open" and began a preliminary scan of the passengers and the train's interior. Despite the locked bulkhead doors between cars and passenger compartments separated by crew operating areas, Jennings could tell there was some sort of commotion on the train. He waited.

Within a couple of minutes, he knew there was unusual activity—"police activity," he correctly surmised. He did not have to wait long. Moments later, officers moved into his car through the train crew compartment at the far end. Jennings's immediate attention settled on the dog, which, seconds after trotting in with its handler, seemed to perk up and glance his way. Jennings's finger hovered over the detonator trigger.

The police dog and the transit officer walked past Denise Richards, who had finally found a seat at Canal St., the first Manhattan stop. Denise, 24, bright, vibrant, and popular, had been on the train for nearly an hour, having boarded at Kings Highway in Brooklyn. She was a bit short—just over five feet—but physically fit. With a pretty face, a great smile, and alluring curves, she dressed somewhat sexily, favoring low necklines and high skirts, though never too flashy. Older passengers would still be waiting for a seat by the time Denise sat down.

Denise was heading to her job near 42nd Street and 6th Avenue, where she had worked for about a year as an "Associate" at a fashion agency—a "dream job" by her own Brooklyn-born standards.

A few seats away was Don Robinson, a 26-year-old attorney at a law firm just a few blocks from Denise's workplace. Don had graduated from Brooklyn College Law two years earlier and, after passing the bar exam on his second try about a year ago, was excelling in his field. He was a decent-looking young man, if not striking, and had boarded the train in Brooklyn at Sheepshead Bay, one stop before Denise. In fact, he had noticed Denise since boarding—and not for the first time. Don was a fan.

His firm served mostly fashion-industry and entertainment clients. He was pleased with his job, good at his work, and recognized for his strong performance so far. Having recently passed the bar, he felt he was well on his way in his career. Spotting Denise again, he began plotting how to introduce himself, maybe hand her his card, and ask for her number. The dog and handler passed Don as well.

The explosives-sniffing dog paused momentarily, turned to look at its handler, then lowered its head, gazing in Jennings's general direction. The dog had picked up the scent of the vest within seconds of entering the car. Its handler, noticing the subtle cue, headed toward Jennings. Glancing briefly at Jennings, he then scanned left and right of the suicide attacker. They were about ten feet away and closing in. Jennings knew.

The resulting explosion hurled the shredded remains of both dog and handler 20 feet backward, slamming them into the far bulkhead door at extreme speed. Their remains spiraled throughout the subway car, mingling with shrapnel and the explosive cloud, recoiling off the walls. In an instant, approximately 40 people— including Don and Denise—were incinerated and flung around the car. In a hellish moment, the blasted subway-car walls burst onto the platform, spraying shrapnel, shattered and burning glass, twisted metal, and human remains into the station.

Passengers on the platform were hurled 15 to 20 feet in all directions, shredded by bomb fragments of superheated metal, glass, and plastic, and doused in blood, human tissue, and burning toxins.

As with the Port Authority blast, a toxic cloud of smoke and debris under pressure plumed up the stairwells and passageways into the terminal. Acrid, superheated air contaminated with explosives residue and an awful mix of manufactured and human materials formed an unimaginable toxic haze that swept through the commuter complex. Horrified passengers and workers ran for the street-level exits, and the poisonous cloud followed them upward.

Across the street, the force of the blast rattled the foundation and support girders of Macy's Department Store. Store fixtures, furnishings, and decorations tore from walls and ceilings, crashing to the floor. Dozens of shoppers and Macy's staff were injured by falling debris, and panic drove everyone onto the street. Macy's would remain closed for weeks while Buildings Department engineers assessed structural integrity and environmental technicians cleaned, tested, and re-cleaned the HVAC systems.

On 34th Street above the station, pedestrians lurched as the horrific explosion shook the ground beneath them. Some fell, some stumbled, while others managed to keep their balance. Many were injured or at least badly shaken. The explosion was deafening below and a tremendous roar above. For a moment, everyone was stunned—

until, suddenly, gruesomely injured survivors emerged from the subway, and terrified, bleeding crowds from Macy's poured into the street. And worse was still to come.

Chapter 30
NYC's Emergency Units at Their Limits

More tragically and dreadfully wounded passengers were assisted up from the railroad level of the station as wailing and flashing fire department, EMS, and NYPD vehicles began to flood the street. The ominous gray-black toxic cloud also settled onto street level. Within minutes, civilians and rescuers alike became sickened by the enveloping poisonous mist. It took several critical moments before the clustered victims on 34th St. in Herald Square were rescued and moved up the block and around the corner from the hot zone.

As emergency service workers were just beginning to arrive in force to assess and manage the mayhem 6 blocks north at Port Authority, a new nightmare unfolded in Herald Square, requiring the same immediate attention as the disaster at 42nd & 8th. The city's emergency managers and emergency service personnel were operating beyond their 'critical' capacity, and the stress level was unprecedented.

Police, fire, and EMS responders had to be directed, and in most cases, redirected to Herald Sq. at 34th St. Some of the responding units were on their third assignment, not yet having arrived at the previous two. NYPD Emergency Truck 6 from Brooklyn was typical of the managed mayhem underway. Initially directed from its regular patrol in the Coney Island–Sheepshead Bay area to respond to the situation at Grand Central, orders then came over the police radio: "Truck 6; you are being redirected to the Port Authority Bus Terminal Train Station for an explosion, reported casualties…"

While en route uptown to 42nd Street, the dispatcher's harried

voice came over the air: "Truck 6, what is your location now?" "Uh…
Westside Highway and 36th Street," came the slightly hesitant reply.
"OK, get off at the next intersection, respond to 34th Street and 6th
Avenue, Herald Square Station 'B' Train Platform, explosion with
injuries, Fire and EMS responding." After acknowledging their third
assignment in 15 minutes, Central Dispatch informed the Truck 6 crew
that 911 was getting calls for an explosion at Macy's Department Store
at that location as well, "Possibly one and the same…" Central
Dispatch intoned.

The Fire Department of New York (FDNY), Rescue
Company 5 from Staten Island received similar instructions. FDNY
rescue trucks, equipped with special gear and manned by firefighters
from the FDNY's Special Operations Command, are specially trained
and repeatedly drilled on the equipment and procedures for handling
a variety of disasters, including terror attacks and frequent emergency
operations involving the NYC Transit System as well as bridges and
tunnels.

Rescue 5, larger, heavier, and therefore somewhat slower than
NYPD's 'War-Wagon' ESU trucks, was just passing through Lower
Manhattan when they too received their third assignment of the
dreadful morning to respond to Herald Square Station. This came after
being redirected from responding to Times Square. Before that,
Rescue 5 had been relocating to the quarters of Rescue Company 2 in
Brooklyn to provide coverage for not only Staten Island but also
Brooklyn, Queens, and lower Manhattan, necessitated by the
extraordinary demands of the day.

News of the explosion at Herald Square stunned the transit personnel at the RTO. Director Randy Black voiced his immediate disbelief. "But the police..." his voice trailed off as his mind grappled with what must have happened. The operator speaking to him began to explain what Black had just surmised: "The police were there, boss. The train was in-station, doors closed. The police keyed on the train and..." Her voice faltered as well, as she described what happened next. "They boarded..." She gasped, "and the train... exploded... Boss, it exploded when they got on..." With that, 47-year-old Rail Transit Operator Ethel Davis collapsed into her seat at the console.

Chapter 31
Courage Under Fire

FDNY Lieutenant Ed Graves had been with the Department 13 Years on the day of the 11/11 Terror Attacks. The last 4 Years of his Service had been at Rescue Co.3 in the Bronx, and he worked as a Department Officer there for the past 2. Ed Graves was one of 17 FDNY African-American Officers in an agency with 14,000 Uniformed Employees, and one of 3 Black Officers assigned to Special Operations.

The Bronx Rescue Company served all of that Borough, as well as all of Uptown Manhattan North of 86th Street. Lt. Ed Graves was damn happy and proud to be an FDNY Special Operations Command (SOC) Officer, and neither very happy nor proud that he worked in a City Department that had only 16 other Afro-American Officers. He'd served the City and Department with distinction and honor, and was pretty much well-liked by friends and acquaintances both in and out of the New York City Fire Department.

In addition to being one of the brightest members of the FDNY and specifically its Special Operations Command, the 35 year-old Graves was physically impressive and agile and was a Co-Captain of the FDNY's 'Bravest' Football Team, in and of itself an Internationally-renowned organization.

One of the ways to reach service in an FDNY elite SOC Unit like Rescue 3, is to actually Rescue people trapped in fires in New York City. While that sounds like a common sense enough of an explanation, it's almost never uncomplicated, and it's not something most people, (including many New York City Firefighters), with good common sense engage in. During the course of his Fire Department career, Lt. Edward R. Graves had Rescued 4 Civilians, and 3 fellow-New York City Firefighters.

When he reached the scene of the Herald Square Disaster, Lt. Graves was exactly the type fellow many of the people there were hoping, and praying to God to send. Rescue Co.3 was just over 10 blocks away from Herald Square, responding to the Port Authority Terminal attack, when they were re-directed to respond in to 34th Street and 6th Ave. for the Herald Square explosion. They arrived within mere minutes of the bombing, suited-up in the CPC Gear, and headed in. Rescue Co.2 from Brooklyn had already arrived On-scene as 'The Members' of the Bronx unit made their way, in full gear down into the Hell-hole of the Herald Square 'B' Train Station.

As Rescue Company 2 arrived at Herald Square under the Command of its new Lieutenant, Tom Reale, the Members donned Chemically Protective Clothing and descended into the Subway. They encountered an unimaginable vision of horror. First came the early Rescuers, Cops, Transit Workers, Civilians, largely unprotected from the Chemical Warfare unfolding below ground. These sickened helpers had dragged along with them the first few victims, located away from the immediate blast area.

The Victims, and their ill-prepared Rescuers were in varying degrees of Respiratory Distress and suffering from blast burns. Lt. Reale and his crew descended into the unholy mess 4 times to retrieve victims, before they themselves, exhausted and traumatized by the work of removing live victims in various stages of dying, collapsed on the streets and sidewalks above the station.

Lt. Reale would himself become sick in the coming days. And in the following weeks and months suffer relapse and remission from Blood Poisoning and then Cancer. Tom Reale underwent trying episodes of hospitalizations, chemotherapy, remission, recovery and relapse. He would die a year later.

Upon arrival, the Haz-Mat detectors on the Rescue Co.3 Rig were in full alarm, alerting the members that even yards away from the Subway Station Entrance, there were dangerous levels of Toxins in the air. Nearby strategically-mounted detectors, as well as those on other FDNY, EMS, and NYPD vehicles were alarming, as waves of toxic vapor began to emanate from the Hellish scene below ground.

The scene 'Below-grade' was horrific. The blast of the Suicide-Vest exploded by Tom Jennings was everything the attackers hoped it to be. The high-charge blast instantly ignited everything and everyone within 15-20 Feet or so of the explosion. So that not only the toxic, super-heated gases of the bomb itself filled the air, but now the ignited contents of the train car also burned, as well as any flammable surface in the station, giving off their own toxic ingredients into the mix.

As the members of Rescue 3 progressed in through the mezzanine and to the stairways down to the train platform, they began to encounter victims, horribly burned, severely injured by flying shrapnel, and choking to death on poison air.

Upstairs, a Command Post was established down the block from the Subway Entrance by arriving FDNY Chief Officers, EMS

Chiefs, and NYPD Commanders. An EMS Triage and Transport Station was being set-up around the corner and down the street from the train station as toxic fumes continued to vent-out into the street. Soon, an FDNY Mobile Command Unit would be On-scene for Officers to direct operations from a more secure and efficient Command Post. For now, they had to operate as best they could, out on the street.

At the Herald Square Explosion the Assistant Chief of Operations Frank Reynolds, a 27 Year FDNY Veteran, was Incident Commander. He was assisted by the Chief of Counterterrorism and Emergency Preparedness, as well as the Queens Borough Commander, Specially Assigned to the Manhattan Disaster.

Ambulances and Mobil Emergency Room Vehicles (MERV's), from around the city converged now, not only at the Port Authority Terminal on 42nd St., but 34th Street and 6th Ave as well. The scene on 'The-surface' appeared hectic and chaotic, and could only be outmatched by the special kind of Terror unfolding 'Below-grade': Ordinary New York City workday commuters as mutilated and poisoned victims of ungodly 'Holy War.'

As Rescue Co.3 Members and other rescuers began to encounter maimed and burned victims, they took control and care of their Patients: First; determine if the Victim has an adequate airway and sufficient respiration. Next; determine if any Bleeding posed an immediate threat, Stabilize any fractures or protrusions. Next, evacuate the Patient to the next-level of Rescue/Evac. And return to search for more Victims.

When Lt. Graves made his way into the now toxic atmosphere of the Herald Sq. Station, respiration and perspiration increased. Not dramatically so, he was in decent-enough shape; but significantly. He was after all, wearing nearly 50 Pounds of Personal Protective Clothing and Respiration Equipment, carrying about 20 Pounds of forcible entry tools and Emergency Medical Equipment, and descending stairs and hallways into a Subway Station. And then there was the factor of a Super-heated, High-velocity and intense, poisonous explosion as well.

As Ed Graves descended this day into his own little personal version of Hell on Earth, his encounters went from uncomfortable, to disturbing, finally to barely tolerable. His first discomfort was the heat and pressure and personal exertion. Then came the tiring slog thru heat and smoke keeping as low as he could, toward the source of the destruction, cautious the entire way down into the depths of the station for unseen obstacles and fleeing victims. The dreadful subway station scene was eerily back-lit by orange and red yellow flame occasionally pierced by sharp blue, lightning-like electrical explosions. This followed finally by encounter with the horribly burned, maimed and poisoned.

Though his perspiration and evaporation clouded face piece, and protected ears, he could began to see, hear, and experience Terror, up close, and, personal. He first came upon a victim immediately as he reached the platform level of the train station. Lt. Graves came into the path of man he supposed was about 25 Years of age. The severely wounded straggler was ashen-faced and bleeding profusely from his lower right arm where his hand was supposed to be. Fortunately, either by survival instinct or instruction, he had his arm bent upwards across his chest and bent at the elbow. Otherwise he would have most likely bled-out before any help arrived. Graves quickly tied- off a tourniquet to just above the injured victim's elbow and affixed a tight sling that secured the shredded limb up around the patient's shoulder and neck. The Lieutenant then passed- off the injured survivor to another Rescuer coming up the line behind him and proceeded onward.

He next came upon a person he surmised to be a middle-age to youngish woman. Because of his restricted visual ability, and her diminished condition, he could only guess.

In the smoky toxic haze, back-lit by the glow and occasional bright glare of the burning surroundings, he saw before him a hobbling, bent figure, stumbling forward. She emitted a chilling guttural wail, interrupted by deep, snorting gasps of inhalation of yet another wave of toxic gas-laced air. Through the seam of light from his portable head-lamp, Ed Graves could make out that her hair and scalp were mostly burned away, her face was a soot covered gray-ash mass of burned skin. She fell to one knee just before him and he could make out her eyes as deep and hollow sockets as a heavy mucus drooled from her nostrils.

His immediate and impulsive intention was to wipe clear her nose and mouth and tears and rip his face piece off for her. That would have most likely resulted in swift-death for him, and done little to help a tragic victim who was already well on her way to death. He did however, immediately scoop her up, carry her about 20 Feet along to the base of a stairway descending from the mezzanine down to the platform, and pass her on to an arriving firefighter.

That rescuer in turn carried the stricken woman along the mezzanine to another stairway which ascended up onto the street. At the base of that stairway, another firefighter in her turn brought the victim up out onto the street. There, 2 FDNY Paramedics and a firefighter carried the woman out another 20 Feet or so away from the subway station entrance to an outdoor initial Triage Station. There, she was lain on a stretcher, examined, pronounced dead, and covered. Thus ended one New York City Commuter's morning workday journey.

Muhammed, al-Marsi, Mehmet and the rest of the al-Nusra Gang could hardly have been more pleased by the results of their evil venture. Not that they had time to celebrate or enjoy the carnage. They were in full and determined flight from their horrific deeds. The controlled panic of escape overcame any enthusiasm for reveling in success. Each, by his own path and mode, was fleeing the United States.

Chapter 32
Triage and Tragedy

In the field of emergency medicine, triage primarily involves categorizing victims of mass casualties into three groups: those who are deceased, those who are likely to die, and those who can be saved. Randy Black faced a similar grim task with the passengers and crew of the New York City Subway. As the Transit Director, he needed to convey this harsh reality to his staff in the Transit Operations Center. It was time for gut-wrenching decisions.

At the Herald Square disaster, the need for decisive action was immediate. Fortunately, Black was not alone; he worked alongside Battalion Chief Frank Watson and NYPD Lt. Steve Palmer. However, the difficult decisions they reached had to be communicated to Mayor Ron Garner and Governor Tom Alexander, and the reaction from higher authorities was uncertain.

"I need everyone to listen up for a minute here..." Black began, addressing the Rail Transit Operators. "Tell everyone on 'the road' to stand by. I need your complete attention." The operators fell silent, awaiting instructions. Black knew they couldn't stop the ongoing attacks. Their best hope was to minimize the damage by strategically placing trains to reduce the impact of potential further attacks.

Suggestions flowed for parking trains in the city's open-air rail transit locations, weighing the risks of explosions in open versus underground spaces. Open areas offered ventilation and the dissipation of toxic gases, while tunnels reduced exposure but nearly eliminated any chance of survival within their range.

The New York City-Greater Metropolitan Area Transit System, including Metro-North, LIRR, PATH, and Amtrak, faced similar critical decisions. Cross-agency conference calls led to a consensus that, if possible, limiting the scope of explosions and toxic releases to underground areas was preferable, tragically dooming those nearby but potentially limiting wider exposure.

The demand for emergency medical services surged unimaginably within 20 minutes. This unprecedented crisis echoed the tragic 9/11 attacks, but with attacks occurring at multiple locations, the challenges were distinct and complex.

By day's end on 11/11, 198 victims had perished, a toll that was expected to rise in the aftermath. The scale of the disaster overwhelmed existing emergency plans, underscoring the enormity of the tragedy that had struck New York City.

Chapter 33
Homeland Security in Action

At the White House, President Lance Bowman had just finished a brief but intense phone conversation with Department of Homeland Security Director Bruce Evans. President Bowman, 58 years old, was a career attorney and politician, now in his 11th month serving as President of the United States and Commander-in-Chief. Holding the office of President is every politician's dream; moments like this are every President's worst nightmare.

From his earliest years—including the gradual incorporation of his middle name, "Lance," as a political brand—everything in Dwight Lance Bowman's upbringing had been geared toward his inevitable and ultimately successful presidential bid. A moderate Republican, Bowman had a well-established reputation for working across the aisle during his time in Congress. He was neither too right-wing to alienate Democrats nor too liberal to alienate his own party. With experience on the Senate Foreign Affairs Committee (as Co-Chair) and on the House Armed Forces and Homeland Security Committees (as Chair), Bowman had a realistic view of both America's threats and its capabilities.

It was fascinating to hear President Bowman summarize, in under a minute, his past year's Middle East national security policy. He and his closest advisors understood that, in every foreign and domestic matter, national security was paramount. Hence, they developed and adjusted, as needed, the U.S. Middle East policy of "support those we favor, challenge those we oppose." One of his most trusted admirals phrased it succinctly: "Cooperate when we can; confront when we must."

Ironically, figuring out exactly whom to support in the Middle East was often more confounding than confronting enemies. Deciphering each group's leadership, goals, and outcomes—and whether helping them would enhance or endanger U.S. security—was frequently more complicated than the actual logistics of supporting or opposing them. During two separate wars in Iraq, the U.S. and its allies had fought both with and against various militias and factions. The same was true in Syria, where alliances shifted repeatedly.

President Bowman preferred to say a group was "presently" operating in support of U.S. security goals (or "not in support of" them) and avoided delving into the detailed politics of battlefield decisions.

When Homeland Security Secretary Evans spoke to the President, they agreed on which actions to take and reviewed those Evans had already implemented. Evans, a Democrat, was a longtime Senate colleague and friend of Bowman's, and their mutual respect and trust ran deep. Secretary Evans had already activated Homeland Security's Nationwide Emergency Notification System, alerting law enforcement and local governments across the country to the New York City attacks. He also suspended all passenger rail service in the Northeast Region. Calling the President, he sought permission to expand this suspension nationwide and to ground all civilian air traffic. The President sighed reluctantly, then concurred. Evans gave a thumbs-up to the DHS staff in his office.

In the next moments, all passenger trains were directed to "hold in place" for inspection and possible evacuation, and all civilian air traffic was ordered to land at the nearest available airport, where they too would "hold in place" for inspection. As on 9/11/01, all international flights were diverted away from the U.S., unless absolutely necessary, heading to whichever airports outside the United States they could reach.

The demands on DHS, the Transportation Safety Agency, and state and local law enforcement agencies would be massive. Inter-city and regional bus service would also be affected. State, county, and local police were instructed, "as feasible," to stop, board, and inspect these buses, along with their passengers and luggage compartments, for any suspicious persons or packages.

Concluding his call with Secretary Evans, the President directed, "We need to speak with Mayor Garner and Governor Alexander in New York forthwith." After relaying the orders through the proper channels, Evans asked the question on everyone's mind, phrasing it in Washington D.C.'s measured language: "I know this is war, sir, but are we 'at war'?"

It was the Secretary's diplomatic way of asking whether the President was about to issue a formal declaration. "Not yet," the President sighed, "but the day's not over," providing Evans with enough information for now.

The United States already had approximately 3,000 military advisors and trainers in Iraq, plus about 200 in Syria. The question loomed: Did the attacks require more "boots on the ground"? Two previous presidents had maintained a "War on Terror" policy; did the current White House occupant need to reemphasize an existing stance, or was something more specific required by Congress?

Before responding, President Bowman paused. "Bruce," he said, "one of the most distressing aspects here is that these barbarians don't grasp the fundamental point of confrontation: forcing your adversary to the table for a settlement. Yasser Arafat and the PLO, Gerry Adams and the IRA eventually realized you achieve more through negotiation than bomb-throwing. But first, you have to stop throwing bombs—carnage buries the message." Evans smiled at the President's insight.

A conference call was arranged with Mayor Garner and Governor Alexander, and Secretary Evans assured both that the full resources of the U.S. government—including the Armed Forces—were available. He also assured them that President Bowman would join the call shortly, confirming his commitment to making all necessary resources available to New York City and New York State.

At the Pentagon, the Joint Chiefs of Staff were summoned for an emergency session. Their main role was to advise the Commander-in-Chief and direct operations of the entire U.S. military. Less widely known was that the Chiefs also served as the board of directors for the National Security Agency (NSA), the so-called "super-secret" intelligence agency. In reality, the NSA was a massive bureaucracy made up of people prone to human flaws, as well as systematic failures inherent in such a large organization.

The NSA's core function was the collection, translation,

evaluation, and dissemination of intelligence gathered by the world's premier intelligence network. The goal was to determine the likelihood of attacks like the one now unfolding, then deliver actionable information to military and law enforcement agencies. The immediate concern at this special meeting was twofold: to see if any fresh intel could expose details of current or impending attacks, and to mobilize the U.S. military at home and worldwide in response to them. The first step was to issue a global alert to every U.S. military unit, warning of the terrorist attacks in New York and the potential for others. They also ordered all units to maintain the highest level of alert and ensure the "complete operational readiness of all units."

The Chairman of the Joint Chiefs of Staff is the principal military advisor to the Secretary of Defense and the President. It was the Secretary who had the "war status" conversation on behalf of the Chiefs, receiving the "maybe soon, but not yet" response. Yet for the Joint Chiefs, another question remained: exactly who, or what, would the U.S. be "at war" with, and what would that actually mean? ISIS was not a sovereign state, even if it controlled significant territory in the failing nation of Syria and parts of Iraq. Was this then a question of going to war in places where the U.S. was already conducting combat air operations and supporting opposition fighters? Things in the region had appeared to be stabilizing, but, as had become the norm, more U.S. ground troops were needed—and soon would be dispatched.

Chapter 34
U.S. and Russia in the Syrian Arena

U.S. military planners were aware of Russia's significant presence in the combat zone. Recently, President Vladimir Putin had deployed Russian combat air operations at the request of Syrian President Assad. So far, these operations had done little to halt ISIS's advance, leaving the bulk of the containment efforts to the U.S. and its allies. Meanwhile, Russian aerial combat missions were significantly weakening the mainstream, non-jihadist Syrian opposition forces. While there was no precise estimate of the number of Russian ground troops in Syria, their presence was notably significant.

Currently, the United States was not inclined to engage with Russian combat forces directly. The next task for the Joint Chiefs of Staff, acting as directors of the NSA, was to assess what was currently known about the ongoing attacks. General Howard Carter, U.S. Army and the Intel Coordinator for the Chiefs, outlined the intelligence priorities: identifying any indicators of further attacks and the identities of the attackers. The issue of identifying intelligence or communication failures that led to the current catastrophe would be addressed later.

In the days before the attacks, there had been an increase in communications intercepted and classified as potentially threatening. The source of this "chatter" was, once again, linked to usual suspects: al-Qaeda and ISIS-linked jihadist groups. General Carter noted, "We've identified some vague information about an operation and celebrations, but nothing specific enough to warrant a particular operation in any specific place."

This NSA notification of intercepts was relayed to the Department of Homeland Security and others for appropriate distribution. Among the recipients were the NYPD and FDNY, as well as major metropolitan area airports including JFK, Newark, and LaGuardia. These agencies were informed of non-specific information indicating possible terrorist activity.

As a result, TSA and DHS officers and agents were already on high alert, and like the NYPD, they were conducting special counter-terror surveillance and tactical patrols. When the notification of the NYC subway attacks reached the airports, they elevated their alert status to enhanced security screening and observation, bringing passenger access to boarding gates to a near standstill. Shortly thereafter, a complete ground stop for all flights was ordered.

This day, the FDNY Operations Center, along with other emergency managers across the city, was engaged in a challenging exercise of triage due to the horrific nature of the attacks. At the Port Authority bombing, the FDNY Chief of Operations was in command, assisted by the Chief of Special Operations Command and the Manhattan Borough Commander.

At the Herald Square explosion, the Assistant Chief of Operations took command, assisted by the Chief of Counterterrorism and Emergency Preparedness and the Queens Borough Commander. The Chief of Haz-Mat Operations commanded the response at Union Square, assisted by the Chief of Safety. The Chief of Weapons of Mass Destruction Preparedness was the incident commander at Grand Central, assisted by the Executive Officer to the Chief of Safety.

At Times Square, FDNY operations were led by the Commissioner's Executive Officer of Department Operations, assisted by the Planning and Strategy Division Chief. The rest of the Department Command Staff Chiefs were with the Commissioner and the Chief of the Department at FDNY HQ at Metro-Tech Center in Brooklyn. According to new department protocols, they too would need to be dispersed to various command centers throughout the city to ensure a sustained chain of command in the event of a terrorist attack on FDNY headquarters.

Besides being livid over the latest terror attacks upon his beloved city, John Reardon, Chief of Department, FDNY, was somewhat frantic that he was being held on a leash at MetroTech while the Department was operating at "all hands" against the ferocious disaster. After the Port Authority explosion, Reardon informed Command Staff that he should respond to the scene. "Negative," came the response from Commissioner DeVito. "I want you here."

When the report on Times Square came in—then Herald Square—Chief Reardon informed all within range, "That's it. I've gotta get out there with the troops…"

"Chief, a minute…?" Commissioner DeVito said, heading toward his office.

"Damn it all, John! I want you here with me, okay? I sent my Executive Officer out and kept you here with me! What does that tell you?"

Reardon paused a beat before replying, "That he's out in the field working even though he has rank and makes more than I do?"

"God damn it, John! I told you the Mayor—"

Reardon didn't let the Commissioner finish. "C'mon, Boss. Let's get back out on the floor. We've got work to do! Why are we dickin' around here in the office?" he said, grinning a winning Irish smile.

"You are a complete ass, ya know that, right?" DeVito said as they headed back out to the Operations Floor.

"Oh, I wish I had a dollar for every time I heard that one—I'd have a lot of dollars by now," Reardon responded. "Maybe as many as the X.O."

They agreed it was time to implement the Command Staff Dispersal phase of that day's counter-terror operations. Commissioner DeVito appreciated the discretion allowed by the Staff Dispersal Plan, while Reardon was particularly fond of the 'Designee' option. Together, they decided how to divide the Command Staff Chiefs now gathered at Metro-Tech. According to FDNY's post-9/11 operations plan, there were three alternate command staff operations sites. In addition to the primary operations center at Metro-Tech, there was an alternate site at the recently reconstructed Queens Communications Center on Woodhaven Boulevard, and one on Roosevelt Island, home to FDNY's Special Operations Command. There were other sites around the city available if needed, but for now, DeVito and Reardon agreed that Queens and the Special Operations Command Headquarters on the Island, as well as Metro-Tech in Brooklyn, would function well.

Some of the top-ranking Command Chiefs, including the Deputy Fire Commissioner – Administration, the First Deputy Commissioner, and the Fire Commissioner's Executive Assistant, would have to be 'scattered' at command locations around the city to preserve the chain of command in the event of continued attacks.

Chapter 35
Deactivating Danger at Union Square

Back at Union Square, the immediate vicinity of the terrorist incident in the station had been evacuated, while the rest of the cross-town transfer station was in the process of being cleared. Union Square Station is a complex hub where six different train lines converge across five platform areas, accessed via eight subway street entrances. The station spans six underground city blocks and houses an NYPD Transit Police District Station, four train control rooms, several train crew rooms, and various railway, station, and revenue department offices, all supported by extensive utilities such as power, lighting, communications, HVAC, and plumbing, all of which required inspection and monitoring during today's attack.

A deceased terror suspect wearing an unexploded suicide bomb vest was at the center of the operation. NYPD ESU initiated the response by confirming the suspect's death. An ESU paramedic checked for a carotid pulse, pupil reaction to light, and any signs of heart or breathing sounds using a stethoscope. Finally, the paramedic pinched the skin and pulled a finger-full of short hairs near the temple to test for reaction to painful stimuli, ultimately declaring the suspect likely deceased. As the paramedic was not a certified medical examiner or physician, this was the most formal declaration possible under the circumstances.

Once the suspect's death was confirmed, the operation continued with the isolation and containment of the immediate area. The first step involved positioning blast-resistant blankets and sandbags around the deceased terrorist, providing enough space for bomb squad detectives to operate safely.

The detective explosive technicians of the NYPD Bomb Squad then took over. Their meticulous task involved examining the suicide explosives for trip-wires, booby-trap devices, and remotely-operated detonators to determine if the device could be safely removed for disposal at an NYPD firearms range.

As this delicate operation unfolded, a specially-constructed explosives transport vehicle was dispatched to Union Square. The NYPD had two such vehicles, and the Federal Bureau of Alcohol, Tobacco, and Firearms had another two available in New York City. Additional vehicles from DHS, FBI, and the Army were also available, a fortunate circumstance given the apparent need for several such trucks on this day of dastardly terror.

Chapter 36
The White House Response
to Herald Square

Once the Herald Square disaster reached the White House Situation Room, deeply ensconced within 1600 Pennsylvania Avenue, President Lance Bowman and his top advisors, including the Secretary of State, Chief of Staff, Secretary of Homeland Security, and National Security Advisor, were immediately mobilized. They recognized they were facing a multifaceted terrorist attack in the nation's largest city, necessitating a coordinated response across various government sectors. In alignment with emergency protocols akin to the FDNY's dispersal plan, the Vice President, Secretary of Defense, and other key officials joined the crisis conference via secure telecom from remote locations.

The initial discussions with Mayor Garner and Governor Alexander facilitated the immediate provision of resources to the city, marking just the beginning of the federal response. "We need to get a handle on this disaster right away; this thing is getting ahead of us too goddamn fast," stated Chief of Staff Jake Thompson, clearly exasperated. Homeland Security Chief Bruce Evans, more seasoned in Washington politics than Thompson, acknowledged the urgency, "We do need to cap this thing off pretty damn soon. The good news, such as it is, is that we have a couple of live perpetrators in custody. The bad news—it's all mostly bad news today—is that it's too soon to know if they can or will help us. But we're moving as quickly as we can, and it's something to present before the cameras."

The pressing issue was that with ongoing bombings and scant new information, there was little the President could offer to a nation clamoring for reassurance. The President emphasized the need to consider the facts: they were up against a terrorist group capable and willing to execute a sophisticated and violent attack on the New York City subway system. The task now was to identify the most likely suspect groups with the capability and presence to carry out such an attack, potentially within the U.S., Canada, Mexico, Puerto Rico, or other Caribbean hotspots.

The conversation, informed by DHS and the National Security Council, quickly narrowed the list of suspects. Through this elimination process, only two or three terrorist groups suspected of being capable and ready for such an attack were identified. Tom Schelling, the President's National Security Advisor, briefed the group on available intelligence: "ISIS-linked cells in the U.S. are primarily involved in recruiting for operations abroad. However, certain Al-Qaeda allies are acting as subcontractors, training fighters and facilitating their return to the U.S. One such group is the al-Nasir Group."

Muhammed's al-Nasir group was suspected of having a presence in the U.S. and had demonstrated experience in orchestrating multi-site attacks in various European and Middle Eastern operations. This information was under further investigation and remained speculative at the time.

Sensitive information like this, intended for inner circles, rarely reaches the public domain. However, as the terror unfolded in New

York City, officials began to suspect connections to the Muslim Relief Agency, long suspected of harboring jihadist sympathies. NYPD Captains Hammond and Martin, and FDNY Commissioner DeVito and Chief Reardon, were not surprised by the suspected involvement of the Muslim Relief Agency and the al-Nasir Front, piecing together the unfolding events and their potential orchestrators.

Chapter 37
In the Crosshairs

In the bustling courier agency where James worked, a somewhat harried supervisor informed Carol that James had taken a few days off but mentioned he'd stop in that morning to make arrangements to get back on the schedule. "Now, Ms. Waters, if you please, this is a very hectic time of day for us..." he said politely but firmly, with a pointed wave toward the door.

By now, Carol Waters was at her wit's end. Wandering out into the street, she absentmindedly descended the stairs back to the Grand Central I.R.T. platform she had just left. A vague notion flickered in her mind—perhaps she could watch the arriving trains and spot James.

She had barely been there a minute when Transit Police began approaching, instructing everyone to leave. "The station is closed," they called out. As Carol looked around, she was struck by the heavy presence of officers, their imposing weapons, and the steady movements of dogs.

Suddenly, an inexplicable impression took hold of her: this had something to do with James. A mother's instinct is intangible yet pervasive, and Carol now felt it fiercely. No matter how irrational or impossible it seemed, she was determined not to leave. The police, she decided, would simply have to deal with it.

This resolve soon led to a heated argument between Carol and members of the Counter-Terror Police Squad on the platform. She was adamant about staying. They were equally adamant she had to go.

At that moment, a train rolled in and discharged its passengers.

James stepped off, and Carol spotted him immediately. Relief flooded her, but in a couple of seconds, Officer Rob Jones spotted him too—and noticed something else: the bulky, awkward fit of James's overcoat.

In that instant, James Waters was one second from eternity.

"Freeze!" Jones roared, the laser dot of his rifle zeroing in on the bridge of James's nose. "Slow now," Jones commanded. "Raise your arms. Slowly."

James stood frozen, paralyzed, struggling to comprehend what was happening.

Chapter 38
Under the Red Dot

Only the sight of his mother's horror-stricken, tearful face and her terror-struck pleas for him to "James, please, for the love of God, raise your hands" kept him from pressing the detonator. Slowly, he raised his arms, the detonator dangling loosely from his pocket. Officer James took a deep breath without squeezing the trigger. "When this is over," he thought to himself, "I'm going to beat the living crap out of this asshole!"

"Steady there, Jonesy, good work, steady as you go," came the calming voice of the Tactical Unit's Sergeant. Sgt. Olsen observed that Jones had relaxed his grip ever so slightly on the trigger, yet he continued to glare at the perpetrator with a menacing death stare. The red laser-dot from Jones's weapon remained steady on James's forehead as he and the other officers approached for a slow and careful takedown.

Sergeant Fred Olsen, a 20-year veteran of the NYPD, spent nearly all his time in the Transit Bureau. Like many officers, Olsen seized the opportunity to expand his police experience when the NYPD absorbed the NYC Transit Police in 1998. However, like many others, he soon grew weary of "above-ground" police work and transferred back to "the hole" of the NYC Transit System.

In the meantime, he had been promoted to Sergeant and was thoroughly enjoying his supervisory role. Sgt. Olsen thrived in moments like this—life and death decisions made swiftly in one of the world's largest and busiest transit systems. He was on-scene managing a dramatic and perilous situation. His task extended beyond merely overseeing his troops; it was to control, as effectively as possible, this critical scenario.

Sgt. Olsen immediately identified at least three potentially fatal factors that needed quick and effective containment. There was James Waters with his suicide vest, Police Officer Rob Jones, who appeared on the verge of firing at the slightest provocation, and Carol Waters. Sgt. Olsen speculated that Carol might impulsively rush to her son, triggering a possible reaction from James and likely Officer Jones. Alternatively, she could become overly defensive and lash out at Olsen or Jones, potentially provoking an immediate response from the officers, which could, in turn, provoke James.

What Sgt. Olsen couldn't know was Carol Walters's mindset at that moment, which was more hopeful than others might realize. Yet, it was a mindset any mother could understand: the most crucial outcome was James emerging unharmed. Carol was aware that James's life would be irrevocably altered by these events, but having him alive in federal prison was vastly preferable to losing him forever. Carol was resolved to do whatever possible to ensure James survived this ordeal, aiming to secure him another day, and then another, and so on—still better than the alternative.

There was also the unpredictable and as yet uncontrolled reaction of the mass of commuters and potential victims on the platform and trains in the station, along with the possibility of additional victims and suspects on any arriving trains or elsewhere around the massive station. All things considered, Olsen and his team were truly earning their pay today.

First things first, and very quickly second, came James and the bomb, and the potentially explosive involvement of Carol Waters. James' eyes roamed the platform, but to Sgt. Olsen, those wandering eyes seemed to be seeing a thousand miles away. "James," Olsen said sternly to capture the young man's focus, "My name is Fred Olsen and I'm a Sergeant with the New York City Police Department—first things first, let's reorient to the immediate details. We've got quite a situation here, James, but so far, no one's been hurt. Let's keep it that way, okay? I'm sure you don't mean to hurt your mom here, right?" Olsen hoped sincerely that this was the case.

As this conversation unfolded, the other officers used hand signals to direct the remaining disembarking passengers around the encounter and on to safety. Among them was Miriam Bednar, who once again came close to disaster but ultimately was spared. She left the station teary-eyed, shaken, and stunned that she had once again escaped unconscionable violence.

Sgt. Olsen needed to draw upon all his training and experience at this moment. "I know we can get through this mess without anyone getting hurt if we work together, okay?" he urged. "Keep the perpetrator focused and engaged, use empowering phrases and questions to give him a sense of choice and control in the situation."

"We can all get through this alright if we stay focused and do what we need to do here, okay, James? You don't want your mom getting hurt, and we don't want anyone else getting hurt—so let's all just take a breath and see what we need to do next. First off, James, we need you to keep your arms raised like that, and please, don't make any sudden moves. We don't need any accidents here, okay?" James nodded absently, still in disbelief that his mother was here—all through his training with Muhammed, in Pakistan, the vest... he had conditioned his mind to ignore her existence. But now, at this critical moment of supreme sacrifice and retribution, she was only a few feet away, and this policeman, this cop, kept pointing her out to him.

Muhammed and the others had drilled into him to ignore the worldly 'distractions'—mothers and fathers, sisters and brothers, friends and lovers—all seen as anchors to drag one down. These earthly distractions were to be shunned to pursue his divine mission. But now, Carol Waters was just yards away, while Muhammed, Mehmet, and the others—the Islamists, the jihadists—were nowhere to be seen. Just this cop, and Carol.

And the cop, continuously using his name—"James, focus... James, be careful... James, no one has been killed..." And Carol. This damn cop. "James, hands up, James, I'm coming over to you..." And Carol. James' mind oscillated between the cop and Carol, mechanically and remotely following the officer's instructions.

Now an NYPD Operations Lieutenant was on the scene, observing Sgt. Olsen's precise and effective interaction with the suspected bomber. He was also coordinating the response of appropriate emergency service resources to address the situation. Once again, Bomb Squad, EMS, Fire Department, and Transit Units all needed to be directed and managed on-scene, along with coordinating the evacuation of this complex and massive train station and the surrounding area.

A female officer on the platform took charge of Carol Waters. Being a mother herself, she understood both the value and potential hazard of Carol's presence. For the time being, the value seemed to outweigh the hazard as Carol, quite emotional, and James, distraught yet compliant, followed instructions. The officer recognized that Carol's presence had a somewhat mesmerizing effect on James. As long as both James and Carol continued to comply, it made sense to keep Carol within close sight and nearby James.

Chapter 39
Strategies in Crisis Management

With James still largely distracted by and trying to comprehend his mother's presence on the scene, the police were managing to get him to comply remotely. "Now, James," Sgt. Olsen instructed, "slowly, hands up all the way now, over your head, straight up, good." Olsen examined the wiring of the vest to see if he could spot any obvious booby traps. Finding none, he realized that there was much about the vest-device he didn't understand. He knew that an explosives technician with more expertise would need to examine the device.

Looking around, Sgt. Olsen once again prioritized his next steps: custody and control, isolation, and evacuation.

Custody and Control – Is the suspect adequately secured? Isolation – Are any more trains scheduled to arrive? Could radio transmission trigger an explosion? Evacuation – Is the entire station being evacuated? Do we have confirmation of Bomb Squad response? It seemed they might already be overwhelmed…

It was then that Olsen spotted the Operations Lieutenant and decided it was time for a consultation. He directed James to slowly lower his arms and instructed nearby officers, including Rob Jones, to maintain control over the suspect.

A brief discussion with the lieutenant determined their next steps: no further radio transmission on the platform. A phone conversation confirmed there would be no more rail traffic into Grand Central. NYPD Special Operations reported that an explosives technician, from either the NYPD or another agency, would be responding shortly. The complete evacuation of the station and the surrounding area was underway. Sgt. Olsen could now return to his conversation with James to explain what would happen next, hopefully within a few minutes, though possibly longer. Olsen did not mention the delay due to other incidents; James seemed to understand why already.

"Now, James," Olsen continued, "we're bringing in some explosives technicians to examine the vest, okay?" "So, we need to know—is this vest booby-trapped in such a way that removing it would trigger an explosion?"

James, overwhelmed by the turn of events, replied distantly but honestly, "I... uh, um, you know? I don't really know. I mean, it never came up."

"Ah-huh," Olsen responded.

Chapter 40
Bobby Wilson's Fatal Error

At Union Square, Times Square, and now at Grand Central, the NYPD, FDNY, EMS, NYC-Metropolitan Transit Authority, and the citizens they serve had been spared diabolical horror, for now. Meanwhile, these agencies were getting a real-time feel for the effects of the already detonated suicide vests at the Port Authority Terminal and Herald Square. No one knew for certain if the remaining vests were booby-trapped against tampering, if they could be detonated by any variety of remote control, or if they had separate time-device detonators. Nor was it clear if the attacks were over or if more were to come. The way things were unfolding in rapid succession, it seemed as if there was no end in sight.

So while things at these locations seemed to be somewhat stable at the moment, the morning's events had, as intended, instilled a dreadful sense of foreboding.

As Bobby Wilson arrived, late, for his appointment with eternity at Penn Station, he was immediately and starkly aware that things were not going to happen as planned. And that was because Bobby had strayed from the plan. He'd begun to have second, and then third thoughts. His delay had caused him to leave late. His hesitation had caused him to exit the 'C' train a stop early at 23rd Street and walk the next few blocks to Penn Station.

Of the various tasks Muhammad and his co-conspirators needed to go right for success in these attacks, none was more important than the first: Stick to the plan. Muhammad and his gang of terrorists knew they would probably not be so fortunate that each of the Western recruits, either by their own doing or some interference, would fully execute a successful mission. Realistically, Muhammad understood that if 2 or 3 succeeded, that was probably about the best he could hope for. Any more than that would certainly be a bestowal from Allah.

He also knew that because of the volatile contents of the vests, interference in an attack did not necessarily mean defeat; they could explode at any moment, still wreaking havoc. Either way, on November 10, he'd be aboard a late-night international flight, praying for the best possible outcome.

So as Bobby Wilson deviated from the plan, it was not anything too unexpected by his jihadi handlers. It was, though, a very big deal to Bobby. Walking up toward the entrance to Penn Station, Bobby knew after one quick look around that any jihadist notions had deserted him.

Bobby Wilson had come into the company of the band of jihadi terrorists more or less by circumstance, rather than any deliberate intention. He soon found among them the attention, and sense of purpose he craved. He'd run into, and had several conversations with James Waters at the Muslim Relief Agency. Bobby was working as a janitor, a minimum-wage, agency 'temp'.

As he became friendlier with James Waters, he began to describe his general dissatisfaction with life, his lack of direction. He told James about his profound sense of disappointment. "James," Bobby would lament after some random discussion, "I just don't get the point, ya' know...?" James, attentive, agreeable, would nod in affirmation. "I mean," Bobby had said, "what's the point of my life? To be a janitor in some building?" Bobby was under a typical misconception—that now was forever. James told Bobby that the fact that he wound up in this particular building, at this particular time, may in fact, have some meaning after all.

As time went on and their conversations continued, James told Bobby about his new friends, and about how his relationship with them had brought about a new and very special sense of direction and purpose to James. Bobby decided to join James for a meeting with his engaging new friends. Bobby was nearly intoxicated with all the new attention, and hooked by the excitement of 'The Teachers'. After a few weeks, Bobby too, experienced a 'Special Calling' to Jihad.

Because he was late, AMTRAK Police and DHS Security Officers were beginning to assemble outside of Penn Station in response to the escalating attacks. Like their law enforcement colleagues at other New York Transit hubs, they bore automatic rifles and were accompanied by dogs. Still a good 30 feet away, and very fortunately for him, downwind of the dogs, Bobby did an abrupt and unobserved about-face to head off in the opposite direction. He decided it was a nice day for a walk; to perhaps, Westchester County.

Almost a block away, he spotted an empty service alley and a dumpster. Unknown to Bobby, he had indeed been spotted. To his continued good fortune, the man who'd seen him was not a law enforcement agent but a local vagrant. From a doorway across the street, the 'un-domiciled' individual watched as Bobby went into the alley.

The person watching knew from his un-domiciled meanderings that there was a dumpster there. He'd scored some decent throw-aways there previously, which accounted in part for his presence at the moment. He'd been astute in his observation that upon entering the alley, Bobby sported a nice-looking overcoat, with possibly some kind of sweater underneath. He saw that Bobby had begun to wriggle out of the coat as he hurried into the alley.

He wondered only briefly about Bobby's rush but was confident with his experience that it would not be the first time he would explain to an officer that he'd found, not stolen, his attire. This experience, though, would be an entirely new and different adventure.

The genteel dumpster-diver was a man in his early 50s, his body, mind, and spirit addled by years of alcohol, narcotic/hallucinogenic/sedative/stimulant drug abuse. His condition was further compromised by years of over-medication on a variety of anti-psychotic and sedative medication. There were frequent moments when he could not be real certain about the reality of what was going on about him. But, by some miracle, he was not quite completely incoherent and delusional, though he had his moments. He had a very strong intuition at this moment, though, that something interesting was unfolding. He was able to remember, and piece together, the sequence of events leading him to where he now stood, waiting to see what would become of the fellow who'd hastened into the alley.

The man he'd watched across the street at Penn Station seemed distracted, and he surely walked away to avoid the police who seemed to be gathering at the station entrance. Yes, some adventure was in play here, he just needed to wait and see what came next.

What came next was very nearly the last thing the homeless man ever saw. A roaring boom, followed by a pulsing cloud strewn with rubbish and the roasted flying remains of one Bobby Wilson came roaring out from the alley and onto 8th Avenue. Only distance and open air prevented instantaneous death for the 8th Avenue vagrant and all of those nearby.

Some surviving pedestrians were sent shooting through the air by the force of the blast venting out under pressure from the tall narrow alley. Five of them died, three on the scene from blunt-force trauma and cardiac arrest, and two later at St. Clair's Hospital from the same symptoms. Over a dozen more were injured, ranging from physical trauma, shock, and varying degrees of poisoning from the airborne toxins. Two of the poisoning victims died within the next 36 hours.

Startled, shocked police officers in front of Penn Station first clenched in a reflexive crouch, then several at once radioed into Command to report the explosion. After the initial confusion of sorting simultaneous radio transmissions, Central Dispatch was able to decipher that there'd been an explosion in an alley up the street from Penn Station and that there were several casualties on the street. This involved more firefighters and paramedics, police officers, explosives technicians, and another specially-configured, explosives transport truck to remove any unexploded remains.

Chapter 41
The High Stakes of
Bomb Disposal

'Emergency Truck Ten, Truck Ten on the air?' Truck Ten was normally assigned to patrol in North Queens. Today, like the other ESU Squads, Truck Ten was interrupted en route to its third Manhattan assignment. 'Truck Ten, respond—8th Avenue, West 34th to West 35th, Midtown and AMTRAK units on-scene, explosion in the alley. Casualties reported, Fire and EMS are responding…' As ESU Truck 10 acknowledged the assignment, they were informed that the 'Next Available' Explosive Tech Unit would also respond.

The vagrant from across the street was transported by EMS in critical condition but survived and was later interviewed by investigators from various agencies to explain what he saw on the street directly prior to the explosion. Although his reliability as a witness was a bit shaky, his account of events basically matched up with the crime scene evidence.

The presence of another one of the multi-lethal, toxic bombs at a transit hub also called for the evacuation of the station and surrounding vicinity. New York's Police, Fire, and EMS Services had yet another complex and truly multi-layered evacuation project to manage, and it was apparent that additional resources were going to be needed.

On this tragic day, the population of New York was at an all-time high; there were approximately 8 million 408 thousand people living in New York City. And this day, it appeared as if every one of them was in grave danger. In addition to a complete off-duty recall of all Police, Fire, and EMS personnel, the State Police and the New York National Guard would now be mobilized to operate in the city. The United States Coast Guard, a key component of harbor security for the Port of New York and New Jersey, was at this point on full alert and off-duty recall, as were New York area units of the U.S. Navy.

The blast that ripped apart Bobby Wilson's body and sent the pieces shooting out of the alley onto 8th Avenue had been detonated by the type of device that had concerned Bomb Squad Techs at the other attack sites. The murderous explosive devices were, as feared, rigged to detonate if tampered with. In this instance, when Bobby removed the overcoat off the vest, it released a pressure-switch trigger on the bomb.

At the time of the Bobby Wilson explosion, it was too soon to determine exactly what had exploded in the alley and how that happened, but officers had significant clues to work with. After literally 'following the trail' of evidence, they were able to draw some conclusions. They knew going in that there were suicide bombers attacking multiple sites in Midtown Manhattan.

Upon arrival at the Penn Station explosion, they knew the initial explosion occurred in the alley off 8th Avenue. Haz-Mat meters immediately alerted them that they were dealing with the same type of toxic bombs as those at the other sites. Probably the most gruesome physical evidence at this site was a trail of debris—bits of burnt, shredded clothing and the remains of the recently departed Bobby

Wilson, from the destroyed dumpster in the alley, along the approximately 20 feet of the alley, and out onto 8th Avenue. This gave investigators enough information to figure out what had occurred—the burned, tattered remains out on 8th Avenue were not too long ago, a complete human figure at that dumpster in the alley.

The subsequent explosion, projecting a trail of evidence, combined with the information from the other incidents, led to the logical conclusion that this smoldering mess in the street was indeed another terrorist suspect.

This explosion now confirmed for Bomb Team Members on-scene with the dead perp at Union Square, and Dennis Harding in custody at Herald Square, as well as James at Grand Central, that there was no room for error in disarming and removal of the suicide vests. While situations at each incident differed according to their particular circumstance, one common component was the very real threat of lethal incendiary explosion.

It all also left no more doubt that New York City, and by extension the United States, was in the midst of a multi-pronged deadly terrorist attack. The people of New York, and the nation, needed to hear from their elected leaders. They needed some reassurance and direction. Reassurance that this catastrophic attack was being contained and managed. And direction on how best to proceed through this dreadful day, and the next few uncertain days to come.

It was soon decided among the powers-that-be, that the people of the City of New York, at the bull's-eye of this assault, should hear from their mayor first, followed very quickly by the governor of the

State of New York. Then, in short order, the entire nation should hear from the president. The very tricky thing here, as with most leadership and political tasks, was timing.

Something, some sort of public showing, needed to happen fairly quickly. It would not serve anyone well then, to give reassurance, to claim control, to imply safety, and then have the attacks continue with more dead and injured. Therefore, the most common type of tactic here was to quickly choose a site, throw together a press conference stage replete with podium, backdrop, a bank of microphones, and then give statements every 5 – 10 minutes or so saying the mayor, or governor, or the president was 'being updated on the very latest information as we speak, and is expected to address the press momentarily'.

In fact, the police department, as well as the mayor's immediate staff, were more concerned with evacuating the mayor from the city to safety, then they were with any public appearances. The mayor, however, was most emphatic in his dismissal of that plan. 'Out of the question, no!' he insisted. 'I will not cower or abandon my post while the city is under attack!'

At Union Square Station at 14th Street, the perpetrator was D.O.A., giving the Explosives Techs there just a bit more leeway in their operation. Only a bit though, as one wrong move, even with a dead subject, could still ignite disaster.

With Dennis Harding at Times Square, the officers were dealing with a suspect who displayed surrender and compliance, but all the investigators there agreed that with his defiant smirk, and less-than-completely cooperative attitude, there was still plenty to be concerned about. Most of the officers on-scene there were certain that one well-placed shot would 'terminate' the terrorist attacker. But no one was certain what the end result of a fatal shot would bring.

The situation with James at Grand Central seemed to be rather favorable given his obviously compliant appearance and behavior, though you had to consider that neither he, nor the vest were completely stable.

At the scene of the first incident at Union Square, the 'subject' had been cordoned off, the evacuation of the station and the surrounding area was well underway, and the disarmament work area had been isolated as well as possible. Now the Bomb Techs needed to conduct a visual safety inspection of the immediate work area, and a detailed and very specific examination of Scott Warren's remains, and the extremely volatile device that was attached to him.

The NYPD procedure at this point was for Bomb Squad Robot 'officers' to conduct as much of the inspection as was possible. And, if feasible, for remote removal of the explosive device. When the operation began at Union Square, NYPD had one Bomb Squad Robot, known as Officer Intrepid, on-scene. A second robot, Valiant, was being transported en route, and a third, known as Officer Charles, was available for backup if needed. As the attacks continued to unfold though, Robot Officer Valiant was redirected. Officer Charles was also given another assignment. Before long the Union Square Techs were being asked how much longer they would need Robot Officer Intrepid.

At Union Square Station, Bomb Squad Robot Officer Intrepid was placed onto the Handicap Access passenger elevator and brought down to the passenger mezzanine level where the very recently deceased Scott Warren lay, adorned in the still-armed suicide vest. Bomb Squad investigators at the scene were familiar with this type of explosive device, as it was a 'popular choice' among terrorists. New York City was a 'high-value target' for terrorist groups, resulting in the NYPD Bomb Squad (a.k.a. Explosives Investigation Unit), being one of the most informed, well-traveled and trained, highly proficient, counter-terrorist operations units in the world. They understood completely what they were dealing with.

They understood that it was most likely that the 'vest' was indeed somehow booby-trapped with any variety of anti-tampering triggers, and that remote detonation of the bomb was a possibility to be considered as well. Being 'below-grade' in a subway station made remote detonation more unlikely, but not, they knew, impossible.

As work at Union Square progressed, the technicians were in the process of deciding upon 'robotic', or 'personal' removal of the device. Having done a visual survey of the scene and device, and proceeding to robotic operation, focus and energy for Bomb Squad operators at Union Square intensified upon hearing of first, the horrific explosion at the Port Authority Terminal, and then the standoff at Grand Central.

As this was being discussed and decided, reports of the explosion outside Penn Station began to come in. This news, more information for the Bomb Squad to consider as they made their next set of decisions.

On the one hand, the fact that a similar device had exploded in an alley near a dumpster, led to the conclusion that the vests were most-likely triggered to explode upon separation from the person 'transporting' the device. This information leaned in favor of robotic, rather than up-close and personal removal. However, given that the vest needed to be moved while somehow maintaining constant contact upon the trigger, seemed to require a finesse better achieved by human touch, agility, and anticipation/reaction more suited to humans, rather than even the very latest in robotic/computer technology. Then again, if one of

the humans attempting removal of the device got tripped up, the result was the loss of human life. If one of the machines were destroyed…well, you could always get another machine.

Still, given all that, if a device were triggered accidentally by either human or machine, there was the ominous menace of death and injury to those in the vicinity, as well as the likelihood of catastrophic destruction of infrastructure and property. When all was considered and rehashed, it was decided that the intricate balance of consistent pressure on a trigger, combined with both agility and instant decision, was more likely to be achieved by skilled and experienced humans, rather than a machine.

Chapter 42
Captain Martin's Critical Choices

NYPD Captain Mark Martin, a 22-year veteran of the department and 16-year member of the Bomb Squad, had spent the last 11 years as Commanding Officer. A third-generation Irish-American, Martin's lineage included service in the NYPD, FDNY, EMS, and Transit. Despite his unimposing physical presence, he maintained a fit, lean figure at 47 years old. Captain Martin quickly assumed command upon arriving on-scene at Union Square. Early on, it was agreed that there would be no remote communication of any type on the mezzanine-level or below at the station, and only broadband email messages using a variety of mixed frequencies were permitted on the surface within three blocks.

This procedure established, when new reports about developing events needed to be relayed to team members below ground, officers from the street-level had to walk downstairs to the mezzanine and signal to whomever they needed to speak. This operation interrupted Captain Martin repeatedly, but necessarily, during the Union Square Station job. Initially informed of the explosion at the Port Authority, Captain Martin was tempted to leave and respond uptown. After some mental triage, he decided that the Port Authority device had already exploded and there was nothing he could do about that.

He informed the detective who had relayed the report of the Port Authority incident to update him if any suspected unexploded devices were found there. Captain Martin then instructed his second-in-command to respond to 42nd Street with a couple of his Bomb Squad detectives to assess the situation there and report back. The next interruption for an update brought different information to consider— a live suicide bomber at Grand Central Station.

Upon being informed of a live bomber being detained at Grand Central, Captain Martin decided to leave the dead bomber and live bomb at Union Square for one of his senior techs to manage, while he responded to Grand Central.

On making his decision to leave the Union Square incident for Grand Central, Mark Martin knew he could not possibly miss the opportunity for discussion with one of the terrorist operators. He knew that any possible information he might get there could prove invaluable to manage the rest of this dreadful day in New York. He was off to meet James Waters.

Upon approaching on-scene arrival at Grand Central Terminal, having raced the nearly 30 blocks uptown in record time, Captain Martin got word that another terror suspect was in custody at Times Square over on Broadway. Upon arrival at '42nd & Park,' Captain Martin quickly instructed an on-scene NYPD lieutenant to send word to other Bomb Squad members to confirm their response to Times Square. Martin was now observing and insisting upon radio silence in the vicinity of the 'Grand Old Terminal.'

Captain Martin completely understood the ramifications of another device just over three blocks away at Times Square. Training drills, site inspections, orientation tours—all had caused Captain Martin and the members of his squad to have walked the railway of the

Times Square Shuttle Train connecting the two stations. He understood the effect of the detonation of another of the powerful and toxic devices nearby. He once again donned his anti-blast vest and grabbed his protective hood and headed downstairs to meet James.

Another NYPD officer who literally could not afford to miss the opportunity of conversation with James was Captain 'Jack' Hammond of the Intelligence Unit. John Hammond, 53 years old and a 30-year veteran of the New York City Police Department, was a lifelong Brooklyn resident and a supervising officer of the Intelligence Bureau since right after the events of 9/11. Captain Hammond had been monitoring the astonishing events of the day on a variety of channels and sources from the unit's secure and secret location just across the East River in Brooklyn.

On the surface, the Intelligence Unit's headquarters appeared as just another run-down warehouse on the Brooklyn waterfront. And actually, the ground floor of the warehouse did not seem to be much more than some sort of NYPD supply and storage facility with a warren of cubicles and offices.

It was downstairs, three stories below-grade, that housed one of the world's best-equipped and ultra-modern counter-terror/intelligence facilities. And it was there that Captain Jack Hammond and his NYPD crew monitored New York, U.S., and international networks and events. The NYPD shared space and expenses here with FBI, DHS, CIA, and NSA. This place was though, very much an NYPD operation. Upon hearing of a live suspect at Grand Central, Captain Jack Hammond and his team were quickly on their way.

One of the Tactical Team members informed Sgt. Olsen of Captain Martin's arrival. Olsen nodded his acknowledgment and turned back to the prisoner. 'James, there's a captain here from the Bomb Squad and we're gonna see if we can get you out of this thing without killing everybody here, okay?' Upon saying this, Olsen gave a distinct nod toward the stairway where Carol Waters still stood, in the protective custody of Officer Tara Wallace.

'James, my name is Captain Mark Martin, NYPD Explosives Unit. You can call me Mark.' This introduction not only identified Martin, but it also began the illusion of friendship between the two men. A suspect was less likely to blow up his new friend Mark than Captain Martin, NYPD. At the same time, the statement identified the authority in the relationship; James' new friend Mark was the NYPD Unit Captain, and James was not.

'Alright, James,' Martin began, 'let's see what we need to do here, okay?' The illusion of friendship, coupled with the fantasy that Martin was completely confident that this operation was going to be smooth and easy, ended in a question that implied permission and participation from James.

Captain Martin continued the role-play of James as a partner in, rather than the subject of, the operation. 'Let's just hang on a moment while we clear some of these folks out of here, James. You just stay just like that, and I'm going to step over here for a minute… and I'll be right back.' Experience, training, and logic had taught defense and police officials worldwide that there should be no unexplained, observable activity with a live bomber at hand.

Martin quickly explained to the on-scene operations lieutenant that everyone who was not an explosives tech or hostage negotiator would have to go 'upstairs.' 'Do you want the mother?' asked Sgt. Olsen. 'Hmm…keep her within reach, but out of the way,' came Martin's reply. Captain Martin was then informed that Robot Officer Valiant had just arrived and was being loaded onto the Handicapped Access Elevator, and that an explosives transport truck had a 15-minute ETA. Also, arriving ESU and Bomb Squad Support Units were being staged on the mezzanine level.

Martin acknowledged the arrival and staging of the additional units and instructed the lieutenant to inform the newly-arrived explosives and ESU techs that he wanted to assemble a portable blast curtain around James, backed by sandbags on the outside of the curtain. All this, of course, would need to be explained, step-by-step to James, to prevent any surprise for anyone.

After confirming that everyone was clear on their instructions and next steps, Captain Martin returned over to James. 'Okay, here we go James, we want to get the vest off of you and get that out of here without anyone getting killed, okay?'

James nodded absently in agreement. As soon as the words left his mouth, Captain Martin had an absurdly simple thought about Union Square. 'Just give me a minute here James, I'll be right back…'

Martin stepped quickly over to the mezzanine stairway and nearly collided with one of his arriving squad members. 'Okay, boss, we're getting set up for the curtain and we're gathering all the sandbags we can find. FD has some here and we've called Highways and

Sanitation…' 'Excellent,' was Martin's reply, but now he had to address an embarrassingly simple question: Where do we stand with Union Square? 'Yeah! There's an idea down there, boss, they want to wrap up the DOA and put the whole package on 'The Truck'…' 'Exactly!' Came Martin's reply; 'Make it happen.'

The next logical progression was that if the DOA perp at Union Square was to be transported with the explosive vest intact, to another location for removal and/or detonation; perhaps that was how they should proceed with James, and the new perp at Times Square?

So there was some discussion. A pro and con debate about the new idea; which had many 'unknown variables'. James could initially agree to the plan, and then change his mind along the way, and try, perhaps successfully, to trigger the bomb. There was discussion that James' mom Carol could accompany them by car, (or in the truck?), as sort of a ride-along hostage. But perhaps interaction between mother and son could fail *en route*, and spoil things dramatically. There was also the possibility that the procession could be interrupted, either accidentally or intentionally, on the way to its destination. The idea was soon dismissed as too risky.

No, it was ultimately agreed to, they would have to work with the removal of the device on-scene. Therefore, the proceedings had to be described to James. Once the police had the more-cooperative James secured and transferring to a remote location, they could focus on the less-reliable Dennis Harding at Herald Square.

'Okay, James. Here we go…' Captain Martin began upon returning to James on the platform. 'Now, we need to be clear here

James. You are not going to trigger the bomb, right?' It sounds like a redundant question, but one that needs to be asked so that everyone concerned is clear on what has been agreed to, and what will happen next. James gave Captain Martin a dull, despondent, 'Uh, right, yeah' in reply. 'James, that did not sound very committed…Have we all agreed you are not going to detonate this thing, or, do we need to talk this over?' Martin responded, concerned.

James sighed – '

No, God, no more talk. We're clear, let's do what we have to do here.' They were the exact words Martin needed to hear—resignation, acknowledgment, and participation. 'Okay, James, very good,' came Martin's response, 'here's how this is gonna go.'

Captain Mark Martin explained that they were going to construct a blast shield around James, called a 'Curtain', and there would be a wall of sandbags around the curtain for protection outside the blast area in the event of an explosion. First, though, they needed to take control of, and as much as was possible, secure the trigger device.

'Alright,' James said when the first part of the beginning of the plan was explained. 'First,' he said, 'we need to get my mother out of here.'

This was a complex dilemma for Martin: He was bound by ethical principle to remove every and all civilians and non-essential emergency personnel. This most certainly included Carol Waters. But to Captain Martin's way of seeing things, James' mom was sort of his 'Ace in the Hole'. He felt as though he had a built-in guarantee with

Carol present; that James was certain to comply for as long as she was nearby. It was unethical and dangerous, but Martin felt compelled to play that out as long as he could. Which, he knew, would not be much longer. But, for right now, he needed at least a few more minutes…It was a good thing he was Commander of the Unit, he thought, because he would not allow such a trick by anyone else.

'James,' Martin began, 'that's going to be a tough one…' 'What do you mean?' James responded, appropriately astonished. 'Arrest her or whatever…take her out of here. You're the police, for God's sake, make her leave!'

'Sure, James. We can do that…' the NYPD captain began to explain; 'We can kick her legs out from under her, and wrestle her down to the ground, and overpower her. Hell, we can mace her or taser her if need be, and then get her all shackled for a ride down to Central Booking and Criminal Court, 'cause we'll have to charge her to cover the injuries… or, we can try and placate her as much as possible, and then persuade her that we've been as nice as we could be…' Martin let James fill in the blanks. 'She wants a minute with you…' Martin concluded.

'Oh God, really?' James moaned, 'you're gonna let her do this?' 'Just for a few seconds James, she just wants to see you, then we're taking her up, one way or another.' Captain Martin replied. It was, Martin knew, his hole card, and he was playing it now for all it could get him.

'Okay, so first James,' Martin began, 'we need to take care of that detonator as best we can. We're gonna need to tape that up, as good as we can, and then secure your hands away from it.' 'I am not going to set this thing off…' James began to protest. 'I know James, I know,' Martin responded. 'But we've got procedure here to follow, and make sure no one gets hurt, okay? We've just gotta go by the book here James, okay?'

'Yeah, yeah, okay,' came James' compliant response. When Martin and the bomb crew had tied up the trigger, and taped it to his chest, a few inches below his chin, they secured his hands behind him. Because of the bulk of the vest, and the overcoat, and the uncertainty of the effect on the bomb, the officers decided to cuff James loosely behind his back, using two separate sets of handcuffs to provide some slack.

Once James was thus secured, Carol Waters, cuffed loosely behind her back, and with an officer on each arm and three more on very close standby, was escorted around the blast curtain, and allowed to see her son, just very briefly. It was a gamble that paid off in the manner Captain Mark Martin had hoped for.

Carol looked directly into her son's eyes –'James, I love you more than you could know. I love you more than life itself…'

James looked down to the filthy subway station floor –'I know Mom, I know, I love you too…'

'I'm begging you James,' she intoned tearfully, 'just do what they say, okay honey, and come out of this alive.'

'Yeah, Mom. Sure.' Came James' reply. With that, Captain Martin nodded and winked at Officer Tara Wallace, and Carol was led away. All that was left was to figure out how to separate James from the vest without killing everyone in sight. The first order of business then, was to reduce the number of people present in the immediate area to a bare minimum, and get on with the 'nuts and bolts' of the operation.

Chapter 43
Coordinating a Citywide Response

As the nearby area evacuation proceeded and escalated, Mark Martin was consistently revising and updating his Plan of Operation. He soon decided that the extended evacuation area should consist of at least two surface area city blocks in each direction around James' underground location. Martin delegated this responsibility to the NYPD Operations Officer-in-Charge of the Tactical Patrol Unit assigned to the Grand Central Terminal area, under the overall command of the Manhattan Patrol Commander.

Capt. Martin then met once again with the Special Operations On-scene Supervisor. "Lieutenant," he explained, "we need adequate Special Operations Command units to maintain the security of the immediate vicinity of the Explosives Mitigation Operation, as well as the necessary technical support for such operations." He then left it to the SOC commanders to sort out the particulars.

Having done that, he refocused his attention, energy, and concentration on how to remove the explosive device without killing himself, James, or anyone else. Capt. Martin too, would be 'earning his money' today.

Keeping in mind the information learned in the blast near Penn Station and the solution reached in the Union Square situation, Capt. Martin began to form the notion that his solution for Grand Central and James was in there, somewhere.

Also, he needed information from his 'in-custody' live perp. He was being coached along these lines by a voice in his head. That voice belonged to Capt. Jack Hammond, NYPD Intelligence Unit, and was transmitted to Capt. Martin via an earbud on Martin's headset.

"OK, Mark, we need to know about the rest of his crew… if he denies knowledge; tell him we already know he's part of a group, and that his 'pals' are active in the city today. He needs to tell us about what's going on, including elsewhere." Mark Martin clicked his mic-switch once to acknowledge the message.

"Alright, James, we need to talk about the others in your group…" James' eyes darted about a bit as he raced to decide how much he would or would not discuss.

"What others?" James replied after a few seconds of hesitation. "James, don't even go there, OK? Don't start playing dumb with me, alright?" Martin replied testily. "You and I have been playing it straight with each other, right?" Martin questioned suggestively. "Uh, yeah… So?" came James' reply.

"So let's not start playing some B.S. mind games," Martin challenged in response.

"There's a lot at stake here," he continued, "so how about we just remain upfront with everything. You and me, James, man-to-man." James gave a near chuckle a bit in reply – "Yeah. You and me, and the entire NYPD, and FBI, and CIA, whoever the-fuck-else is listening?" "Tell him yeah, OK, we're all listening," Jack Hammond instructed in Martin's head. Martin and Hammond had worked together before, they'd participated in endless training sessions and exercises together. They each had a sense for how the other was thinking, and where they were going with something.

"That's right, James. The gang's all here," Martin answered. "So let's not screw around, and bullshit and play games… We know what we know, and you know what you know, so let's talk." James paused a moment and was reminded of Bob Dylan's song – "When ya' got nothing, ya' got nothing to lose. You're invisible now, you got no secrets to conceal." "Sure," James said, "Let's talk…"

"Alright then, James," Martin began, "we know there are several teams in this operation. We have a couple dead, and a couple in custody. My question – exactly how many teams are operating today?"

James paused, took a deep breath because he knew Martin was not going to like the answer: "I really, and I mean really, Captain, don't know." James was right about one thing, Martin did not like the answer.

"God damn it, James!" came the heated reply, "I thought we were being honest with each other?" The sad truth was that James was now being completely honest with Martin; he did not know exactly how many other teams were operating. He of course knew there were others; he'd met and trained with some of them. And Muhammad told James there were a couple of others. One reason for this was that Muhammad was fairly certain, mistakenly, that James would carry out his suicide mission to completion. It was just an instinctual reaction he got from the ever-serious, studious, and attentive James. And if it hadn't been for Carol at Grand Central, Muhammad would have been correct.

Another reason was that Muhammad also sensed that James needed reassurance, as the other 'recruits' did, that he was part of something larger, more involved, and with more impact than just James. And if it hadn't been for Carol...

So Muhammad had reassured James over the last few days leading up to 'The Mission', that there were in fact others. "His jihad brothers," Muhammad had said to James, would serve notice this day. They were to forever change the face of jihad, "bring it furiously home into the midst of the infidels' world."

So James could only tell Captain Martin what he actually knew – that there were others. As for how many, and where and when, he really couldn't say. James began to explain – "I know there are others, but I don't know how many, Muhammad didn't say... I know one's supposed to do a job at Union Square, and probably another at Times Square, and me... You said there were a couple dead, and a couple in custody, that's four, and me, wow, five? I didn't know there were five."

Martin's head was full of Capt. Hammond – "Muhammad? Who's fuckin' Muhammad? No, wait, let him finish, don't interrupt. Who the fuck is Muhammad?"

"OK, James, let's talk a bit more about Muhammad," despite Hammond losing it in Martin's ear, he sounded, as intended, cool and casual when asking the question, like he, James, and Muhammad were all good friends. "Where was it you ran into him?" As if Captain Martin and NYPD knew all about Muhammad, he just needed to be reminded of where he and James met...

"Muhammad?" James replied, "Well, I knew him from school, and then I volunteered at The Muslim Relief Agency..."

"Those fuckers!" Hammond gasped, "It figures." Hammond

got onto his own network- "All units, everyone available, get over to those rat-bastards at Muslim Relief, full precautions! Detain everyone in sight, goddamn it! We should have done this weeks ago!"

Previously, the intel unit of NYPD had gotten several tips about the Muslim Relief Agency being something more than a nonprofit, social welfare charity.

Suspects arrested on

unrelated charges, jailhouse informants, even ostracized members of the agency itself, had informed various law enforcement agencies, including NYPD, that the MRA, located on the West Side of Manhattan, was a fundraising 'front' for Islamic terrorists.

At the time of the attacks, there were over 800 Middle Eastern refugees in the U.S. whose status was 'unconfirmed', meaning it was not yet determined which of these refugee-immigrants were in the U.S. legally, or if these individuals were law-abiding citizens or wanted criminals. Most, but not all of these 800 'unconfirmed' individuals, were in some sort of 'custody'. Just over 400 were actually incarcerated, many of these at the Metropolitan Corrections Center in downtown Manhattan. Others' degree of incarceration ranged from 'housing' at various other local and federal prison facilities to community halfway houses, to supervised apartment programs, to permission to live with family or friends in the community. Those not actually incarcerated in prison were under varying degrees of house arrest.

The remaining 'detainees' were, in theory anyway, under strict federal supervision/observation. The actual facts of the matter, though, were that federal probation officers, Immigration and Customs

Enforcement (ICE), as well as U.S. Marshals officers, all responsible in varying ways and means for custody/immigration detainees, were already 'up to their ears in alligators', and were now being tasked with custody and supervision of an additional 800 persons.

Chapter 44
Tracing Ties within the MRA

Of this new batch of 'refugees,' at least 40 were on international counter-terrorism watchlists and no-fly lists. This was the status and backlog of counter-terrorism cases under active investigation on November 11th.

Previously, law enforcement agencies in New York and Washington, D.C. were notified that the Muslim Relief Agency in New York had been mentioned several times in various conversations with suspects and witnesses. In D.C., this information was escalated up the chain of command to the National Security Council and the Attorney General's Office. Feedback to the investigators in New York was vague and slow, indicating that other sources had also mentioned the MRA.

Subsequently, the NYPD, including Jack Hammond, and several federal law enforcement agents gathered significant but ultimately unsustainable evidence confirming such reports. However, decisions at various government and law enforcement levels were made not to move from investigation to prosecution. The reasons ranged from political correctness to anti-defamation concerns. Yet, suspicions were once again confirmed this day.

Capt. Hammond and members of his squad in the Intelligence Unit, along with NYPD detectives from the Counter-Terror Unit, FBI, DHS, and U.S. Secret Service, conducted various surveillance operations and had conversations with MRA officials, members, volunteers, and visitors. The MRA complained of harassment to congressional representatives, senators, White House staff, the

Department of Justice, the Governor of New York State, and the Mayor's office, claiming to be a legitimate, professional humanitarian relief agency repeatedly faced with unfounded allegations by law enforcement officials.

"Kenny, go to 'The CTC,'" Hammond commanded, "there'll be a warrant there for you, damn it all!" 'The CTC,' to which Capt. Hammond referred, was the Federal Counter-Terror Court, where Hammond and various colleagues had previously been rebuffed in their criminal pursuit of the MRA. However, this day was dramatically different—there were bodies in the streets, and blood ran down the drains of Manhattan like rainwater. This day, when the streets of the city resembled Baghdad during the war, there would be warrants.

"What is his name, James, Muhammad, what is his name?" Capt. Martin asked during the impromptu interrogation at Grand Central. Capt. Martin knew, as did Capt. Hammond, that there were about 30 men named Muhammad who were members of the Muslim Relief Agency. Detectives and federal agents working in New York had heard these names in connection with the MRA several times. Getting hands and eyes on that information had required imagination and significant government pressure on various sources.

Further investigation identified Muhammed Anwar as a potential radical and possibly a recruiter. Occasionally, there was mention of an associate named Mehmet as well. Investigators needed to obtain a copy, or at least another look at a copy, of the membership list of the MRA.

"I heard Mehmet once called him 'Anwar,'" James replied.

Chapter 45
Human Cost of Counter-Terrorism

CTC was consulted, and the appropriate warrants were issued. Upon their arrival at MRA Headquarters on 12th Ave, NYPD and various federal agents were uncertain about the conditions or resistance they might encounter. The standard operational procedure was applied: Hope for the Best, Expect the Worst. On a day filled with explosions and fire, maimed bodies littering the streets of New York City beneath a fine mist of lethal toxins, expecting the Best seemed unlikely.

Just as James, Jennings, and others who had accompanied Muhammed and his group in combat operations in Pakistan and Iraq had done; so too, had the Counter-Terror Troopers operating in Manhattan this day experienced 'Live Combat'. Many of the operators on this very mission had tasted, if not the Worst, something very close to it. The most harrowing of combat consequences is the loss of a Comrade-in-Arms. Some present on this day knew such pain personally.

In other operations, mostly abroad, particularly in the Middle East, and often with Israeli operatives, some of these troops had encountered significant resistance to attack/capture. Some had seen action either as U.S. military personnel or as law enforcement operators trained by Special Forces to U.S. military standards of combat engagement. All this training and practical experience came at a price.

In various operations, against a variety of opponents, U.S. and allied forces, including U.S. Counter-Terror Ops in-training, had routinely encountered defensive tactics, including the regular use of suicide bombers. One moment you're marching along the road, in-force and attentive, the next, an approaching passenger car explodes, killing and maiming your comrades. This type of horrifying defensive measure is something some terrorist groups employ. This mindset permeates the troops in action.

Typically, after sufficient 'credible intel' had been gathered against a target, operational plans were designed. This 'credible intel' was almost always the result of a combination of human information, some form of documentation, and observation. Observation could mean anything from a few hours of reconnaissance, to weeks of on-the-ground surveillance, to the often-favored aerial reconnaissance. Though aerial recon was often the least clear and reliable form of surveillance, it almost always ensured that no one got hurt.

A recent example of such a sequence of action was a devastating blow to ISIS in Iraq. Mosul, the second largest city in Iraq, had been under ISIS control for over a year at the time of the joint Iraqi/U.S. combat forces operation there. Information, combined with prior knowledge of the layout of Mosul, led the joint forces to conclude that a particular building in the city was being used for high-priority activities. The al-Zuhour bank in eastern Mosul, previously an office of the Iraq National Bank while under Iraqi control, was reported to be used as a cash depot for ISIS, primarily for payroll and payoff purposes.

Covert observation by drone, another favored type of reconnaissance, confirmed freight-transfer activity, presumed to be cash, at the facility. Although joint Iraqi/U.S. forces had no available 'boots-on-the-ground' observers, they did have an informer on the inside.

Several types of attack and pilferage operations were designed and subsequently dismissed. It became clear that planning an operation against a heavily fortified facility, deep within ISIS-held territory and frequently patrolled, would require lightning-quick, precisely controlled infiltration and egress deep behind enemy lines. While such an elaborate operation was within U.S. capabilities, the complexity and execution risk were high, and the likelihood of successful completion was low. A much simpler and highly successful alternative was chosen.

In the pre-dawn hours, a drone flew unseen several hundred feet above the target, streaming live, night-vision television views and precise GPS coordinates to a U.S. Air Force F-18, miles away and thousands of feet above the target. Below, back down on the surface of the Earth, a 38-year-old ISIS stalwart stood sentry at his designated post. The Iraqi Muslim had been a 'combat insurgent' of one type or another for nearly 20 years. He'd fought against Saddam Hussein's troops, Shia militia combatants, U.S Marines and Army, British Airborne Special Forces, and the latest iteration of the Iraqi National Army. He'd murdered, raped, and pillaged across and around the Middle East at the behest of various terrorist armies throughout his adult life. He was among the earliest members of the radical Islamist group now known as ISIS.

And now, as his just compensation for all his 'struggle' here in this life, he stood guard duty at a well-protected bank building deep within the city of Mosul. Just as dawn broke, he thought he sensed a distinct shift in the morning breeze. Suddenly, he heard the shrill screech of a rocket zoom past his ears. Seconds before, all the correct data had lined up for the U.S. F-18, and two laser-guided, two thousand-pound bombs were launched at the al-Zuhour Bank. In practically the same instant, millions of dollars in ISIS funds were destroyed in a flash, and the sentry was rocketed into eternity.

When Muhammed Anwar later heard of the destruction, his own cold heart ached. It seemed unlikely now that he would be paid the highly-touted, and hard-earned cash bonus he'd been promised for the New York attack.

Chapter 46
Retaliation Across Borders

Shortly after the airstrike on the al-Zuhour bank in Mosul, Abdullah Hakim, a 24-year-old Syrian, strolled the grounds of the Sultanahmet district, near the famous Blue Mosque in Istanbul. Hakim was cautious yet confident. Like his fellow operators in New York, he had to stifle anxiety in order to avoid drawing attention. As he approached as close as he dared to the heart of the site, he decided the moment was upon him.

As a group of sightseers, mostly Germans from a particular tour group, approached, the Syrian ISIS operator closed his eyes in prayer and detonated his vest. Along with Abdullah Hakim, eight of the twelve German tourists were killed instantly or very nearly instantly. The remainder of those nearby were horribly maimed. One more victim succumbed to her injuries some 18 hours later, while the remaining victims learned to live with some degree of lifelong disability.

There was speculation in certain circles that the Istanbul bombing was in retaliation for the Mosul Iraq National Bank air raid. While there was no direct link to Turkey in the destruction of the bank, it was well-known that Turkey frequently supported U.S. air combat operations in the region.

Although the aerial destruction of the Iraq National Bank building in the enemy-held city of Mosul was not typical of the kind of operations the Joint Combat Forces-Mid East were used to, it was not exactly an unknown type of operation, especially in the gathering and evaluation of 'Actionable Intel.' Nearly every member of the team of counter-terror operatives moving against the Muslim Relief Agency Office on Manhattan's West Side had spent hours of 'Observation' of 'Potential Targets' in Middle East trouble spots. And most of those had participated in follow-up operations against such sites.

As the officers and agents proceeded against the MRA Offices, it quickly became clear that, as far as combat was concerned, they would encounter the best scenario—no resistance. The suspects and evidence that federal and city anti-terror police sought had vanished.

There were a variety of booby-trapped IEDs throughout the complex, but these were identified quickly and either isolated or otherwise avoided. Disarmament and inspection of the office suites would take days, but a fairly thorough 'toss' could be managed quickly.

As far as intelligence was concerned, it became apparent that they would face the worst scenario: little to none in the way of suspects, evidence, or clues.

Still, as often was the case in such matters, whatever 'ancillary' digital hardware and software had been left behind were confiscated. Frequently, as was the case in the 10-year hunt for Osama bin Laden, such scraps yielded more interesting morsels, which occasionally led to useful information.

In the notorious bin Laden case, continuous sorting and sifting through such information finally led to a clue. In repeated review of the bits and pieces, a name consistently reappeared. Investigators asked each other, 'Who's this guy? Do we know who this is? Why does his name keep popping up? Where is he? What's his story?' Such persistence led investigators to a man who led them to the man. One never really knew for sure in this business; you just keep running down leads—one thing leads to another, often for naught. But every once in a while, 'hey, you never know.'

Hopefully, James had informed the 'Appropriate Authorities' of a name, which might develop into some 'Actionable Intelligence'. Meanwhile, there was the matter of getting James out of the vest.

Chapter 47
Constitutional Rights in
Counter-Terror Operations

As the NYPD/DHS Joint Task Force now had some names to work with and investigations to pursue, it dawned on some of the sharper legal minds that James had not been advised of his Constitutional rights as a suspect in the U.S. It was a common misconception that 'terrorists', especially those born outside the U.S., were not entitled to standard Constitutional rights such as legal representation during questioning and the right to refuse to speak to prosecutors or police. Recent court rulings had affirmed that even foreigners in custody, including places like Guantanamo, were entitled to certain U.S. Constitutional rights.

In the rush and excitement of the day's events, no one had informed James of his rights. So far, it had been mostly 'no harm, no foul'. At this point, James could be sentenced to life, or perhaps face the death penalty, based on the evidence that was in 'plain sight' and easily observable by the police or the public. His possession of 'weapons of mass destruction' was evident, with or without his cooperation. But now, as he began to converse with the police, the situation was moving into a new area.

Up to this point, James could legitimately deny having said anything about Muhammad, Mahomet, or the Muslim Relief Agency. That was of little consequence when James was apprehended wearing a suicide vest on a day in New York that such vests had killed and maimed hundreds.

The only legal concern so far was that James had named others without the benefit of having been advised of his legal rights. This might become a concern if government prosecutors pursued a conviction on conspiracy charges. James had informed police that he had met and spoken with others about circumstances currently under investigation, without being formally advised that he was not required to do so. Also, because he had not been warned, he could not be charged with conspiring with others to commit felony offenses.

This meant little to those who were named, as their failure to be named had not, at least up to this point, been used against James. But now, indeed, the situation had begun to delve into murky legal waters. It was time to address the issue.

A voice clicked on in Martin's ear— "Captain Martin, this is Robert Pelham from the D.A.'s office. Can you read me okay?" Martin quickly clicked his mic once. Captain Hammond nodded to Pelham to continue. "Captain, I just spoke with the District Attorney and he wanted you to know that Mr. Miranda called. Do you understand, Captain?" Again, Martin quickly clicked. Mr. Miranda was, of course, a reminder to Captain Martin to read the well-known recital of James Waters' Constitutional rights while he was in police custody and being questioned.

"James, there's some formal business we need to clear up before we go any further here," Captain Mark Martin spoke to James. "Ah, yes, Captain. I was wondering when and if we were going to get to this," James replied, fully anticipating what was coming. Before

Martin could begin, James interjected: "You know, I could legally deny anything we've discussed up to this point..."

Even as Captain Hammond began to coach into Martin's headset, Martin responded—"That's right, James, you are correct. So where does that leave us? You could deny having said anything about Muhammad and the Muslim Relief Agency. What does that get you? The opportunity to explain why you were traveling in the subway wearing a weapon of mass destruction on the very same day that hundreds of New Yorkers were killed by terrorists using these same deadly explosive vests."

"Easy, Mark, don't back him into a corner..." came Hammond's voice into Martin's ear. "Now James, remember, we've all agreed, you and I and your mother, Carol, that we want to move on from this mess without more bloodshed, right?"

There it was again, James thought, Carol. At that point, Captain Martin proceeded with the formal 'Miranda Warning' for James.

Chapter 48
The Mechanics of
Bomb Disarmament

The plan for safely removing the vest from James crystallized in Capt. Martin's mind once he stepped back to gain a more objective view of the situation. When up close and personal with the problem, Martin couldn't see the solution. However, as he engaged in conversation with James and Hammond about other matters, the answer became clear.

The bomb had a pressure-switch trigger set to detonate as soon as the pressure was released. This was how the Penn Station bomb had exploded, tragically sending Bobby Wilson into the fatal aftermath. Such an outcome was imperative to avoid with James at Grand Central and Harding at Times Square.

To counteract the pressure-switch, continuous pressure had to be maintained on the trigger to prevent its release, contact, and subsequent detonation. The challenging part was extracting the person from the pressure trigger while still applying pressure to the switch. Martin thought, if we could slide a board under the individual while maintaining pressure on the switch, we could remove the person strapped into the vest as long as we maintain pressure on the board.

The next question for Martin was how to maintain enough pressure on the board while extricating the bomber from the bomb. He reasoned that the board should be louvered, angled toward the trigger, allowing downward pressure to be maintained as officers slid the board into place, while simultaneously lifting the bomber slightly upward onto the board. The front end of the board would need to be generously lubricated to facilitate sliding the body onto the board, but not so much that it might cause the individual's body to slip around on, or even off the board, potentially causing chaos for everyone involved or nearby.

If this worked, as Martin hoped, they would have the bomber on a board, separating him from the trigger. The officers would then continue to slide-step along the board, positioning themselves as the bomber was removed up and away from the board and the bomb.

The next step was inspired by a lesson learned from a deceased bomber at Union Square: the bomb techs there discovered that by using duct tape to secure the dead weight to the trigger, the package could be transported away from the incident scene. This provided another learning opportunity for the bomb squad techs—they could test their theory in a controlled environment before attempting it live. If it worked in practice with the late Scott Warren at Union Square, then it could be implemented in real-time with the remaining devices. If not, well, that's a risk bomb techs must occasionally face. If you can't deal with that possibility, then you should find another line of work.

Chapter 49
Vest Removal Protocol

The latest of the explosions was the one near Penn Station, which had incinerated Bobby Wilson and an unfortunate few nearby innocent bystanders. That had occurred at approximately 8:45 AM, 10 minutes after the Herald Square explosion at nearly 8:35, and 25 minutes since the initial explosion at the Port Authority Terminal at just after 8:20.

James Waters had arrived at Grand Central Station at nearly 8:20. Dennis Harding had surrendered at Times Square at 8:38 AM. So things had begun blowing up in New York City at about 8:20, continued until 8:45, with a couple of potentially disastrous stand-offs and a fatal suspect shooting in between. Meanwhile, no one knew if the attacks were over, or how the stand-offs would end.

As 9:30 AM on 11/11 passed without incident, all parties concerned with the safety of New York City's residents and visitors, as well as those residents and visitors themselves, began to hope that perhaps, maybe now, they could experience some relief from the madness.

As The President addressed a nervous Nation, as well as a worldwide variety of concerned parties, the NYPD Special Operations Bureau continued its precarious set of tasks. Immediately upon them was the removal of the Explosive Vests from Union Square, Times Square, and Grand Central Subway Train Stations. Operations which also involved securing passage to, and securing and isolating, Rodman's Neck in The Bronx, as well as Floyd Bennett Field in

Brooklyn. Also on the agenda today for NYPD SOD was the ongoing evacuation and inspection of the city's Trains, Train Stations, including also Train Yards, and Lay-up Areas.

Foremost of these operations, for now, being the 'Packaging' and Removal of the late Scott Warren from Union Square to Rodman's Neck Range in The Bronx. There they would conduct Capt. Martin's improvised Removal Method, and, once successful, hopefully, they could remove James from his device, and send that God-awful package to the Bronx Range. At which time, if all went well, James could be transported to the 'Nearest appropriate NYPD Facility' to have his Name and other Personal Information, along with the reason (Charges, if any) for his Detention.

'The Nearest appropriate NYPD Facility' would be the NYPD Transit Bureau Station at Grand Central. Because Grand Central was being evacuated at the time James was taken into Custody by NYPD, this then gave them some leeway as to what the 'Most-Appropriate' and Nearby Facility was. Capt. Hammond of NYPD Intelligence, as well as some other Top-Guns at NYPD, including the Chief of Detectives, the Inspector In-Charge of Special Operations, the Police Commissioner and others, decided the Chief of Detectives Office at Police HQ at One Police Plaza in Downtown Manhattan would be as good a place as any.

This, of course, infuriated the FBI, DHS, ATF, and a few other departments and agencies with three-letter names, but for now, NYPD had the Suspect In-Custody, and until a Higher Court ordered them otherwise, in NYPD Custody he would remain.

At Union Square Station, the Explosives Techs working there did a fine job of securing Scott Warren's bullet-eviscerated body onto a standard E.M.S. Backboard with thick, wide, heavy-duty Duct Tape. The pressure from the tape pressing Warren down onto the contact-trigger provided enough gravity to prevent inadvertent detonation. More tape secured sandbags atop Warren and ensured that Warren remained secured to the Backboard for his final ride up to The Bronx.

A police caravan, consisting of Motorcycles and 'Fly-Cars' of the NYPD Highway Division, a couple of Emergency Services Division Trucks, an Aviation Division Helicopter overhead, along with some of the 'Bomb Squad' Detectives, ATF Bureau, FBI, and Homeland Security Agents in various vehicles, made the 16-mile trek from Union Square Station in lower Midtown Manhattan to the Rodman's Neck Firearms and Explosives Range out in the far end of The Bronx. Offshore of the Rodman's Neck Range, NYPD and USCG Boats secured and isolated the bay.

At Rodman's Neck, apprehensive but cautiously confident New York City Police Department Explosives Unit Detective Technicians, accompanied by U.S. Alcohol, Tobacco, and Firearms Agents, carefully but with determination, removed the 'packaged' remains of Scott Warren, whose life came to a sudden and certain end by two expertly placed, instantly fatal gunshot wounds fired by an NYPD Sharpshooter. Warren's torso remained well-bound by duct tape to a Backboard, pressure being maintained on the contact-trigger the whole trip from Grand Central.

It was now time to put Capt. Martin's theory to the test. The sandbags remained in place atop Warren's chest as the Techs cut away the duct tape securing him to the Backboard. There was some discussion of removing the sandbags before sliding Warren off the Backboard.

The 'Pro' side of taking them off was that Warren's dead-weight (literally) had sustained enough pressure on the contact-trigger without the bags, and it would be easier to have them out of the way, instead of having to work around them. The 'Con' side of the discussion being, that perhaps the extra weight of bags had locked the pressure switch down enough into a new position, and taking the sandbags from Warren's chest would jiggle the switch and thereby set off detonation of the Bomb. When Capt. Martin posed that theory, he was told by one of the Bomb-Squad Detectives that he 'Sure knew how to kill off a lively discussion.'

It was then decided to let Robot Officers from the Squad handle sandbag removal while the others watched from a safe distance on Remote-TV. Once the sandbags were removed without any 'fireworks', the Humans once again resumed operation.

While a 'fair amount' of pressure was sustained manually by Squad Officers, that being just enough downward push to maintain some pressure down onto the Contact-Trigger, the front of Warren's Suicide Vest was opened, and the Velcro straps tying Warren into the deadly device were cut away. Then came the most precarious and nerve-wracking phase. As manual pressure was maintained, the louvered board was slid down into place between Warren and the Contact-Trigger, downward pressure being pushed down onto the board as Warren's torso was simultaneously slid out of the Vest. At this point, the Bomb Officers involved each silently wondered if they would be around later to tell the story. Some asked themselves how many missions like this one they had left before good fortune finally abandoned them. Then they took another breath, prayed a silent prayer, and did what was next.

As this was done, the sandbags were smoothly slid into place atop the louvered board over the Pressure-Switch Contact Trigger. Once again, Duct Tape was applied to secure the sandbags to the board in place over the board atop the Contact Trigger, and then again to stabilize the entire 'Package' in place.

Scott Warren's remains were subsequently sent to the Office of the Chief Medical Examiner's Lab for further Examination. The Detectives of the Bomb Squad quickly agreed that any further examination of the Suicide Vest could best be done by a couple of the Robot Officers transmitting Digital Images to Humans working further away at a much more reasonable distance from the Explosives.

The first utilization of the 'Vest Extraction Operation' having been successful with the deceased Scott Warren, the next customer was James Waters at Grand Central. In the street above the Subway Station, Rescue Techs of the NYPD and FDNY worked together to custom-cut an E.M.S. Backboard into a louver-pitched plank for use in the Extraction Operation.

The louver-cut board, angled down onto the pressure switch, was slid into place, the Officers side-stepping onto the board, as James, lying on his back in the Vest, was gradually eased out of the Vest. 'Wait!' intoned Capt. Martin urgently, 'There's a wire…'.

Chapter 50
One More Goddamn Thing

With Bomb Squad and Emergency Services Officers holding James' body about eight inches above the backboard over the Contact-Switch Trigger, Mark Martin spotted a coated wire trailing from along James' back, down onto the Vest back toward the Contact-Trigger.

One of the Bomb Squad Officers was using a hand-held Digital Camera, recording the Operation and relaying images to a Command Desk on the Mezzanine Level. At 'The Desk', a Squad Member sighed half-heartedly – 'there wasn't a wire on the other one…'. To which Mark Martin, exasperated, retorted – 'Yes, Well, there is most certainly a wire on This One!'

'Oh, Now there's a wire,' James Waters lamented mockingly. 'All this elaborate bullshit and drama for nothing… 'cause Now, there's a wire. Looks like we're all going to Hell after all!' The remark tweaked Capt. Mark Martin's last nerve.

'Listen Up James, pay very close attention. We now have control of the Bomb, O.K.? Not You, Us. And in case you haven't noticed, We have Complete Control of You. Also, upstairs we have Custody of your Mother Carol, and your Girlfriend Joann. Muhammed is probably half-way to Pakistan and couldn't give a Rat's-ass about you anymore. Got it? Me and You buddy. If you say just One More Goddamn Thing I don't want to hear, I Am going to Shoot You Dead and The City will give me a Medal, and Name a Street for me.'

As Capt. Martin finished telling James Waters where things stood, Capt. Hammond gave his immediate critique: 'Congratulations

Mark, you just told a man who has nothing left to live for that you're gonna' shoot him. I'm sure we'll get his cooperation now.'

James too jumped at the apparent gaffe. 'Oh, Oh, you're going to shoot me?' Look around Captain. Does it look like I have a whole lot to live for?'

'Did I mention that we have Carol and Joann upstairs?' Martin quickly responded. 'You might survive this to explain it to them, or I could tell Carol that you loved Muhammed and the things he did, more than you love her and all that she does. You tell me Slick, which is it gonna' be?'

James had gotten about half-way through his 'I don't care even a little...' speech, when Martin carefully and quickly drew his 9mm weapon from its hip-holster, pressed its nose into James' temple. 'Say bye-bye James' in a rather menacing guttural semi-whisper. 'Oh this is going well,' Capt. Hammond in Martins head, 'what are you going to do now Mark, Shoot him?' Those nearby to Hammond simultaneously held their breath, each heart missing a beat, gawking at him in stunned disbelief, waiting for the now inevitable gunshot.

Similarly, those on the deck with Mark Martin were also shocked in complete silence. James lay cradled in the stern grasp of the Squad's Officers, wincing deeply with the gun barrel pressed into the side of his head, nearly hyperventilating through clenched jaws, awaiting the shot. 'Mark?' Martin's Squad Sergeant asked steadily yet anxiously. 'Quiet' replied Martin. Martin pushed and slightly twisted the gun into James' scalp. 'Say it, James. You're going now, say bye-

bye'. James inhaled, paused, and yelled – 'Someone get this lunatic Bastard away from me, he's crazy!'

With this, Capt. Mark Martin, NYPD Bomb-Squad, took a step back and re-holstered his weapon, winking at his Sergeant, Bob Miller and nodding almost imperceptibly at James. 'Now James,' Sgt. Miller began, 'we're gonna' let Capt. Martin step back a bit here and catch his breath and cool down. And while he's having his break, why don't you tell me about this wire on your back here?' Extreme Bad Cop / Good Cop.

Chapter 51
The Anatomy of a Booby Trap

The Saudi bomb-maker, al-Marsi, had incorporated an additional anti-tampering device into just two of the suicide vests, which booby-trapped any unintended separation of the bomb from the bomber. Despite the dangers, he pressed on with ferocious intent, driven by his lifetime obsession with destroying his adversaries. To al-Marsi, these were fairly new developments, and he had only managed to include them in the last two devices. Ironically, those two newly-improvised devices were the ones James now wore at Grand Central and another attached to Dennis Harding at Times Square.

"Look, uh, Officer...," James began. "I'm Sergeant Bobby Miller, James, NYPD," the sergeant introduced himself. "Yes, well, here's the thing, Sergeant," James replied, "Muhammed pretty much insisted that I wasn't supposed to know too much about the bomb at all. I swear to you, Sarge, that's just the way things were. Whenever he brought the vest over, he just had me put it on and fuss with it, whatever... But whenever I asked him about it, he told me all I needed to know was how to use the trigger, and that when I did, all the infidels around me would be blasted into hell and I would be rocketed to heaven to be with Allah and the Prophet. If I ever asked about the vest, that's what he would tell me, that I only needed to know about the trigger."

This response, as disappointing as it was, seemed perfectly logical and reasonable to the agents and officers on scene. The more experienced among them knew that this was fairly standard operating procedure for terrorists worldwide. In most terror groups that counter-terror agencies had managed to infiltrate or apprehend, standard practice was to inform mission operators only of their role in the mission, and if questions persisted, suspicion was aroused.

Now, Captain Hammond's voice came over the net to Bobby Miller, "Yeah, yeah. That all sounds about right; we won't press him on that right now. Let's hear more about Muhammed bringing the vest over—where, when, with whom, was anyone else at all ever there or mentioned?"

James tried as best he could to recall and explain that mission security was repeatedly emphasized by Muhammed. "Not so many questions, Young Warrior," he would say. "Your role as a Vessel of Justice is to deliver and detonate the device. Don't concern yourself too much about me or any of the others. Do your part, Noble Soldier."

While this conversation progressed, the Explosives Squad Team had a back-channel discussion about the wire. Naturally, the purpose of the wire needed to be understood. Was it just an 'Ordinary/Normal' piece of wiring of the bomb's operation, or did it have a special function, such as anti-tampering? Was it, in fact, a booby trap? Consensus among the technicians concurred it most likely so, with one abstention.

The abstaining squad member was Rick Brown. Detective Rick Brown, 40, just a bit overweight but basically physically fit, maintained a decent crop of bushy black hair and a moderate handlebar mustache. He had been a New York City cop for 10 years in the Patrol Division, occasionally being assigned some 'Clothes' work (a term used by uniformed cops for 'plain clothes' cops), before being promoted to detective.

During those 10 years, Brown maintained his interest in electronics and computer technology and, as well as vocational trade courses, had qualified for certification in certain aspects of the trade. His hope after NYPD retirement was to run a 'Geek-Squad' sort of business on his own.

In fact, several months after his promotion to detective, he was assigned to assist with the investigation into crimes involving cyber-fraud and other digital crimes. His prowess in electronic technology came to the attention of those within NYPD concerned with such matters, and after his first year in the Detective Division, he was recommended for the 'Bomb Squad.' So, Detective Rick Brown left 'police work' and joined the Bomb Squad.

There's a time-honored tradition in the NYPD that when an officer transferred to certain special units, such as Aviation or Harbor, the 'real cops' referred to them as 'no longer doing police work.' The Bomb Squad fell under that category.

Detective Brown was quite the stickler when it came to the finer points of electronics. He explained to his teammates that the stray wire on the bomb attached to James might indeed be an anti-tamper booby trap. His point, he explained, was that they did not know for certain. The difference being that if it were a wire that delivered a charge to an explosive after ignition, then they could 'probably' cut it. If, on the other hand, it was a booby trap, then they needed to somehow neutralize it to get James out of the vest.

Brown suggested that they photograph the wire and its 'destination' on the device for digital comparison in international databases maintained by various counter-terror agencies worldwide. "I bet the Israelis know that wire," he stated.

"That's gonna' take some time," Captain Martin replied. "I don't know how much time we have left with this thing..." Martin had several dreadful considerations in mind: These bombs were battery-powered. As the batteries drained, this could cause an interruption or surge which would result in detonation. Also, the cops did not know for certain if the devices were on timers, or if remote detonation was still a possibility. The other squad members were aware that a variety of ugly outcomes were still possible.

"Thirty minutes at the most," Rick Brown said, "let's get some pictures and get 'em out on the net while we consider our choices." "Yes, let's," came the captain's reply. Although Detective Brown knew from past experience that Israeli counter-terror units were probably the best informed and most responsive resources available in this particular line of work, he also understood that other NYPD/USA anti-ISIS partners such as France, Great Britain, and Germany were extremely helpful. And that was only a partial list of partners. Other contributing and helpful allies included Australia, Italy, the Netherlands, and some very helpful but deeply confidential information came in from Saudi Arabia, Jordan, the United Arab Emirates (UAE), to NYPD via anonymous, deniable back-channels, from DHS, NSA, Defense Dept., and the like. All working if not exactly together, at least mostly with each other, united, to ultimately defeat ISIS, al-Qaeda, and other terror groups.

Chapter 52
Nets and Nerves

All the while, for several minutes, a team of officers held 195-pound James Waters over the board atop the Pressure Switch, and he was growing heavy. No one spoke; no one wanted to be the first to break the silence. After a few minutes, one of the larger team members remarked, "Well, I'm having a real swell time, how about you guys?" Another replied, "I think we should stop hogging all the fun and let some of the others get a turn..." Consensus: it was time for a shift change.

Sgt. Miller suggested, "Maybe we could get a net..."

NYPD ESU and FDNY Rescue trucks are equipped with cargo nets, commonly used for moving obese persons into ambulances. A net was retrieved to place beneath James, and a new team rotated into position. The incoming team carefully gripped the cargo net and positioned themselves on the louvered board atop the Pressure Switch Trigger, pondering, "How many times am I gonna get away with this?"

Placing the net beneath James, with the wire leading up from his back into the vest, proved tricky. Momentarily, the wire shifted, perhaps stretching, and everyone held their breath, braced for an explosion. None came. The net was in place, the wire intact and stabilized by tape.

Sgt. Miller continued his conversation with James, while the squad discussed their next move. "The only way to proceed," Capt.

Martin stated, "is to treat the wire as a booby-trap." He looked pointedly at Det. Rick Brown, who nodded in agreement. "How can we defeat it?" Martin continued, noting the wire's path from the detonator to a contact on James's lower back. "If we move him out of the vest... ignition?"

"Maybe, maybe not," Brown replied. "We operate on the assumption of ignition. Our focus is bypass. Can we safely install a bypass wire? Has it been done before?"

Miller engaged James in conversation, carefully balancing casualness and interest. "So James, did Muhammad ever have others with him when he visited? Where was that?" James appreciated the distraction from his predicament.

"He came to see me at The Cave," James replied, explaining he was instructed to view his single-room occupancy as a "Warrior's Cave." He provided the Bowery address and recalled Muhammad's 5-6 visits over five weeks. On two occasions, Muhammad wasn't alone - once with one man, another time with two.

When pressed, James described these companions as fellow "Warriors," Arabic or Middle Eastern, around 25-30 years old. No names were mentioned during these visits.

Chapter 53
New York's
Finest in Action

As intense activity unfolded at Grand Central, elsewhere across New York, police, firefighters, medics, and transit workers continued their efforts to rescue, treat, and transport victims. The New York City Emergency Medical Services System was operating just beyond capacity and had activated its Regional Mutual Aid System. This brought in not only municipal volunteer and commercial emergency medical providers but also assistance from New Jersey across the Hudson, Westchester County to the north, Long Island communities to the east, and the Rockaways in Queens and Nassau Counties on the Atlantic shore to the south.

For only the third time in recent history, the FDNY had enacted the Emergency Mutual Aid Program, with previous activations during the 9/11/01 suicide attacks and Superstorm Sandy. With mutual aid activated, fire departments and emergency squads from surrounding communities were arriving via well-guarded routes in Manhattan and the boroughs. Their task was to provide either direct response to assist at the scene of the bombings or to respond to specific FDNY firehouses to provide coverage for any other emergencies that might occur while the New York City Fire Department was engaged in this colossal disaster.

Chapter 54
President Bowman's Address

Before much longer, the time came for the Man in Charge to address a frightened and anxious nation. President Bowman appeared at the podium not in the White House Main Press Room, but from the Oval Office, which provides easier access to the reinforced passageways leading to the elevator to the Sub-ground Situation Room.

From President Bowman's address: "This horrid savagery once again brings an ancient and tribal battle to our shores. I cannot declare 'War'; we are already at war with these maniacs, who seek to destroy our nation and our way of life. These are the same savages who murder innocent schoolchildren, claiming it is God's will. These thugs are not about religion; they are about power.

In response to this heinous act of barbarism, we shall use all available resources to gain whatever information we may glean from this disaster and use that to track down and destroy our enemy. Make no mistake. We will not be intimidated. We may be battered; we will not be beaten. We can, and shall, prevail."

With that, the President of the United States added a few more comments about the dreadful injustice of it all, and that 'we will be safe and strong.' He concluded his remarks, which included some not-too-subtle reminders for America's foes; the final comment among the most pertinent—'We are the U.S.A., and we are everywhere. We have the technology and the intelligence to find and track you. And, we have the resolve to destroy you once we meet. God bless those who suffer and those who mourn. And, God bless the brave men and women of the United States, everywhere."

It was precisely the message confused and anxious citizens of the U.S. needed to hear; "We are the U.S.A.; we are mighty and able, we will not be defeated—and, of course, we will find you, and you shall pay."

Although President Bowman went before the American people and said the words they needed to hear, once he was away from the microphones and once again secure in the bunker several stories deep below the White House, he could voice aloud his most pressing thoughts: "Have there been any more explosions?"

"No, Mr. President," Chief of Staff Thompson responded, "Nothing further has happened." "Well," the President sighed heavily, "Thank God for that." It was, for President Bowman, his first heartfelt genuine relief all day. There was work ahead and he and his National Security and Homeland Defense staff could not bear the burden of more murdered Americans. They had to now, somehow, find a way to make this stop. For all the talk of identifying the killers and delivering justice, that was all secondary until this turmoil stopped.

So while his remarks to the public hit all the right marks about identification and retribution for the terrorists, and strength and God's blessings for the U.S.A., he avoided any specific reference as to who might be to blame, and when the attacks would stop. Basically, it was the job of the President's National Security Council (NSC), to direct the effort to identify and locate the perpetrators of this God-forsaken devastation. It was the task of Homeland Defense (DHS), to direct operations concerned with casualty and damage control. Another function of DHS was to ensure the security and safety of incident sites, in order to preserve the crime scenes, and ensure the legal and appropriate evidence collection for investigation and any subsequent prosecution.

Both the NSC and DHS, therefore, have affiliations with the U.S. Attorney's Office, and naturally, great interest in the investigation into, and the prosecution of the 11/11 attacks case. And this was yet another consideration for the NYPD as well; another set of interested 'partners' to deal with.

Chapter 55
Innovation on the Front Lines

Behind the horror of 11/11 in New York lay years and years of international intrigue, revolt, and religious and racial hatred. The appalling devastation of the New York City attacks, as horrendous as they were, was yet just another episode of seemingly endless Middle East strife. The newest twist in this age-old animosity was the recruitment and utilization of disgruntled, aimless, malcontent Westerners as suicide bombers unleashing such shocking destruction on U.S. soil. This repulsive event, being a chapter of a much larger story, inevitably required the helpful participation of those who were extensively involved—and unfortunately, all too familiar with the murderous fanatics responsible.

At the moment, the current partnership with international agencies was paying off. Both Pakistan and Israel replied to the NYPD's overseas inquiries. Both nations' counter-terror forces had encountered the explosive devices described in the NYPD bulletin. Each nation had had its own experiences with the device and had arrived at common observations and solutions regarding these particular bomb "booby-traps."

Examination of such devices by the two separate departments had led to shared findings about overriding the anti-tamper features. The sum of each agency's work led to these conclusions: as menacing and intricate as the devices appeared, they were actually fairly typical and crudely constructed products of bomb makers. Although the devices were somewhat sensitive, they were not overly reactive to minor movement or adjustment. Given the mission conditions under which the bombs were operating, they could not be too finely tuned to slight movements and position changes.

This was encouraging news for the NYPD Explosives Units. The Pakistani explosive technicians had devised a taping method to temporarily mitigate the wire's function, and the Israelis had developed a simple bypass circuit device, which worked as long as it was correctly installed and stabilized.

The Pakistanis' tape solution seemed to require a lot of careful movement and precise tape placement that looked rather tricky; the Israeli method appeared simpler, more straightforward, and slightly less risky.

It was therefore agreed that the Israeli bypass device would be recreated by the NYPD. A solution was possible and, if successful, would give NYPD negotiators more of an upper hand in dealing with the snarky terrorists.

The Israeli device was simple, and in fact, it already existed. To apply this bypass, the squad technicians needed to adapt splicing equipment that was widely available—and in fact, already in stock in the Bomb Squad's extensive supply inventory. The procedure involved installing a mini splice box to provide a consistent current to the detonator while the vest was removed from the bomber.

After just a few minutes of intricate recreation of the Israeli device, Detective Rick Brown had assembled a remarkably similar model. "So, this is it, right?" Captain Martin asked, seeking confident assurance from Brown. "That's why we get the big bucks here in

Explosives, Cap," came Brown's characteristic sarcasm. "We're all about to find out." Martin gave Brown a glare carrying an unspoken but very clear response. "We're all good here, Cap," Brown reassured. His confidence covered that nagging one percent of doubt that the unknown always brings. "This damn-well better be it," Brown thought to himself, "or we'll all have nothing to worry about, ever."

That unsettling thought aside, Detective Brown proceeded downstairs to the Lexington Avenue Line platform to see if he could install the bypass without killing everyone. "Yeah…" he thought, "the big bucks…."

The moment of confirmation had arrived for the NYPD, for James, and for the Lexington Avenue Subway Station at Grand Central. Captain Martin and his squad returned to James's position on the train platform—another shift change for the net handlers.

As Detective Brown arrived to perform his precarious task, protocol dictated an introduction and explanation. After introducing himself, Brown said, "James, you know we're concerned about this loose wire here that we've found…"

James nodded, wearing a nonchalant smirk that Brown noticed but dismissed. "So we consulted with worldwide bomb experts about the wire…" That earned a quick glance of interest from James before he returned to mock-disinterest. "And we've come to agree," Brown went on, "that this is something we've seen before and can easily bypass." Brown then held up the device.

"So," Brown continued, "we're just gonna install the bypass, stabilize it, and remove the coat from the vest. Then we can get a better look at the vest and compare it to our model"—this comment drew another quick flash of interest from James—"then remove you from the vest," Brown added, "send it out to wherever it needs to go, and we can all get the hell out of the subway. Sound okay, James?"

"I guess…" James replied, still feigning indifference. "Look, James," Detective Brown said, "this is some serious shit we're into here, amigo, and you need to cooperate so nobody else gets killed." This was the official acknowledgment to James that people had, indeed, been killed.

James contemplated that, then asked, "You have a model?" "Yes, sir, we surely do," came Brown's reply. James considered briefly asking if they had a prisoner but knew it would be pointless. The police wouldn't reveal any more than that. "So, this bypass thing works on the model, then?" James ventured. "Absolutely," Brown lied brazenly. "Alright, let's do it," James consented.

After just two minutes of meticulous, deliberate work, Detective Brown installed the "Israeli bypass" onto a wire leading to the pressure-trigger booby-trap. A green indicator light on top of the device confirmed a continuous electric flow to the detonator, preventing ignition of the bomb. All this time, the net handlers maintained a sturdy, stable grip. With that phase of explosives removal complete, the net handlers prepared for a shift change.

The next step was to reexamine the overcoat for any more stray wires and confirm that all wires leading out of the detonator were accounted for. All leads went only into the vest. Therefore, the coat could be safely removed from over the vest. Only the actual removal of the coat would confirm these conclusions.

Thick, sturdy diamond-tipped scissors were used to cut away the shoulders of the overcoat up to the collar. Then, while Bomb Squad technicians held the cut shoulders and collar, the sleeves were individually cut away. Every inch of cutting presented an unknown risk. The intensity of each move in this life-or-death operation was breathtaking. At every snip, as each piece of cloth separated, no one could be certain whether the next move would result in an explosion— or nothing at all, which would simply allow for another cut.

In the end, the coat was successfully removed with no casualties. This, of course, meant it was time to remove James from the vest, yet another potentially fatal undertaking.

With officers standing on the board to maintain contact on the pressure-switch trigger, and the Israeli bypass providing a constant electric signal to the detonator, theoretically, nothing prevented James from being removed from the board, the coat, and the "device."

Another moment of putting theory into practice: when the officers helped James up and away from the bomb, nothing happened. Many things occurred, of course, but thankfully none involved a detonation.

First off, those closest to the bomb exhaled and resumed breathing. James was swept up into the anxious arms of Captain Martin, Sergeant Miller, Detective Brown, and others. "Subject in custody—repeat—subject in custody!" Sergeant Miller shouted to police officers stationed on the stairway up to the mezzanine. Word of mouth spread quickly throughout the 6-Train station and up to the street, where the message was broadcast over the secure Special Operations network.

As breathing resumed and radio announcements were made, James was indeed in NYPD custody. The first phase of taking charge of the prisoner meant ensuring security—not only for the prisoner but for those who had him in custody. This involved a quick, preliminary strip search of James and his clothing; a more detailed examination awaited him soon enough. For now, on the subway platform, there was a quick but careful removal and inspection of his clothes as he was almost simultaneously outfitted in a bright yellow, government-issue jumpsuit. Across the back shoulders, in large bold letters, was "DHS," and directly below it, "PRISONER." On the left-front chest patch, the Homeland Security emblem bore the letters "DHS," and directly below, a large capital "P," announcing James's new status as a federal terrorist prisoner.

Handcuffed, James was quickly escorted into an unmarked NYPD detective radio car—one of a handful of marked and unmarked NYPD, FBI, and DHS vehicles arranged to dazzle and confuse any bystanders or lookouts. The procession ended in the basement of One Police Plaza in downtown Manhattan. There, James rode the express elevator with his handlers to the offices of the NYPD Chief of Detectives and the Major Case Squad. He was officially read his Miranda rights and subsequently "booked" into the Police Department information system as Prisoner #1111-0122, indicating date, police precinct, and arrest number for that day.

Later on, James would be taken for arraignment in U.S. Federal Court in Manhattan and into the custody of DHS and the FBI. For now, however, he was a "guest" of the NYPD. Carol Waters, in a separate vehicle and away from the "downtown convoy," was also hustled to One Police Plaza. Captain Martin, as well as the officers in the Counter-Terror/Intelligence squads, recognized the value of her presence. She had a somewhat calming and cooperative effect on James.

The vest James had transported along the #6 Lexington Ave. Local from the Bowery to Grand Central was ready for transfer on the platform. Captain Martin had complete confidence in the Bomb Squad crew on scene to remove the device to the Rodman's Neck Range.

On the subway platform, it was time once again for a series of decisions: humans or robots? One robot or two? Stairs or elevators? Captain Mark Martin left Sergeant Miller to supervise explosives removal at Grand Central and raced, lights and sirens blaring, the four-and-a-half blocks crosstown on 42nd Street to Times Square.

Sergeant Miller was fortunate that he had a successful model to follow from the Union Square incident. In that case, an effective procedure had been implemented: Bomb Squad robots, assisted by human officers, loaded Scott Warren and the backboard "package" onto a handicap-access elevator, brought the deadly cargo up to street level, and onto the Explosives Transport Truck.

At Grand Central, Sergeant Miller had three 50-pound sandbags duct-taped in place on top of the board over the pressure switch. This monstrously fatal device was then cautiously loaded onto the elevator and brought up to the street by Robot Officer Valiant and placed on an awaiting ATF Explosives Device Transport Truck. Once it was securely aboard, another caravan proceeded from midtown Manhattan out to the Bronx.

Chapter 56
The Port Authority Blaze

This left the NYPD with the matter of Dennis Harding at Times Square. It had been decided early on in the disarmament process to first concentrate on James Waters at Grand Central, where they had a seemingly genuine cooperative perpetrator. Harding's status as a cooperative prisoner was frequently uncertain.

Now, cooperative or not, it was time for Captain Martin to remove the bomb from Harding. Once James was on his way to headquarters from Grand Central, his job with James was done. Martin's job was bombs; James was no longer a bomb. He was a bomber, so further conversation might be necessary, but he was no longer a bomb. Dennis Harding was; that was Captain Martin's next order of business.

Meanwhile, the fire at the Port Authority Terminal on 8th Avenue continued to burn through the underground infrastructure, taxing the resources of the New York City Fire Department. It is known but unspoken in the FDNY that by the time you reach a seventh alarm for a fire, you're just sort of making things up as you go along, trying as best as intellect and imagination will allow, to place adequate fire department assets on the scene of a major disaster. Then try, as best possible, to assign something resembling adequate fire department coverage for the rest of the city. The seventh alarm had been recently transmitted for the Port Authority Terminal fire while Captain Martin left Grand Central for Times Square. The Herald

Square explosion was already at fifth alarm status and was also entering into FDNY imagination management as the multi-site, multiple disasters continued to unfold.

New York City Fire Department members who had the distinct honor and unfortunate assignment to the Port Authority incident had borne witness to an unseen vision of hell. The 9/11 attacks and subsequent fire and collapse of the World Trade Center towers bore some resemblance. Something of this magnitude that was completely underground, however, had not been seen in New York City since 1964. Most of the firefighters at the Port Authority had not yet been born by that time, but a few of the senior chiefs there knew 'old-timers' who were working for the department then.

On April 22, 1964, there were two historic events in the city: the opening of the New York World's Fair, and early on, an underground fire the likes of which no city had seen before or since. Thankfully, the World's Fair opened without too much acrimony or disruption, which was not certain given the racial tensions and disturbances of the times. And the subway fire occurred at almost 5 AM, just prior to the onset of the morning rush hour.

The 1964 New York City subway fire took place, appropriately enough, at Grand Central Station. That fire burned so hot for so long that below grade the steel girders supporting 42nd Street and Lexington Avenue buckled and twisted so badly that streets were closed for weeks as repair and replacements were made. It was later determined that faulty wiring had 'cooked' for a while, then igniting combustible material surrounding the wires. That was a sixth alarm fire bringing over 40 FDNY units and 200 members to the scene. Just one alarm short of making things up.

The Port Authority fire on 11/11 was in the 'imaginary' state of the 'seventh alarm', and the day, and the fire, and the mayhem and dying, were not yet over. As the man-made explosion and fire took hold of the IND Subway Station at 42nd Street and 8th Avenue; the already existing 'combustibles' began to burn having been, as designed, ignited by the super-heated, explosive propulsion of the suicide bomb vest.

As intended, the burning and propelled magnesium from the bomb incinerated plastics, rubber, polyphosphates, and magnesium materials in the subway train cars and the station itself. Temperatures at the hottest points of the fire, where the blasted train cars met the station platform, and areas close to that point exceeded 2,500 degrees. At this point, everything within reach of that stage of the fire, whether artificial or organic, either burst into flames or melted, or both. Firefighters in full protective gear, attempting to advance hose lines, could get nowhere close enough to that hellacious inferno, as steel columns began to twist and bend, and water vaporized upon leaving the nozzles of fire hoses. Only a combination of high pressure water and foam operations would be sufficient to smother these super-heated flames.

In Midtown Manhattan, the New York City Fire Department has strategically located high volume/high pressure engine companies for fighting intense high-rise fires. These engine companies have unique multi-stage pumps to increase water pressure/volume needed to pump water at sustained pressure up into high-rise buildings. Also, their crews are specifically trained in the operation of high pressure mechanics and logistics, as well as foam operations. Special, large diameter hose (LDH), carried in bulk by certain special units of the FDNY, was used to transfer the high-pressure, high volume-pumped water. This involved the appropriate alignment of high-pressure engine (pumper) companies with the correct hydrants, using a massive outlay and operation of sufficient amounts of LDH, into the fire building and ultimately, onto the fire. All companies involved in this special operation were well-drilled and well-practiced in these operations.

However, the actual logistics of such an operation took even well-supervised and well-practiced crews more than just a few minutes. The LDH is thick and heavy and unwieldy. It requires several teams of three and four firefighters to maneuver the stuff when it is empty ('light', or dry), and even more teams of five or six or so, to move it when it is carrying water (charged).

As in good business, the rule is location, location, location. With fire, every second counts, and a few minutes is too much. Upon arranging all the appropriate units with the trained and practiced personnel, in tandem with the high pressure water supply system, LDH can be usefully deployed and operated. Also, the city's DEP (Water Supply) has to monitor and ensure a steady high-pressure supply. With the extra-high temperature fires burning super-hot below ground level and far removed from the pumpers, only high pressure-LDH lines would be of any use at all in the hellacious inferno that roared below, and up into the Port Authority Terminal.

As designed by Muhammad and his gang of murderers, with the explosion and fire at Herald Square also presenting a very similar hell-on-earth situation, FDNY high-pressure pumpers, and LDH special units city-wide, as well as Manhattan's water supply system, were being pressed to the absolute max.

Chapter 57
NYPD's Hostage Negotiation Tactics

Edward Reynolds was a 43-year-old working-class White male who grew up in a stable, working-class, mostly White neighborhood. He was nearly 6 feet tall and weighed 234 lbs. Reynolds grew up mostly well-behaved, moderately accomplished in academics at Grammar and then Catholic High School, and noteworthy for his athletic performance in Football and Baseball. He excelled in all fields, both Mental and Physical, at the NYPD Academy.

He was a 21-year veteran of the New York City Police Department and had personally witnessed more Black-on-Black violence than most of the 8 million people of New York, Black, White, or otherwise.

He worked at maintaining a fit physical condition and a sharp mind. For most of his NYPD Career, he intended to put in his 20 years, grab his pension, and work on a second career. After 14 years he was promoted to Sergeant, which prompted him to recalculate his pension at that pay grade. As a result, he decided to stay on a few more years. Then he got a very interesting opportunity that kept him on the job even longer.

Sgt. Ed Reynolds had always excelled in the Social and Psychological Sciences he'd studied, and that interest continued through his Police Career. This included additional Professional Continuing Education Courses and various Certificate Studies. He thought that perhaps after NYPD, he might pursue a career in the Social Sciences, maybe as a Certified Counselor.

Growing up in a mostly quiet and steady environment, the violence he was called upon to address, mitigate, manage, and intervene in aroused a psycho-social professional interest in him. Becoming somewhat a familiar face at the NYPD Academy, the John Jay College of Criminal Justice in New York, and in some Brooklyn College Certificate Programs, he was noticed in certain circles within NYPD. This led to the interesting opportunity: Hostage Negotiation.

Thus, on 11/11, Sgt. Ed Reynolds, NYPD Hostage Negotiation Unit (HNU), and Dennis Harding, a 'wanna-be' Suicide Terrorist Bomber, were engaged in conversation at the Times Square Subway Station, awaiting the arrival of Capt. Mark Martin, NYPD-Explosives Unit.

Just like James, Harding too had posed the thinly-veiled threat of Detonation. Sgt. Reynolds, being more finely tuned and experienced in the art of Negotiation, was able—unlike Capt. Martin—to manage that threat without drawing his weapon. But one thinly-veiled threat was as good as the next, so Reynolds dropped a few vague hints of his own, causing Harding to wonder. Sgt. Reynolds talked to Harding about snipers being deployed, and about how sometimes NYPD had been able to disable bomb electronics with microwaves.

Capt. Martin, upon arrival after his swift trip from Grand Central, sent an encrypted text to Sgt. Miller to send the Unit's special equipment to Times Square as soon as it was available. He wasn't certain how Sgt. Reynolds and Dennis Harding were getting along, but the fact that everyone at Times Square was still alive and the station intact boded well.

After all the dramatic distractions with James at Grand Central, Martin was pretty much spent. He hoped Sgt. Reynolds was making better progress here than Martin had with James, and that they could wrap things up fairly quickly. 'Yeah,' Martin thought cynically to himself, 'that'll probably happen…'

Sgt. Ed Reynolds had in fact been making slow, but nonetheless steady, progress with the egotistical, sardonic Kevin Harding. Harding, a pathetic, maladjusted chronic loser, compensated for his caustic shortcomings by imagining himself omnipotent— common among Hostage-takers and other Anarchists. This was well understood by Students of the Human Psyche such as Hostage Negotiator Sgt. Ed Reynolds. The fact that Harding had a bomb and was virtually holding the most monumental city in the world hostage fed his delusions of grandeur.

He could not fathom the notion that his makeup and behavior were typical of a particular class of maladjusted malcontents. His imagined supremacy left no room for the idea that Sgt. Reynolds had a clear sense of the lunatic he was dealing with, and was initiating an evolving plan of action. Harding was seriously outmatched and outwitted, with no room to even consider that possibility.

Sgt. Ed Reynolds, on the other hand, fully understood the very perilous nature of the present situation and the fact that Harding currently held the upper hand—at least for now. Well-armed with actual facts rather than a mind-tripping fantasy of phenomenal power, Reynolds was able to employ a plan of action based on Logic and Tactical Thinking. That plan was being developed, and the groundwork laid, as Reynolds' conversation with Harding progressed.

The first stage of such Negotiation began with listening, hearing, and understanding. As the conversation continued, Reynolds needed Harding to realize he was indeed being heard and understood. Reynolds accomplished this with a lot of nodding in agreement, and simple repeated statements like, "I hear you," "I understand," and "Yeah…"

There was no actual agreement with Harding's complaints and bold proclamations, just confirmation that they were heard. Because Harding's Complaints and Anti-Social Proclamations were simply hysterical statements, Sgt. Reynolds only had to listen, appear empathetic, and propose an alternate way for Harding to get out of the corner he'd painted himself into without killing anyone. With an egomaniac psychopath like Harding, that included offering a way for his Complaints to be publicly aired without detonating any bombs.

Since Harding, deep down in his cold and damaged heart, didn't really want to kill himself, he was slowly, painfully accepting such a plan. Reynolds repeatedly emphasized to the aggrieved egomaniac that his bold and daring actions had indeed stunned and dazzled millions. Sgt. Reynolds explained that Harding had already brought the World to a standstill to pay attention. Reynolds assured him that this kind of attention wasn't going away anytime soon, and that journalists, authors, and all kinds of sympathetic parties would be beating down doors to hear more from him. Harding had already achieved what he set out to do—stopped the World and got its attention without setting off any bombs—so why not proceed safely from there? Slowly, simply, calmly, and repeatedly, Sgt. Reynolds planted this seed in Harding's mind and continued to nurture it until it could take root. Deep down, Harding hoped they would indeed be able to do exactly that.

Thus, the stage was set for Capt. Martin's arrival. He was The Man with The Plan for Harding's extrication from the mega-lethal Suicide Vest, and for its safe removal to a location where it would do no harm. The Poison Cloud that would be released by detonation posed an additional challenge for the Explosives Squad and related experts, but that would be dealt with later. For now, the challenge was at Times Square.

As standard practice, any Officers within a certain range— and certainly those close to a Terrorist Bomber—wore Blast-Resistant Protective Gear. In a show of Trust and to inspire cooperation, those negotiating with "The Perp." typically removed their headgear, which also allowed for clearer communication. So, as Capt. Martin arrived on-scene with Harding and Sgt. Ed Reynolds, he, too, removed his Headgear.

As he did so, Sgt. Reynolds began making introductions. "Dennis, this is Capt. Mark Martin, NYPD-Explosives Unit, the Bomb Squad. He's here to determine how we can separate you from that device without any more people getting hurt."

"Wait a minute!" Harding protested. "No one's gotten hurt here. Now you're telling me someone's been hurt? Oh, no. No, no. Nobody's been hurt here, and you're not about to blame me if someone's been hurt somewhere... Nobody's been hurt here." Harding maintained his defiant, defensive stance even in the midst of surrender.

Reynolds needed to pause, start at the beginning, and clarify his remark about people being hurt. "Dennis, I did not say you hurt anyone. Nor did I say you're being held responsible for anyone who's been hurt elsewhere." (That blame, Reynolds thought to himself, would be addressed at trial.)

That comment, however, did acknowledge that people had in fact been hurt elsewhere in the city, placing Harding on notice that the NYPD believed he was not completely uninvolved in the day's events. Sgt. Reynolds thought it best not to mention the scale of death and destruction inflicted upon the city at this time. Disclosing the full extent of ruin and suffering could drive Harding from cooperation to desperate despair. Better now to "keep the peace" and maintain compliance.

Reynolds wondered if this latest discussion had calmed The Subject—whether Harding now grasped that no one here was focusing on any Blame. Outwardly, Harding appeared as if he was "with" the team on the current goal: never mind all of that, let's just get you out of that Bomb. Despite appearances, no one—perhaps not even Harding—could be absolutely sure his mind had fully changed from hopelessness and attack to compliance and surrender. Only time, and the next set of decisions and actions, would reveal if Harding would follow directions and surrender or recognize the actual hopelessness of his situation and detonate the Bomb.

It was therefore imperative that Sgt. Reynolds and Capt. Martin draw on all their training and practice to establish and maintain an atmosphere of cooperation and continued progress toward a safe resolution. Accordingly, Capt. Martin reiterated his introduction in a calm, confident tone.

"Dennis, my name is Captain Mark Martin, NYPD Explosives Unit. You can call me Captain Martin." Unlike the situation at Grand Central with James—where Carol Waters had some influence—Martin knew things with Harding at Times Square were different. There would be no casual first-name friendliness with a hardened career criminal, a convict, and a true loner. These types had to be handled with a stern approach. "What we need to do now, Dennis, is remove you from that Bomb Vest and get you out of the damn Subway."

"And into a cell to await execution?" Harding replied. As Martin drew a breath to respond, Sgt. Reynolds cut in, "Dennis, you're getting ahead of yourself. Of course, you'll be taken into custody—no one's going to pretend otherwise. But this Execution stuff, man, that's way down the road. First off, as you said, no one's been hurt here, so there's no reason to assume you'll be held responsible for anything like that. Secondly, you know how Plea-Bargaining works. You are still alive. You have information the United States Government desperately wants. You get to play the game, man. Nobody's gonna execute you while you hold such valuable information."

Truth be told, Sgt. Reynolds did not know for certain if any of that was true—though it was possible. One of the advantages in negotiating with Terrorist Bombers is that you're allowed to lie, provided it's believable. This one was, and Reynolds was doing a good job selling it.

The actual facts, however, were somewhat at odds with Reynolds' statement. Dennis Harding had already committed multiple Capital Crimes that could easily result in execution. He had borne a Weapon of Mass Destruction into the New York City Subway System at the peak of a weekday A.M. Rush, so he was already "Executable." The fact that others like him had, on this very day, detonated their bombs—killing, maiming, and poisoning hundreds, perhaps thousands, of innocent people—didn't help his case. The U.S. Government might well decide not to "Bargain" at all and push for his execution. But Reynolds and Martin couldn't mention that possibility or even hint in that direction.

"Dennis," Capt. Martin said evenly, "you have the choice to end all this madness and come out of it alive. That's all we're trying to do—get you, and everyone else, out alive. Can we go ahead with that now?"

"Agh, ahh, ah, Man!" Harding's guttural wail made everyone in earshot draw a sharp breath and murmur a final prayer. It sounded much like a madman's final cry.

"All right, all right, Goddamn It All, let's get this thing wrapped up!" Harding exclaimed, as though consenting.

"We're clear, then, Dennis, right? We're gonna get this Bomb wrapped up and be on our way, yeah?" Martin sought confirmation.

"Yeah, yeah, Goddamn it! Let's go!" Harding replied.

This greatly relieved Capt. Martin, who proceeded to examine the Vest. He knew there was a "Truck" upstairs to transport the Bomb, and a convoy was being assembled.

Already, two extremely powerful Suicide Vests were "on-the-ground" at Rodman's Neck, packing enough explosive potential and poison to make everyone there very uneasy. Two separate convoys, using different routes, had traveled to the Range. Anyone tracking those convoys by Television or other Surveillance would have seen both routes, giving them some familiarity with approaches to that facility—making NYPD and Federal Officials apprehensive.

It was decided, then, that Dennis Harding's Vest from Times Square would undergo the procedure at the NYPD's Special Operations Base at Floyd Bennett Field on Brooklyn's South Shore at Jamaica Bay. That facility was also used for NYPD Highway, Emergency Services, Aviation, Harbor Patrol, and the U.S. Coast Guard. The demand on these and all other City, State, and Federal Agencies continued to exceed capacity.

Chapter 58
Neutralizing a Live Threat

Capt. Martin did not yet have his robots at hand, but he knew that they, along with some members of the Squad, would be arriving momentarily. In the meantime, he used this interval to conduct a thorough examination of the vest, paying very close attention, of course, for any 'strays' which had nearly ruined his day earlier.

Upon initial visual inspection, he could see no stray leads that might be part of 'The Wire.' He knew, however, that the wire on Woods' vest at Grand Central had been on his back, and only became visible as Woods was being separated from the vest. Martin understood that just because he did not see a wire did not necessarily mean it was not there; it simply meant he couldn't see one. He carefully moved Harding's arms, turned him slightly from side to side, all the while looking intently.

As his crew began to arrive, Capt. Martin now took the lead in conversation with the perpetrator. Sgt. Reynolds remained visibly present should things take an unexpected turn.

As at the Grand Central and Union Square incidents, a wall of sandbags reinforced by blast-resistant blankets and surrounded by a shock-restricting curtain had already been constructed around the area where the suicide bomber and his attendants conducted negotiations. Into this restricted space came Detective Brown, Sergeant Miller, and the rest of 'The Unit,' bearing the equipment they would need. Several of the heftier Special Operations Officers present were carrying a cargo net. The robot officers of the Squad were arriving and were being brought down into the subway station via the passenger elevator.

A greased backboard was slid under Harding's back, and the officers strapped him onto it. They held him in place against the board, just as they had done with James at Grand Central, to maintain contact with the pressure switch trigger as they slid the board to the ground.

As per protocol, they instructed Harding to remain lying on the board and explained to him that an officer would keep a hand on his chest to prevent any unintended movement. While Harding was attached to the first board, they would be able to slide the louvered board into place to maintain contact on the pressure switch. Then again, as before, they could lift Harding off the bottom board as they stood atop the board to maintain pressure.

As this was done, the officers took particular notice of Harding's back and flanks for any stray wires. To their mild confusion but great relief, there were none. With this assurance, they were able to quickly take the prisoner into their personal custody.

As Harding's clothes were quickly stripped away and replaced with the DHS PRISONER jumpsuit, sandbags were placed atop the board over the pressure switch and secured with heavy-duty duct tape. It was now time for the removal of the prisoner, and the transfer of the bomb to NYPD's Special Operations Quarters at Floyd Bennett Field in Brooklyn.

Upstairs from the station at Times Square, once again, there was a massive array of local, state, and various federal law enforcement vehicles with lights flashing and sirens beeping. Adding to the confusion, by design, were NYPD, Port Authority, U.S. National

Guard trucks, armored cars and personnel carriers, and fire engines, and predominantly, the NYPD explosives transport truck.

Only Hostage Negotiator Sgt. Reynolds, Capt. Martin of the Bomb Squad, and just a few others knew exactly which vehicle was intended for Dennis Harding. Again, another circuitous route downtown to Police Headquarters from Midtown Manhattan. There, Harding, like James Waters before him, was 'booked' into the New York City Criminal Justice System. Now there were two terrorist prisoners in custody to be shepherded through the system.

Chapter 59
Determining Detainment
for a Terrorist

Arrangements for James Waters' "in custody" status were nearly as dramatic as the process of taking him into custody. After the harrowing, very touch-and-go situation at Grand Central, appropriate detention matters needed to be decided. Initially, there was a brief, intense power struggle among law enforcement agencies over who exactly the prisoner belonged to. New York City authorities presented a quite proper and valid argument that the perpetrator's crimes had all occurred under New York City jurisdiction, and that it was, in fact, New York City law enforcement that had responded to, managed, and ultimately resolved the deadly crisis.

Furthermore, it was the City of New York, the city's transit, police, fire, and EMS systems, and ultimately the citizens of New York City, who were the 'most aggrieved victims' of the crimes.

While that was all certainly true and valid, there were a few things working against the city here—first being that the New York City Police Department, and the New York City Department of Corrections did not have an appropriately segregated and distinct detention facility for such a high-profile and high-risk prisoner. There is a very high-security detention facility at NYPD Headquarters at Police Plaza downtown, but this was not intended or designed for prisoner lodging of more than 24 hours. Nor did the NYPD want 1 Police Plaza to become the scene of the media circus arrests like these create. Similarly, the NYC Department of

Corrections did have some accommodations that could be pressed into service for these special inmates, but in the long run, this too would be more than city authorities really wanted to get too involved in.

They would have to seek such arrangements from either state or federal agencies before long anyway. Then there was the matter of the multi-faceted, wide-reaching, and quite likely international aspects of the obviously intricate conspiracy. As the smoke began to clear, it was obvious this was a federal case.

In New York City, federal terrorist suspects are held in custody at the Metropolitan Corrections Center, Manhattan (MCC). Despite its very municipal-sounding name, the MCC is actually a federal facility. As a matter of professional courtesy and recognition, due respect would be accorded to New York City law enforcement authorities, and each prisoner was to be 'booked' into the NYC Criminal Justice System at 1 Police Plaza, before transfer to the MCC.

As soon as it was established that there were in fact 'live' terror suspects in custody in New York City, MCC was placed on immediate 'lock-down', and a high-alert security sweep of the facility itself, and the surrounding vicinity was enacted by the U.S. Bureau of Prisons, U.S. Marshal's Service, NYPD, and the FBI.

Of course, New York City investigators and prosecutors would be included as a vital component of the government proceedings. But when all was said and done, the U.S. Department of Justice, along with the CIA and FBI were the lead agencies in the proceedings. This proved bitter yet inevitable medicine for NYPD Counter-Terror Police and for prosecutors for New York's District Attorney's Office, but such was the way of things.

Also to be decided was the matter of the prisoner's defense… In the U.S., citizens have the right to an attorney, and a proper and vigorous defense, even if they cannot afford it. In high-profile cases such as this, that right is observed in a variety of interesting ways—the court hearing the case, finding that the government has construed an elaborate and intricate prosecution, such as was sure to be the case here, can provide for appropriate defense beyond that which can be afforded by the defendant.

Also, there is the curious American yearning for the national spotlight, which has compelled America's most prolific defense attorneys into cases of national prominence. Such was true again here and resulted in visits to James by a couple of the finest U.S. defense attorneys in recent history. This all made James Waters a very popular, if notorious young man.

In short order, a defense team consisting of a high-ranking administrative attorney from the American Civil Liberties Union was appointed, along with the lead attorney from the New York City Legal Aid Society. R.F. (Robert) Huntington, a top-dollar, high-powered defense attorney who'd offered his services pro-bono, was also approved for the team.

Chapter 60
Times Square Problem

Another route was planned for the Explosives Truck, stretching over 13 miles to Floyd Bennett Field on the South Shore of Brooklyn at Jamaica Bay. In the 1920s and '30s, Floyd Bennett served as New York City's first municipal airport. Over the years, it has functioned as a U.S. Naval Air Base, an Army Training Base, and a Coast Guard Air and Patrol Boat Base. Since 1938, when the NYPD initiated its Aviation Unit there, it has maintained a presence through various changes.

These days, the New York City Police Department maintains its Aviation Unit Headquarters there, along with an Emergency Vehicle Operations Training Ground, and a base for the Special Operations Division and the Emergency Services Unit. The field is part of a National Parks Recreation Area, though the NYPD controls a significant portion of the 321-acre field. On November 11, when the city was under attack, NYPD control of Floyd Bennett Field was not in question.

The New York City Police Department, FBI, DHS, and ATF, as well as the U.S. National Parks Police, had full access to the field, with nearly a mile of open space at their disposal. Near the southeast end of the field, the NYPD Special Operations had a dug-out, 15-foot berm for the disposal of firearms and explosives. Fortunately, on this day, the prevailing wind was from the northwest, blowing southeast over Jamaica Bay and out to the Atlantic Ocean. Even if there were a wind change, Floyd Bennett is primarily surrounded by Jamaica Bay and largely uninhabited highway space. It was therefore decided that the final explosive device of the day would be detonated there.

This would involve closing the FDR Drive in Manhattan, the Brooklyn Bridge, and surrounding streets in Brooklyn, as well as the Belt Parkway along Brooklyn's western and then south shore. Also, the south end of Flatbush Avenue leading to the Marine Parkway-Gil Hodges Bridge to the Rockaways, and Beach Channel Drive in Queens to the south side of Jamaica Bay. The distance from the Flatbush Avenue perimeter of the field was nearly a mile from the Explosives Pit. It was just over 240 yards across Jamaica Bay to Beach Channel Drive. With the prevailing winds and the depth and strength of the berm, there was practically no risk at all from the vest's detonation.

Having secured Dennis Harding and removed him from Times Square, it was now time to remove the Bomb Vest. Fortunately, this procedure had gone picture-perfect at Grand Central after James Waters' apprehension. What the 'Bomb Squad' had to do now was simply replicate the process at Times Square. The only caveat being that there was never anything simple about bomb removal.

The procedure itself had been mapped out and successfully executed at Grand Central, so there was a plan to follow. The plan mainly involved two robots, the Subway Station Handicapped Access Elevator, and the Explosives Container Truck. Ancillary support included the helicopters, boats, and escort vehicles for the trip to Floyd Bennett.

The first robot was sent down to the platform level of the station, and the elevator sent back to street level for the second one.

The first robot traveled down the length of the platform, from the elevator to the spot where the squad members stood inside the explosive-resistant wall that surrounded the bomb. When the robot arrived, the sandbag, explosive-laden backboard was affixed to the robot vertically. The robot's powerful arms and vice-like 'claws' tightly secured the 'package'.

The squad had decided it less risky to transfer the 'package' to the second robot already on the elevator, than trying the tricky manipulation involved in having the loaded first robot maneuver onto the elevator. This was the method that had been executed flawlessly at Grand Central.

At Times Square however, the hand-off did not go as smoothly. The second robot aboard the elevator seemed to be having some difficulty in retracting its extended arms holding the 'package'. The number of humans present at this most precarious moment of the operation had been extremely limited to the absolute minimum necessary just in case something went wrong, and the bomb exploded. It had been decided there would be two 'Handlers', one for each robot, and two 'Assistants', for a total of four persons. The planning that decided upon this number was for the minimum number of 'Hands on deck' in case there was a problem with the robots. At the moment, there was very clearly a 'problem' with one of the robots. This was disturbing on several levels.

The Explosives Squad Robots on-scene were the newest the Police Department owned, and of the latest technology available. These exceeded the lift capacity, maneuverability, and dexterity of older model robots operating in counter-terror work in the Metropolitan Area. Any problems with the newer, high-tech models was a bad omen.

The first time a handler, using a controller, instructed the robot to retract its arms, the arms retracted a couple of inches and stopped. Previous, less sophisticated bomb robots had a one-arm claw, a less complicated, but also less effective, arrangement.

'Not good', said the handler into the mic in his blast-resistant helmet, alerting all involved. Communications here among the Bomb Squad were conducted via scrambled Ultra-Low Frequency that had a range of barely 15 feet or so, and were extremely unlikely to register sufficiently to activate any radio-sensitive 'hardware' on the vest.

Capt. Martin was the C.O. of the operation, and he was on the platform as one of the assistants. 'Okay', came Capt. Martin's reply, 'What is the problem? Do we have a malfunction?' 'Unknown', the handler, Sgt. Miller replied, 'There is no trouble indication...it all seems good, it just didn't fully retract'. 'Alright', said Martin, 'Let me do a visual'. Martin and the other 'Humans' stood a good 25 feet or so away from the elevator, partially shielded by the platform's steel girders, which provided protection that was probably only minimally helpful. The four men on the subway platform, and the couple of dozen or so officers up on 6th Avenue, were now in a standoff with two robots and a devastatingly-explosive, poisonous bomb.

'This is going to be alright....' Martin thought to himself as he walked toward the robots and the bomb, 'I just need to see what's wrong and get it fixed'. There is no other mindset one can have in order to do the kind of work the men and women under his command do. In doing so, his mind ran through the possibilities of the 'problem', and what his experience and knowledge could help him with. In explosives, there was no other way to go.

Mark Martin approached the stalled robot officer and the deadly vest bomb with an air of extreme intent and focus, as well as some serious apprehension. He conducted a visual inspection of all the immediately visible elements of the puzzle. He fully understood that he needed to lift a portion of the vest here and there to see if it had somehow jammed the robot's ability to retract its arms. As he moved each piece of the vest, and put hands-on parts of each of the robots, he knew that slipping or fumbling at all, was absolutely unacceptable. One even small mistake, would end not only him, but all those around him. Concentration, attention, and patience prevailed for Capt. Martin and his squad as training and experience kicked in.

Upon painstaking and occasionally breath-taking observation and inspection of every visible aspect of the operation, he could find no apparent cause of the hang-up. He returned to his previous post behind the girder, and reported his findings, or rather, lack thereof. Capt. Martin, and his crew, came to the unspoken conclusion that there was one certain way to see where they stood with the non-compliant robot and the bomb – try again. And when the robot was sent the signal to retract its arms, everyone held their breath. And it worked.

'Onto the elevator'? Sgt. Miller asked into his headset. 'Ah-frim', replied Martin, 'onto the elevator'. And when robot officer

Charles, NYPD 'Explosives', was instructed to wheel back into the elevator, it did so. Martin, Miller, and the others quickly ascended the two flights of stairs to street level. There was an officer posted at the elevator stand on 42nd St. & Broadway. Capt. Martin gave him the thumbs-up signal. Upon seeing this, the officer pressed the elevator call button to bring it up to the street. And as instructed, she then quickly paced to a position on the other side of the 'Bomb' truck.

The elevator arrived, now on street level. With this Det. Rick Brown took over control of the second robot. Brown looked over to Capt. Martin. Once again, Mark Martin gave the thumbs-up signal, and Brown directed the robot to exit the elevator. An approximately 6 or 7-inch high border constructed of sandbags and two-by-four planks outlined a path from the elevator to the bomb truck parked on 42nd Street east of Broadway. This path was not intended to contain any explosives damage, rather to prevent the robot from straying off course.

As directed by Det. Rick Brown, the robot rolled fairly smoothly along the path to the truck. All along the way, at each and every crevice and crack, lay the possibility of accidental detonation and a hellacious explosion. All around this scene, breath was held and prayers were offered.

Robot officer Charles came to the end of the path and was now to wheel right, out onto the street and up to the truck. This the robot performed without incident. When it came time to make a second right-hand turn toward the rear portal of the bomb truck however, officer Charles balked.

As Det. Brown signaled the instruction to the robot to make the turn and maneuver toward the truck, the robot's wheels turned in the correct direction, but there was no further movement. While

Capt. Martin pondered another walk-up to do a visual, Rick Brown posed a suggestion. Brown spoke into his headset mic., 'I think if we back it a bit to the left, he can make the turn'. The Explosives Unit's members considered the robot officers their very valuable partners on the squad, and referred to them by name, or called them 'he'.

Capt. Martin did a quick surveil of the surrounding perimeter before replying. He then waved back a knot of officers standing nearby, gawking transfixed on the stalled robot officer. As they backed, some taking cover, he returned his attention to Det. Brown and officer Charles. 'O.K.' Rick', he replied, 'Go for it'. Another deep breath, another quick prayer, and Rick Brown 'went for it'. Officer Charles backed a half-turn to the left in response to Brown's command, paused, wheels right, and then forward toward the bomb truck.

A deep exhale and Rick Brown speaks, 'O.K., Boss, looks like we're good to go here'. 'Stand-by', replies Martin as he has another, final look around and at the robot with its 'package'. Satisfied, Martin speaks, 'O.K., here we go'. 'Roger that', replied Brown. Det. Brown then signaled the robot to move to the truck and this went smoothly. The next maneuver for the robot was to extend the bomb onto the tray to be rolled into the truck. This too, was accomplished without difficulty.

The next two-part move was more than just a bit nerve-wracking. Robot officer Charles had to release its grip on the bomb, retract its arms, and back away from the truck. All this too, went without incident. Next, an officer positioned away from, but facing the rear of the bomb truck, used a cable remote control to engage the bomb trucks' conveyor belt system to draw the tray holding the bomb into the explosives-suppression chamber. As the conveyor brought the bomb into the chamber, it would also draw down the hatch to close the chamber portal. The officer activated the switch to engage the conveyor.

The explosion that followed decapitated officer Charles, the blast shearing-off the robot's headpiece, the unit atop the robot containing a camera and transceiver. The hatch door to the truck's portal had not yet fully closed and locked. The force of the explosion then, rocketed the 45 lb. door from the truck at 100 mph. Fortunately, cautious planning paid off, there was no one or nothing in its path as it roared, under pressure and burning magnesium, south on 6th Ave, nearly a full city block to 41st Street.

There was indeed, a booby-trap wire on the Dennis Harding bomb that went undiscovered by the explosives techs. The various maneuvers of the device in getting it onto the elevator and up to street-level prevented it from functioning properly. When it was finally laid-flat in the truck, it fired and ignited the bomb.

The horrendous roar shattered windows and cracked facades on the 54-story Bank of America Tower, the 50-story W.R. Grace Building, and other buildings surrounding the blast area.

Falling glass and debris from the buildings fell from 100 ft. above on 6th Ave from 42nd to 41st Streets, as well as a bit north on 6th Ave toward 43rd Street and east and west on 6th Ave. The shattered glass flew down toward the street gaining speed and momentum as it cascaded down onto firefighters and medics, officers, agents, and a few press members on the sidewalks below. Fortunately, most of the witnesses to the spectacular debacle were shielded by protective gear they'd adorned in precaution. An unfortunate few who were not properly equipped, or had missing or misplaced gear, were brutally lacerated.

The bomb truck was severely damaged, but as by design, largely intact. A horrid toxic plume however, roared out of the blasted portal hatch and leaked out of the cracked seams of the explosion-suppression unit.

A cry to 'mask-up!' came over the NYPD radio for the units at Times Square and similar instructions quickly came across FDNY-EMS airwaves, as the deadly-poisonous cloud spread over the area. The toxic plume leeched out onto 6th Avenue and all around the crowd rapidly dispersed in all directions, seeking safety in nearby buildings and fleeing down into the subway.

FDNY transmitted a 10-80 code 3, for 5 or more contaminated patients; bringing a full decon task force to the poisonous scene. Men and women sheltered where they could as the ominous cloud of toxins dispersed and settled onto the vicinity of the explosion. A few of the victims began to gag and choke as the potentially fatal poison took hold. Fortunately, there were enough rescuers present with enough of the right equipment to prevent any deaths, although some of the victims were, and would continue to be, quite sick. Those attending to the afflicted had to patiently and purposefully, take the care and attention to 'mask-up' and 'suit-up' properly to prevent becoming victims themselves.

The signal for a 'mass-decon' task force also included additional ambulances and the establishment of a decon/triage, 'clean-zone', for treatment and transport of victims. Because planning and foresight had gone into arranging the scene prior to the bomb being brought from the subway up to the truck, close to a bare-minimum of emergency personnel were stricken. As often is the case though, there were a few more than the bare-minimum present, resulting in 18 police, fire, medics, transit emergency and press, who'd become victims. Of those, 8, were in 'critical' condition, including 1 cardiac arrest, and the remainder in varying degrees of 'stable' condition. All 18 victims arrived alive at various hospitals in the area, and remained that way days and weeks later.

Also days and weeks later, was left the destruction and contamination of properties and infrastructure of Times Square. The first step of restoration was decontamination. Contractors and DHS workers, New York City Department of Buildings, New York Environmental Protection Agents, sanitation, transit, FDNY, NYPD workers, all in personal protective equipment gear, scrubbed, removed, inspected, and tested surfaces, windows, doors, ceilings, walls, and floors throughout the infected area.

Major structural repairs to buildings, streets, and sidewalks, and the subway, would all have to wait until final decon, inspection, and testing were complete.

Chapter 61
Legal Eagles and Last Hopes

As the work to restore Times Square, The Port Authority Terminal, and Herald Square to something resembling normalcy progressed, so too did the work to prevent the execution of James Waters and Dennis Harding. Like the work on the City's devastated infrastructure, the effort to save the defendants' lives would involve careful planning and implementation.

The U.S. Government had succeeded in providing a stellar collection of the top legal minds in the country to defend the terrorist attackers. The first order of business, and the more promising case, was the first prisoner, James Waters. Consensus for his defense was reached quickly among these top 'Legal-Eagles', and the strategy was soon presented to James and Carol.

It was Muhammad, Mehmet, ISIS, al-Qaeda, al-Nasir, bin-Laden, it was Scott Warren, it was Tom Jennings, it was the Unknown Port Authority Bomber, it was Dennis Harding and/or Bobby Wilson; it was because of his father and/or mother, it was anyone and everyone except poor, miserable, misguided, abandoned/smothered James' fault. All this misdirection was intended not for a Not Guilty verdict— that was probably never going to happen. Rather, all this convolution and diversion would hopefully generate enough distraction to get the prosecution to consider taking the death penalty off the table, and spare James' life.

James, being the noble soldier he imagined himself to be, would have none of it; James was the master of his destiny. James was completely responsible for, and accountable for, his own choices and actions. This led his legal team to threaten him with the possibility of posting an insanity defense. Surely, they explained to him, anyone who declined to participate in his own defense and willingly subjected himself to capital punishment had to be insane. And it was that which had led to James' dreadful plan. Not some noble, dramatic strike against injustice. 'No, Your Honor, Ladies and Gentlemen of the Jury...' one of his attorneys play-acted for him, 'No, this was all a case of psychotic delusion'. This too could spare James capital punishment, and achieve a result the defense hoped for.

That last ploy made a considerable impression. It was though, the women—and the endless pleadings of Carol and Joann to please follow the lawyers' instruction—that eventually caused James to cave and allow the defense team to proceed as they would. Not that any of that brought any guarantees for survival. The government prosecutors could still take a hard line and tell them: 'Sure, sure, bring it all. We'll take our chances and see if we can exterminate the bastard.' And if they got before a federal judge with no compunction about executing terrorists, things could go very badly for James and the people who loved him.

Chapter 62
Dueling Strategies

So, that became the proposed theme for the defense - tie them all together; one elaborate, complex terror plot, involving many players and moving parts. All of which needed to be identified, located, and presented, in order for the defendants to present an informed defense resulting in a fair trial. Failure to permit this, the defense maintained, would be to deny a fair trial. This would of course involve extensive, intricate international investigation. It would also mean the exploration and investigation of government information related to the case.

The 'ringleader' Muhammad, it turns out, had been on DHS/Customs & Immigration watch-lists. The defense team was able then to propose an elaborate tactic - How then, and why, was he able to move in and out of, and about the country unimpeded? Was that a matter of pure incompetence, for which the defendant was now being held liable? Or, was there something more convoluted about it all, involving government collusion in some sort of undercover operation?

The presiding federal judge admired the ploy, but didn't buy the basis as valid. She did concede though, that the defense maintained the right to examine any evidence, and cross-examine any witness, referenced by the prosecution. As promised, the defense filed appeal on the ruling.

Also they contended; there was the complex matter of James' intricate psychological condition. The defense, they informed the court in a variety of filings, was preparing to assemble and establish a detailed historic profile of the dysfunctional development of James's early and adolescent persona, and present all the professional testimony and appropriate authoritative documentation relative to how this resulted in James' extremely vulnerable emotional state, which was recognized and manipulated by the Jihadi terrorists. Anything less than such a vigorous and detailed defense, they argued, was automatic grounds for appeal.

Here, the judge reserved decision, but indicated that such evidence might be considered for admission later into the proceedings. It was a hoped-for result. The defense team knew such a finding could produce a lengthy delay which the prosecution may seek to avoid through negotiation.

* * *

The prosecution, in direct opposition to the defense strategy, aimed to keep the proceedings as clear-cut and straightforward as possible: KISS; 'Keep It Simple-Separate'. Charge each individual defendant with the individual crimes/individual acts of terror they had committed. Federal prosecutors had no doubt there was indeed some larger, diabolical conspiracy involved here. They'd decided that a conspiracy case was for another trial, at another time. No, that discussion need not see the light of day in the present proceedings.

They argued in their motions before the bar therefore, that those details concerned other individuals, and other crimes. There may be some ancillary involvement, but that is not urgently significant to the matter at hand here. An empathetic federal judge ruled in their favor.

When the prosecution heard of the subsequent decision to consider mountains of evidence and a long parade of expert witnesses however, they had a new series of difficult decisions to manage. Everyone on the government side of the table knew that removing the death penalty would most likely inspire a guilty plea. Now they had to decide if that was in fact acceptable in light of the horrid turmoil inflicted by the attacks.

In thinking it through further, the notion that the previous ruling had cleared the way for individual trials, and thereby placing the responsibility for the devastation on the defendant present at trial, could outweigh the implications of all the conspiracy theories posed by the defense. However, all the psychological evidence could make the entire procedure much more convoluted, lengthy, and tedious. It could wear-out a jury, and quite possibly actually invoke mitigating circumstances, eliminating a death penalty sentence in the end anyway. The possibilities of non-jury, or bench trial as they are called, needed to be considered as well, both by defense and the prosecution.

Judges are fairly well paid, highly educated and well-steeped in the law, and usually patient. Practicing attorneys, for the most part, understand this. This understanding then, sets the tone for lawyers presenting their case. When, as was the example here, the defense were interested in presenting large doses of professional psychological/psychiatric issues to consider, they would have to stick to the pertinent stuff, and keep it limited. However, they knew it was most likely to get a considerate, rational review from the judge, rather than the emotional reaction of a jury.

Juries overtime, have become famous for short attention spans, short trial memory, and a profound desire to drop a verdict, and be on their way. Keen attorneys have incorporated these traits into their trial practice, with substantial success. Trial before Your Honor, however, takes a bit more 'lawyering' than being keen. It means being practiced, careful, and precise. While the prosecution here had the advantage in unlimited resources in being precise, the defense team held the edge in being practiced and careful. The prosecution too, had been forewarned, any intricate and/or 'sensitive' information they may uncover, had to be shared with the defense, who also reserved the right to cross-examination.

All things considered, the defense leaned in favor of an intellectual and evidence-based verdict, rather than the almost-certain more emotional and panicked result from a jury. A jury peering across the courtroom at the likes of Dennis Harding or James Waters, listening to the testimony of law enforcement agents and survivors, would tend to seek revenge. A professional jurist however is compelled, and more likely to think – which laws have been violated, according to the relevant evidence, and what is the appropriate punishment?

Although the prosecution was certain that executing the defendants was popular at the moment, how eager would the public be in another couple of years, after prolonged, complicated motions and testimony, to send these Americans, who hadn't actually killed anyone, to the death chamber? True, Harding's bomb had in fact exploded, after being placed in the 'bomb-proof' truck, but the detonation had injured police, firefighters and medics, as well as civilians. The bomb-truck explosion had also destroyed property, and released some of the deadly toxins of the vest bomb into the atmosphere in Times Square, causing considerable danger and extensive decontamination work.

This in turn led to further consideration of an offer for Harding. Further examination and deliberation regarding his affairs exposed his recent accomplishments: He was a 3-time convicted felon and inmate. Upon his last prison release, he'd come to New York City, affiliated himself with a terrorist group, and executed an attack in the transit system. This begged the question of if an offer of a life sentence was appropriate for him. After further deliberation by prosecutor's staff, it was agreed upon that in fact, a death sentence was more appropriate for him.

It was decided then the convict felon Harding, whose bomb eventually exploded, would not get an offer of a life sentence in return for a guilty plea. James Waters, the wandering, angry, college student, no criminal record, family present and publicly and privately pleading for his life, would get an offer.

Keeping that in mind, that the public was now eager, but may eventually lose enthusiasm, the offer was put forward as a one-time only, take it now, or 'forever hold your peace', deal.

Before this seemingly generous offer was proposed though, everyone concerned with the deal knew there was a significant price of admission. Everything, absolutely everything, everyone, everywhere, every who, what, when, where and how, every detail James could even fathom about this monstrous terror attack, everything and anything James could provide; he must. Normally with such plea-deals there is also a significant deal-killer: If at any point during investigation, or any subsequent investigation, facts are uncovered that the defendant knew of but did not disclose, or, facts which the defendant "reasonably" could have or should have known, the plea deal becomes invalid.

Chapter 63
The 24-Hour Challenge

The defendant was offered a deal at lunchtime on a Monday, and told that it expired in 24 hours.

After lunch on the day of the offer, James' defense team met with him at the Federal Metropolitan Corrections Center in Manhattan and informed him of the deal. Upon hearing the details, James had already begun to shake his head in disagreement. It was at this point in the conversation that the attorneys reminded James of the plan to proceed with an insanity defense if he chose not to cooperate in saving himself from the execution chamber. James countered that he would fire his lawyers and inform the court that they were not representing his wishes in the matter.

They in turn, explained to James that he would have to persuade the judge not that they were not doing what James wanted, but that they were being incompetent and unprofessional. This, they assured James, was not at all the case, and that the judge would almost certainly agree that they were doing everything possible to provide James with nothing less than an adequate and vigorous defense.

About an hour later, James had a visit with Carol and Joann. Yet again, the women pleaded.

Chapter 64
A Defendant
Without a Cause

Huntington and the Defense Team then went to meet with Dennis Harding. Harding had come to his 'Jihadist Awakening' as the result of a life marked by failure, frustration, and abandonment. His father was a drifter who had gotten his mother pregnant just before serving a 7-10 year sentence in an Oklahoma Penitentiary for his third conviction for Assault & Robbery. His 22-year-old mother gave Dennis over to foster care when he was 4, as she was sentenced to 5-9 years for her fourth felony conviction in 5 years. While she was 'inside', there was an incident; she was charged and pleaded guilty to an attempted murder rap and was given another 5 years to reconsider her behavior. After that, Dennis was lost to the state system.

Eventually, Dennis Harding made his way to New York. After just 2 years, Harding came to reside in a quaint Hudson River Village north of New York City known as Ossining, at a state facility called 'Sing-Sing'. Having spent nearly 3 years as a 'guest' of the state, he found himself in a work-release program with his new Islamist friends at the Muslim Relief Agency. The rest is jihadi history.

Unlike James, Dennis Harding did not seem to have any supportive and encouraging family and friends ready to rally to his side and promote his well-being. Despite research and outreach efforts by the Harding Defense Team, no one who had been located showed any enthusiasm for getting involved in Harding's latest anti-social endeavor. There was an ex-wife who said she 'supposed she could make the trip' from Oklahoma to New York, provided all expenses and 'arrangements' were covered. A former cohort of nefarious character made a similar offer. It was agreed that, other than a couple of sympathetic companions seated behind the defense, these allies added no persuasive value to the defense. There were no children, relatives, or friends who seemed to care much at all about Harding.

Upon hearing about the prosecution's decision from his attorneys, Harding initially played the 'tough guy'. "Oh, so you want me to plead, huh?" he snapped. "Yeah, well, fuck that! You know? They wanna do me in—they're gonna have to do the work! Screw them!"

"Well, Dennis..." Huntington replied after Harding had unleashed his initial rant, "that's where things stand for right now. We don't have to respond until tomorrow. Let's put this aside for right now, and we'll take it up again tomorrow. Keep in mind though, the prosecution doesn't seem to mind at all about 'doing you in' or 'having to do the work'."

Chapter 65
Plea Deals
and Punishment

In the days following the massive destruction of the attack and the suffering it brought, the presiding Federal Judge, U.S District Court Judge Helen Moynihan, was involved in a conversation with a staffer. The legal assistant had some troubling news for her boss about rumors of a plea deal.

Judge Moynihan was deeply disturbed at the prospect of Dennis Harding getting a plea bargain and avoiding the death penalty. She was already having regrets about sparing James Woods, and now she was hearing 'murmurs' about Harding having been offered a deal.

"Who offered a deal?" she wanted to know. Having served on the Federal Bench for seven years and being in the Circuit for years before, she knew U.S. Assistant Attorney Peter Stemple. She had an idea of how he thought about the law. She could not wrap her mind around the notion that Stemple was about to spare Dennis Harding. If so, she might have to intervene and overrule the prosecutor. Still, she could not see Peter Stemple going that route.

A junior clerk had come to Judge Moynihan after having heard the story from a clerk in the prosecutor's office. According to the story, she explained to her boss, a cop negotiating with the defendant in the subway told Harding that he could work a deal for information.

"A cop? In the subway?" Helen Moynihan gasped in response. "Talking to some lunatic strapped to a bomb vest in the subway? I beg to differ! That offer does not make the grade in my courtroom. That officer is a hero. Give him a medal and a promotion. But his offer of a deal carries no weight here. And I doubt very much that it's going to carry any weight with Peter Stemple!"

The senior assistant U.S. attorney for the New York City office of the Northeast District was Peter Stemple of Rapid City, Iowa. Rapid City is a city of approximately 68,000, and an elevation of 3000 feet in the Black Hills Mountains. It is said there are thirty or so sunny days each year there whether you want them or not. Stemple was a brilliant legal mind and practitioner. He had served in his present assignment in New York for the U.S. attorney for 11 years, five of those as senior assistant attorney. Basically, he was the chief prosecutor for the U.S. attorney general in the New York City area. He was 51 years of age, had attended the University of Notre Dame at South Bend, Indiana for two years before moving on to Harvard Law in Massachusetts, where he achieved his law degree.

Stemple himself was no stranger to municipal disaster. In 1972 when he was 13, a massive flood from the nearby Rapid Creek struck the Rapid City area, killing 250 people, including Peter's uncle and a cousin. Over 3,000 people were injured, including family and friends of the Stemples.

At Notre Dame, he'd excelled in both the public law and criminal law programs, and continued his focus there at Harvard. Stemple was deeply troubled by the prospect of the perpetrators in this case receiving life sentences. Upon considering the prospect of 'dealing' with both James Waters and Kevin Harding, he had this thoughtful observation:

"One of the many disturbing aspects of this case is that it is most clearly a capital case, yet no one is to receive capital punishment? That can't be right. Especially given the devastating nature of these terrorist crimes! No, it's not justice when these heinous, dastardly acts are perpetrated against us, and none of the attackers is being made to pay the supreme price. Hundreds of our citizens were killed and maimed, and poisoned and horrified on their way to work, in the place that they live! No. No, someone has to pay. We cannot just 'let this be'."

"So, what do we do?" he continued. "James Waters, he's never been arrested. He's a college student. His mother is here publicly and privately pleading for his life, along with his sister and girlfriend. He has agreed to be completely cooperative in the investigation.

This Harding—is a three-time convicted felon. After serving his third prison sentence, he gets himself involved with a bunch of Islamic jihadist terrorists, and attacks the New York City subway. The bomb he brought to the train station actually exploded upon removal, causing injury, damage, and danger. No, I cannot fathom not getting the death penalty for this marauding lunatic. He is most certainly out to get us. No, no. There is a war being waged. Harding has brought this war, again, to New York. He should be dealt with accordingly. He's death penalty eligible under U.S. Code Title 18 Part II, aggravating factors—he's been previously convicted of two violent felonies.

We have substantial planning and premeditation—to cause the death of a person or commit an act of terrorism. And, multiple attempted killings—he intentionally attempted multiple killings. He gets the chamber."

Later that afternoon, Judge Helen Moynihan's assistant phoned the U.S. attorney's staff to inquire if attorney Stemple could be available for lunch with the judge the following day. There was a matter of 'some urgency' the judge would like to discuss. After just a brief pause, the lunch date was confirmed.

Their lunch was held at one of the more distinguished dining rooms on Worth Street, not far from the U.S. Courthouse at Foley Square in Lower Manhattan. The area was 50 city blocks from the monstrous devastation that had been wreaked upon Midtown, and the neighborhood, spotted with moderately elegant restaurants and taverns, had resumed its normal ebb and flow.

"Judge Moynihan," Peter Stemple said, patting her arm as they took their seats. "We're at lunch, Peter, you may call me Helen," she said with a smile. They brooded briefly over menus, ordered drinks, and discussed news, sports, and weather as they awaited their meals. Upon being served, attorney Stemple asked Judge Moynihan, "So to what do I owe the pleasure of such a lovely lunch date?"

Helen Moynihan finished a bite of her marinated scallops, dabbed at her mouth with her napkin, and responded. "Peter," she began, "I feel somewhat foolish discussing some low-level office gossip with you, however the nature of the aforementioned gossip is rather disturbing…" "Please, Helen, feel free…" Stemple said. "Well, what I'd heard from an aide, was that she'd heard from one of your aides, was that an offer was being considered for Harding." At this point, Helen Moynihan held up a finger, and continued quickly. "I didn't say I believed it. I just said that I'd heard it and it was disturbing. Something to do with negotiations that took place with the police…"

"I'd heard the same thing," Stemple replied right away. "In fact," he went on, "I spoke to the officer in question about it, and he gave the absolutely correct explanation. He said to me 'Counselor, really? He had a bomb, we were in the subway, people were dying all around us. I was sure I was not obligated to honor such a ridiculous offer. In fact, I said that you might make him an offer. If you don't well, then shame on me.'"

"Shame on him indeed," she responded with a pert smile. "I'll tell you," attorney Stemple continued, "this decision did in fact cause me some distress. My initial instinct, of course, was that this act of terrorist violence was a clear-cut capital case; for both defendants. Then I realized of course, that was an emotional, gut-reaction, to a devastating tragedy."

Helen nodded in agreement, and in appreciation of the prosecutor's wisdom. He continued, "I knew I needed to take a calm and more objective look at the actual facts yielded by the investigation. This then, led to further stringent consideration. Without discussing the particulars, prior to the case being brought before you, I can say as a straightforward matter of procedure, that after consultation with my chief of staff, and my assistant prosecutor, and of course the AG, that this office has accepted a guilty plea offer with a life sentence, pending your approval of course, for the defendant James Waters. We will seek the death penalty, without an offer, for the defendant Dennis Harding.

We can expect, I'm sure, an appeal in the penalty phase for him. And I will of course, explain the details of these decisions, as troublesome as they were to me, in court."

"I must say," Helen Moynihan replied, "that was pretty much what I expected to hear you say. With regard to Harding anyway... I'd heard 'whispers' about the Waters situation being different. But, as you say, these are 'particulars', are better discussed in the courtroom. I want to thank you first, for being so quickly responsive to my invitation, and secondly for being so frank, as usual, in your thoughtful conversation. So, enough 'shop-talk'. How are your lovely wife and daughter?"

Chapter 66
Navigating the Legal Labyrinth

Dennis Harding, upon learning that no plea deal would be offered to spare him, opted for a not guilty plea and a trial. His defense team had repeatedly tried to persuade him that this was virtually useless since the evidence and testimony against him was overwhelming. Thinking he had nothing to lose, he remained stubbornly defiant and insisted on a trial. "Hell," he thought to himself, "I'm already a dead man, I might as well drag this out as long as I can. I'll be a celebrity—Dennis Harding, the notorious terrorist."

This case was hardly Robert F. Huntington's first rodeo. In fact, it was his twelfth capital case. He had come to understand the mind and tendencies of condemned criminals. He also understood a basic tenet of defense in death penalty cases which was very much in sync with the condemned: Delay, delay, delay, and hope for a misstep by the prosecution, or a dream-come-true ruling from a sympathetic judge or jury. He knew that neither of those circumstances were likely in this highly charged and emotional case. His approach was to briefly placate Harding in order to gain his confidence so he could then persuade him to give it up. After a few weeks, Huntington gradually shifted from acquiescing in delay tactics to moving Harding into a state of acceptance of the inevitable. Harding, however, did not shift.

Huntington knew it was time for some hardball persuasion. "Mr. Harding," he began very formally, "this is my twelfth capital case. I've been able to obtain five suspensions in death penalty cases. Four of my capital case clients remain on death row, and two have been executed. I know all the ins and outs and ups and downs of death penalty cases. I'm certain that if you persist in delay and demand a trial, you will indeed, eventually be executed. We've already tried twice to transfer jurisdiction from federal court to New York State, which has no death penalty. Both times we've been refused, and our request for an appeal has been denied."

"Your only hope, really, is that you agree to waive the trial. I'll make a very strong argument in your favor about how you are being completely reasonable and prudent in sparing the government a great deal of time, effort, and expense, and hope that Judge Moynihan will appreciate the gesture and spare your life. And if not, we will of course appeal the sentence. That'll go on for years. I assure you, you will be much older by the time this thing is finally decided."

Harding thought for a moment, then spoke, "Yeah, that's great, fantastic. Thanks for stopping by. You can go now, leave. You're fired."

Thus ensued two hearings before Judge Helen Moynihan where Harding made two feeble attempts to dismiss his entire defense team. At the conclusion of the second hearing, the only thing dismissed was Harding's motion. "Mr. Harding," Judge Moynihan explained, "you have the extreme good fortune to be represented in this most critical case by some of the finest legal minds in not only the State of New York, but the nation. You failed to persuade me that they are providing anything less than the finest legal representation available to you in this dire situation. Consider yourself in the best possible hands.

Your motion is dismissed." "It's over, Dennis," Huntington remarked, "let's move on. We have to arrange the appeal of the sentence. This is going to require your cooperation."

After ten days of fuming and sulking, Harding relented. "Alright," he later told Huntington, "let's get this over with."

In one of his final meetings with his client before sentencing, Robert F. Huntington tried once more to persuade him to cooperate with authorities in the investigation. Harding remained adamant in his refusal. "I've told you a hundred times," Harding said, "If and when they take execution off the table, I'll cooperate. If not, no dice, I say nothing." Huntington exhaled deeply and replied, "And each time you say that, I try to explain to you, once you agree to cooperate, then the government will be more likely to offer a deal."

"Yeah, more likely..." Harding responded, "Always good to see ya there, R.F., thanks for dropping in. You know the way out, right?"

Chapter 67
The Fates of Harding
and Waters Decided

At the foot of the Manhattan side of the Brooklyn Bridge, just north of City Hall Park and opposite Police Headquarters at 1 Police Plaza, lies Thomas Paine Park in Foley Square. Originally named after the famed American Revolutionary, the park was colloquially known as Foley Square Park until the city officially adopted the name in 2000.

It was now mid-October, nearly a year after the horrific jihadist, multi-site terror attacks of November 11. Foley Park, a surprising contradiction amid the manufactured concrete canyons of New York City, offers a break from the relentless traffic and claustrophobic crowding. This triangular oasis of open space is sprinkled with trees and benches, where, on this October day, the sparse remaining leaves had turned from green to a bronze hue.

Surrounding the park and Foley Square is the very seat of New York City, New York State, and the United States' criminal and civil justice systems. Among the neighbors here are the FBI, U.S. Attorney's Office, the New York County District Attorney, and the United States District Court for the Southern District of New York. It was here that Dennis Harding and James Waters were to hear the formal pronouncement of their fates. Various hearings and appeals had wound their way through the courts, and it was now time for formal sentencing. This event, too, would inspire another round of motions, appeals, and hearings. It was not the end for the defendants, but it was very much the beginning of the end.

Adjacent to the various prosecutors' offices and courthouses was the U.S. Bureau of Prisons Metropolitan Corrections Center, the latest home of the two defendants. Each, in his turn, would be shunted through a maze of passageways and tunnels for his appointment in federal criminal court.

As the final legal matters came to a conclusion, Dennis Harding was nearly done with his defiant, tough-guy stance. He'd begun at last to personalize that the rest of his life, really, finally, was about to be decided, without Dennis having much say in the matter. This realization somewhat subdued his noisy, jeering persona. In the end, Harding's tough-guy stance faded, just as it had in the Times Square Subway Station.

He did not, however, move off his stance of not cooperating in the investigation. He still stood firm that he had to be spared before he cooperated, not after. This pretty much sealed his fate.

James, on the other hand, was saving his most stinging protest for last, in a moment of extreme poor judgment and profound bad timing. Judge Helen Moynihan's court on sentencing day was just not a good choice for Waters to demonstrate his defiance. He could have at least waited until Judge Moynihan pronounced sentence before demonstrating his glib indifference to the proceedings.

It came to the point in the proceedings where Judge Moynihan had the charges read back to James Waters and his defense counsel, and asked if he understood "the full and final implications" of pleading guilty to all charges. Appearing unconcerned and inattentive, staring vacantly into some space off to his right, pausing just long enough to be annoying but not quite audacious, James absently replied, "Yeah, whatever."

Prosecutors, defense attorneys, investigators, and police, bailiffs and clerks, all take court proceedings and the sanctity of a judge's court very seriously. None, however, more so than the presiding judge, especially presidentially selected, senatorially-approved U.S. federal district court judges such as U.S. District Court Judge Helen Moynihan. Her eyes went wide and vengeful as James' words registered.

Fortunately, really, for all present, Attorney Robert F. Huntington was as attentive as the best of them, and quicker than most. He immediately placed joined hands directly beneath pursed lips as in prayerful repose, his head bowed just slightly toward the floor in respectful remorse and looking up into Judge Moynihan's face with just the right touch of graceful pleading, and in perfect timing, uttered the words that possibly saved James Waters from capital punishment: "Your Honor—with your permission please, can you allow us a moment?"

"It'd better be a remarkably quick moment, Mr. Huntington," came the reply.

At that moment, Robert Huntington had had about all he could take with James Waters. The attorney came to believe that James was not much more than something of a spoiled child who'd very nearly killed and wounded a thousand people. Huntington understood, though, that his personal opinion of his clients was largely irrelevant; it could easily prevent him from providing his best work, thereby failing to provide his best defense.

R.F. Huntington respected the seriousness of the judicial process, not nearly as much as Judge Helen Moynihan, but enough so that he too was annoyed by Waters' lack of respect. As such, Huntington had all he could do to maintain a discreet volume in addressing his client with an urgent tone of emphasis: "James— don't even try to pretend that everyone in this courtroom doesn't understand precisely what that smart-ass response to the judge meant. We all 'get' that you don't approve of us, or all this... But you gave your word, James."

"You gave your word, James, not only to us but to Carol, and Joann as well. Now, does that count for nothing? Is making promises to people who love you something you do on a whim, or does it really mean something?"

Robert F. Huntington wasn't always right; just frequently. This was one of those frequent moments, he'd struck just the right chord with James. James sighed and exhaled deeply. There it was again, thought James; Mother. Carol. She was the reason he did not ignite the vest and murder hundreds. She was the reason he was still walking and talking and breathing. She was the one person James had any real respect and love for. He was now aware of humiliation, deep shame, for his dramatic, brash remark.

James thereupon addressed Her Honor, with appropriate remorse and regret. "Your Honor, I beg your pardon... Please excuse my rude response, to you, to the Court. I appreciate and respect the conditions I've been granted here. I apologize."

Judge Helen Moynihan once again addressed the defense:

"Against my personal preference, which would have seen you on Death Row, which remains a possibility, if you fail to continue to provide complete and unconditional cooperation with investigative and prosecuting authorities, I, being fully empowered by the President and Congress of the United States, do hereby sentence you to incarceration by the U.S. Bureau of Prisons, and any and all appropriate authorities for the remainder of your life, whatever that may be, without the possibility of parole."

Judge Moynihan's next statement was dismissive— "Hearing nothing further, this court, is adjourned." With that, James Waters' life was spared. For the time being. If he reneged in any way, all deals were null and void.

Chapter 68
Confrontation at the Edge

Just a few days after his sentencing, Art Mandell, an assistant to Peter Stemple, met with Dennis Harding at the MCC. Harding was set to be transferred the next day to a maximum-high security facility in Colorado to await execution. Mandell, a 34-year-old, ten-year veteran of the U.S. Prosecutor's Office, was determined to persuade Harding to reconsider his refusal to speak to investigators about an alleged Islamic terrorist plot.

"What do you think happens after this?" Mandell asked, gesturing broadly.

"After this?" Harding responded angrily. "You strap me to the table and inject poison into my veins! That's what happens!"

"And then?"

"Then what?" Mandell pressed. "Then it's over. Dead."

"Are you sure? Are you absolutely certain?"

"Yeah, man. That's it. It's over."

"You don't really know, though, right? For thousands of years, people have believed there's something more after death."

"Ah, man, that's nonsense. There's nothing. It's over."

"So for thousands of years, millions of people have been wrong?"

"Yeah, man, they're wrong. You're dead."

Mandell paused, then replied, "No, not me, Dennis. I'm still very much alive. You're the one who's dead. I'll still be having my morning coffee, kissing my wife and kids, petting the dog, going to work. You're the one who's dead. Then, you find out if millions of people over thousands of years are wrong. What if it's the other way around? What if they're right and you're wrong?"

"Well, then, I suppose I burn in hell. Can't be much worse than it's been here," Harding said, sweeping his hand dismissively.

"Yeah, I hear that a lot from guys like you. But really, it could be quite a bit worse than anything you've experienced here."

"Ah, man. You're just spouting nonsense. Get out of here. Your visit's over. Go. C.O.! On the gate!" Harding called the Corrections Officer to his cell.

Mandell just laughed. "What's funny?" Harding asked.

"Harding, take a look around. Where the hell do you think you are, the Waldorf? You think you're calling a bellhop to your room? You're in my house now. They come when I call, not you. I decide when the visit is over, not you. See? Wrong again! What if you're wrong about the other thing too? What if, just like right now, I'm right and you're wrong?"

"Man," Harding moaned, "now you're just annoying me, okay? Now you're just pissing me off with your preaching, okay? I guess you can force me to sit here and listen. 'Your house' and all..." Harding made air quotes with his fingers.

"Oh, no. No, no," Mandell replied, "Perish the thought, Dennis. I was just asking some questions. Think about them, don't think about them, that's your call. It doesn't really matter to me. I'm going home to dinner with my family. And you? You have a date with the needle. I'm just saying maybe you want to rethink some things, that's all."

Then, the conversation ended. Mandell signaled for the officer to come to the gate. Harding made a show of dismissing Mandell as if nothing had changed, but a troubling seed of doubt had been planted.

Epilogue

It took five months for U.S. authorities to catch up with Muhammed in Libya. The U.S. Joint Counter-Terror Task Force assembled an action team that included not only U.S. Special Forces but also, in a gesture of reconciliation, members from the FBI, DHS, NYPD, and NYPD Transit Counter-Terror Teams.

The outcome for Muhammed was grim. During the encounter, there was disagreement among the team members: some insisted that Muhammed had drawn a weapon, while others did not see a gun, and some were unsure. Regardless of the conflicting accounts, when the smoke cleared in the room that day in Libya, Muhammed was quite dead.

Further Reading

Terrorism and Security

- Greenberg, Karen J. - Director, Center on National Security at Fordham University School of Law
- "The Muslim Brotherhood: From Hassan al-Banna to the 'Great Arab Revolt'" - Historical analysis of the organization's growth and influence
- "Joint Statement on Counter-ISIL Cooperation" - Defense Ministers of Australia, France, Germany, Italy, the Netherlands, the UK and US

Historical Events

- Israel-Palestinian Letters of Mutual Recognition (September 1993) - Jewish Virtual Library
- "The Eleventh Day" by Anthony Summers and Robbyn Swan (Doubleday, 2011) - Comprehensive analysis of terrorism and intelligence
- Chicago Tribune (April 22, 1964) - "Subway Fire Jams N.Y. Traffic":
- New York Times (April 22, 1964) - Coverage of the Times Square-Grand Central subway fire

Legal Framework

- United States District Court for the Southern District of New York - Jurisdictional overview and procedures
- House Permanent Select Committee on Intelligence - Overview of intelligence oversight
- Select Committee on Benghazi - Investigation findings

Emergency Response

- FDNY Tiered Response System - Technical rescue and victim-removal protocols

- NYC Emergency Room capacity and response capabilities
- HazTac paramedics and EMTs operational procedures

Note: Some of these sources may have been updated or archived since their original publication. Readers are encouraged to verify current availability.

www.ingramcontent.com/pod-product-compliance
Lightning Source LLC
Chambersburg PA
CBHW071308101025
33774CB00008B/118